PRINT EDITION

Exile: Unreachable Skies Vol. 2 © 2019 by Mirror World Publishing and Karen McCreedy
Edited by: Robert Dowsett
Cover Design by: Justine Dowsett

Published by Mirror World Publishing in September 2019

Mirror World Publishing

Windsor, Ontario, Canada
www.mirrorworldpublishing.com
info@mirrorworldpublishing.com

ISBN: 978-1-987976-58-8

For Dianne, and in memory of Philip. Love always.

EXILE:
Unreachable Skies

Vol. 2

By Karen McCreedy

M|W mirror world publishing

With best wishes for a happy Christmas 2019,

Karen

One

"If you go through the Deadlands, you will all die."

As I picked my way between strewn belongings, and smouldering campfires that did little to warm the icy dawn, it was the voice of Shaya, the Chief Hunter, which carried to me above the sound of breaking waves, whimpering younglings, and complaining females. Just two days ago, every wingless youngling, and every female who had produced one, had been sent into exile by our Prime, Kalis, urged on by his favourite adviser, Fazak. Yet already the arguments had started!

My nose alerted me to the stink of a shallow waste-pit and I edged around it, stepping over a broken beaker, and continued on toward the squabbling voices. As Kalis' Fate-seer I was expected to return to my dwelling on the *Spirax* peninsula, a few nines of wingbeats across the bay, but a Vision had shown me that my future lay with the exiles and, after visiting my Dream-cave, I had flown to their makeshift encampment.

The females, their wings broken by Kalis' new Elite Guard, had been netted over the river along with their younglings, and had been left on the claw of reed-tufted sand that jutted into the ocean from the Manybend estuary's north shore. As I'd circled over the nines of fires, their spiralling layout had shown that someone had taken charge of setting the camp properly, and my sole concern had been finding somewhere to land without being seen. In the end I had set down on the beach to the north, wetting my feet as I landed at the edge of the incoming tide. Taking care to make sure I would not leave any traces of my approach, I had walked along the tideline till I reached the promontory at daybreak. I had intended to find my friend Doran and make myself known to her, but the sound of raised voices had drawn my attention, and I had instead made my way across the camp to the ridge of snow-covered ground that separated the hook of sand from the mud of the Deadlands. I smelled cooking – branmeal bubbling in a pot to my left, meat patties warming in a pan to my right. My stomachs rumbled a protest that I was not stopping to eat, but my attention was on the group at the foot of the slope where Shaya stood, and the arguments that I could now hear more clearly.

"The Deadlands are frozen, Shaya, just like everywhere else. I don't see why we can't walk straight across them to the Ambit river. We can head for the Eye, or even the river upstream from there where it narrows and will be easier to cross."

I didn't recognise the speaker, though I knew from her copper tunic that she was an Artisan. As Shaya set her ears to a more aggressive angle and began to explain the dangers of the Deadlands – the thin ice masking mud that was deep enough to drown in, brambletrap that would feed on any creature living or dead – I spotted Doran's russet fur and green-and-black Healer's tunic amid the crowd. Forgetting that I had changed my appearance by dyeing my fur and changing my tunic from Fate-seer black to Trader blue, I made my way over to her and said, "Doran, what's going on?"

She twisted an ear my way, gave me a sniff, and looked me up and down. "I'm sorry, do I know you?"

I took a quick look round. Nineties of females were attending to their younglings, cooking meals, or still rolled in blankets, sleeping. Those in the group surrounding Shaya had their attention on what she was saying. Only Doran had an ear twisted my way. "It's me," I hissed, "Zarda. I promised I would join you, didn't I?"

"But you're…" she said as she waved a paw from the neck of my tunic to my feet, "you look so different." She sounded disappointed. "I've been waiting for you to come. I thought that having Zarda the Fate-seer join us would help all these drax to face what lies ahead. But if they don't know it's you…"

It had not occurred to me that I might help anyone's morale. "I came because I Saw that I should," I said, "and because Kalis no longer listens to me. Besides, if Dru is to fulfil his destiny and defeat the Koth, he'll need help and guidance from a Fate-seer, especially—" No. Only members of the council knew that Dru had the Sight, and we had agreed to keep it secret for the moment. Doran had no need to know – not yet. I dismissed what I'd been about to say with a flick of an ear that told Doran it was of no importance, and spiralled a paw across the front of my tunic. "I can't be Zarda here. I know Kalis isn't interested in anything I have to say, but he is a stickler for tradition. I've left him without a Fate-seer and he won't be happy. He'll send the Guardflight to look for me – maybe even his new Elite Guard. And I think we can both guess what will happen to me if they find me." As I finished talking, I turned my head to indicate the pathetic figure huddled in a blanket, sitting alone in the shadows beyond the encampment fires.

Doran flicked an ear in sympathy – the other was still turned toward Shaya and the ongoing argument – and ran a paw over her tunic. "I never liked Varna, but to lose her wings like that…" She shuddered, then leaned toward me to confide, "She howled through the entire first day. Only subsided to a whimper when Limar threatened to bind her mouth shut. Dru kept taking her beakers of soup from Limar's cauldron, and showed her things he'd found on the beach, but she snapped and snarled every time he went near her. In the end, he stayed by the fire over there with Limar." Turning back to face me, she waggled an ear in apology. "I suppose you're right, you can't be seen to have joined us. Not yet, anyway. I just hoped…" she said, indicating the group arguing with Shaya. "Perhaps if the Fate-seer had been able to step in, these silly females wouldn't be proposing to cross the Deadlands on foot."

I turned my gaze from Doran to the arguing group and then down to the laden carry-pouch that was still strapped to my shoulders. My black tunic was in there, buried at the bottom beneath cold patties, jars of healing herbs, bags of avalox for tea, a second blue tunic, a blanket, several beakers, knives, spoons, and a bag of precious spirelles which I had found in the Fate-seer's dwelling a few ninedays ago. Could I – should I – pull out the tunic and join my voice to Shaya's? As I hesitated, she climbed part way up the slope, sending snow and sand tumbling beneath her feet as she took the high ground in typical hunter fashion. As she turned to face the crowd again, I saw that there were five other hunters with her, standing at the foot of the slope. All of them had a defiant set to their ears and one wing apiece half-extended while they joined their arguments to their chief's – "the ice is thin," – "there will be quickmud," – "there will be nowhere you can rest in safety."

Shaya raised her arms and her voice once again: "And if none of that worries you, then the brambletrap should. Just because there's snow on the branches doesn't mean it's safe."

I eased my pouch to the ground, still uncertain what I should do. As I straightened up and rolled my shoulders, I almost forgot that I was supposed to have a damaged wing and started to give them both a stretch. Only when they were partly-extended did I remember. Giving what I hoped was a convincing yelp of pain, I winced and pulled one wing in.

No-one noticed. All attention was now on the females who wanted to leave the main group. They had heard all the arguments, all the reasons why they should not try to cross the Deadlands. A few moved away, ears drooping, muttering to each other as they shuffled back towards the campfires. But a female in the brown tunic of a farmer stood her ground and I recognised her as Colex, one of the first females I'd attended, along with my teacher Vizan, when her youngling hatched without wings. She had been stubborn and angry then, and sounded equally stubborn and angry now as she barked: "We'll all die if we go the way you are proposing. So the beach runs north – so what? There are dunes and rocks and cliffs before you even reach the Cleft Rocks.

And you can't stay on the coast much beyond them, because the Ambit peninsular juts east, and if you go east, there is nowhere left to go except to turn and head back along the estuary. Even if your wings have healed by then, it will be difficult to carry all the younglings over the water there. Much better surely to go north and west through the Deadlands, and make for the narrower stretch of the Ambit west of the Eye."

The Eye was a small, vine-strewn islet that divided the Ambit's flow in two for a few spans, giving the river the appearance from above of looking back at you as you flew over it.

"That's a long way upstream from the estuary," Doran murmured. "We were west of that, I think, when we flew to the Forest that day, remember?"

"I'll never forget it," I replied, my voice low. "You were bitten by a vine-serpent, and I nearly got eaten by a mouldworm." I also remembered that it had taken us the best part of a day to fly there. How long would such a journey take us on foot? Especially if we took the longer but safer route along the coast and over the peninsula? Kalis had set no deadline for us to reach the Forest, but I was sure that he would not wish us to linger in his territory any longer than we had to. "It is a long way," I said, answering Doran's original point, "but at least by going along the coast there's a chance of reaching it. Anyone going through the Deadlands has no chance at all."

I twisted my ears back in Shaya's direction as I heard her make the same point. "At least wait a few days—"

"What for?" Colex extended a paw in the direction of the encampment as she spoke. "We haven't moved since the guardflight netted us here. I say we move now, and quickly, so that we can cross the Deadlands while they are still frozen." She turned in a slow circle, ears alert, nose busy sniffing for support from those surrounding her. "I'm leaving now, with Lexon," she added, placing a paw on the wingless shoulders of her offspring. "Get your carry-pouches if you're coming with us."

Doran gave me a sideways look and another quick sniff. "Are you going to say anything?"

I looked again at the carry-pouch in which I had buried my Fate-seer's tunic. Lexon had hatched before most of the other wingless emerged from their eggs. Only Colex's stubbornness had kept him alive when everyone else was urging that she left him in the foothills for the Koth to take. Back then, before it became clear that every female who had recovered from the Sickness would produce such offspring, even Vizan had suggested that the hatchling would be better off dead. He'd actually brewed a deadly mixture of zenox powder and rotberry juice, but Colex had knocked the beaker out of his paw. She had refused to listen to him, just as she was not listening to Shaya. "Colex won't heed anyone's advice," I said. "She certainly won't listen to me."

"Some of the others might," Doran retorted, indicating the group of several nines who were collecting their carry-pouches and their younglings. "They'll die if they go into the Deadlands. You know that, Zarda."

I did know it, but a glance round at the still-whimpering Varna reminded me again of what awaited me if Kalis found his errant Fate-seer. My wing struts developed an itch at the mere thought, but still I sniffed the air to discern how Colex's supporters truly felt. There was not so much as a whiff of doubt among them – only determination and a degree of sorrow. I looked around at the nines surrounding us, listened to the shouts of their younglings, and smelled their fright, pain, and doubt. I saw Dru, my reason for joining this exile, bound across to Shaya's side and heard him try to reason with Colex. "I'm not a Fate-seer," he shouted, his ears erect, and his white mane blowing in the breeze, "but I have the Sight. Shaya is right. If you try to cross the Deadlands, you'll die!"

Colex snorted. "I'm not going to stand here and listen to a pup tell stories. Get along with you, before I nip your snout, young Dru. It's your fault we're out here at all – don't pretend you can know what will happen to us when you couldn't even See what would happen to you on the Night of the Two Moons."

"That's not fair!" Limar, a pink-clad, fluffed up bundle of indignation, pushed her way to the front of the crowd, brandishing a ladle from the branmeal she had been preparing a few spans away. "None of this was Dru's fault, he did exactly what he was supposed to at the Two Moons ritual. It was Fazak finding some ancient scratching that said everyone had to be airborne that spoiled everything."

"Doesn't have the Sight, though, does he?"

And for that, Limar had no answer. Though she was Dru's half-sibling and nest-nurse, she had not been told that a visit to the Dream-cave with me had awakened his talent. Of those within earshot, only Shaya, Varna, and myself knew he was speaking the truth. Shaya had been on the council when it was agreed to keep Dru's abilities secret, and whatever had happened since then, I was sure she would not betray that trust. As for Varna – well, she was in no fit state to do anything, and was certainly not about to rise to her pup's defence.

Nor could I, not without revealing who I was.

As I'd flown south during the night, the Great Spiral itself had parted the clouds to send me a sign that my decision to join the exiles was correct. Those same clouds, edged with pale gold in the east, now hid the Spiral from view, but I sent a prayer skyward anyway: *"Tell me what I should do!"*

This time, there was no answer, no sign – just a memory of my own Vision of crossing the Ambit's mudflats with the wingless. The mudflats lay to the north, along the coast on the far side of the Ambit peninsula. If I was to cross them, I had to survive to travel with Shaya and the nineties with her. I couldn't risk putting on my black tunic. Even if no-one betrayed me when Kalis sent the Guardflight to look for me – and he would – we were just a short flight from the *Spirax* where the Elite Guard now flew. It was unlikely they would spot one single black tunic amid the myriad colours that surrounded me, but it was not impossible.

The scent of Doran's disappointment was overwhelming, and I looked up from my carry-pouch to see her ears and whiskers twitch with disapproval.

"I can't save them, Doran." My voice sounded hollow. "But if you want me to try – if you want me to risk my wings by speaking up – then tell everyone right now who I am, and hope that no-one betrays me when the Guardflight come. Because come they will, I guarantee it."

She half-turned away from me, getting as far as opening her mouth to call to Shaya and the others before I scented uncertainty. She looked back at me, then at the set of Colex's ears as the farmer picked up her carry-pouch and set her snout north-west. "I can't be responsible for you losing your wings," she said. "Come on. We're supposed to have nine round each fire, but with all this upset no-one will worry about an extra one sitting at ours." Turning away from the sight of a line of females and younglings scrambling up the sandy, snow-lined ridge to set out across the Deadlands, she led me through the encampment to a warm fire where her youngling, Cavel, was stirring a pot of hot branmeal. "I suppose we'd better think of something else to call you," she said.

Two

The camp was a mournful place. It seemed to me that the distress went deeper than the hurt of betrayal, exile, and broken wings; deeper even than the sadness of leaving home, friends, and nestmates for ever. There was a hopelessness in the way ears were set and in the scents around me that indicated no-one expected to even reach the Crimson Forest, let alone survive it. Perhaps I should put on my black tunic after all. Perhaps…

But no. What good would it do if, in a few days, the Guardflight or the Elite Guard came to find me? I doubted that it would do anything for morale if these exiled females saw the Fate-seer dangling in a net, which was what it would take for the guards to take me back to the *Spirax*. No – I would have to find some other way to make these drax believe they had a future.

"So, Shaya and her hunters have taken charge?" I murmured to Doran, as I spooned branmeal from my beaker. It was thin stuff, and bland, but it did have the virtue of being hot.

The set of Doran's ears made it clear that despite her earlier words and the bowl of branmeal, she was still not entirely reconciled to my decision to remain hidden.

I licked my spoon and beaker, and looked around at the others who sat by our fire. Apart from Doran in her healer's tunic, and Cavel in his yellow-and-white stripes, they all wore the pale blue of Traders, though the only ones I knew were Jonel and her youngling Manda, who had once welcomed Dru and me to their dwelling in my hatching cluster. Neither of them had shown any sign of recognition when Doran introduced me as Thyla, and I'd said that others from my campfire were going with Colex. They'd shrugged, acknowledged me politely, but exhibited an uncharacteristic lack of curiosity that reinforced my belief that everyone was shocked and numbed almost beyond caring.

"We need to find something to do," I said, stuffing my spoon back into my carry-pouch and tying the beaker to a strap. "Us traders, I mean."

"We've got something to do," said Jonel, giving Manda a lick and handing the youngling her toy egg. "We've got to travel to the Forest, and we've got to keep our younglings safe and fed. Isn't that enough?"

"No." I waved a paw in Doran's direction. "Doran here and the other healers, they know they can help with our broken wings, or with any other injuries we might pick up along the way. The artisans have all sorts of skills that will be useful – weaving, making, wood-shaping, building, dyeing. The hunters and fishers know how to find food where most of us would starve. But what do we have to offer? We'll travel together from here, we're one big cluster – no-one will need traders to get what they need, they can just ask each other."

Jonel looked, if it were possible, even more depressed. "I hadn't thought of that."

"Nor had I." Flori, a slight, dark-furred female who had no youngling at her side, looked as though she was preparing for her last nest. I assumed her youngling had not survived its first days, and she doubtless assumed the same about me since I had no pup either. Neither of us remarked on it, or asked about it. Missing hatchlings had long since ceased to be mentioned. "We're worthless out here, aren't we?"

"We're not worthless," I said firmly, setting my ears to a resolute angle. "No-one is worthless. There must be something we can do. I'll ask Shaya."

As I made my way through the camp, fluffing my winter fur against the biting wind, I could scent fear and despondency from every group I passed. Here and there, healers were smearing more salve onto broken wing struts, and I wondered how long their supply of pain-easing ointments would last. There would be precious little camyl along the shoreline and none at all while the snows persisted. I sniffed the breeze, hoping for a hint of a change in the weather, but there was nothing save salt, seaweed, and a faint tang of ice from the southern mountains. The females would, it seemed, have to learn to live with the pain while their broken wings healed. The younglings, though not in physical pain, were clearly subdued and unhappy. Few of them had strayed further than a wing-length from their dams, and the noise of their complaints about the cold, the food, and the makeshift nests on the ground followed me right across the camp. There were fewer younglings than there were females, a sad reminder of how many of them had been disposed of before Dru's hatching. Killing them had not saved their dams – the clusters had abandoned them to their fate as soon as Kalis' decree of exile 'beyond the Forest' had been heard. I had been the one charged with issuing that decree from the *Spirax* balcony, and it had been me who had warned them that their wings would be broken prior to exile. On reflection, seeing me in my Fate-seer's tunic would likely not have helped at all.

As I approached Shaya, one of her fellow hunters hurried over to her, the set of her ears indicating that she had important news to impart. "Chief," I heard her call, "we have the final numbers."

Shaya, sitting by the fire that marked the centre of the camp, licked her spoon and bowl and put them aside, then stood up as the hunter reached her side. "Well?"

"Colex took fifty-two adults and twenty pups with her to the Deadlands, including all but two of the Fishers and most of the Clay-shapers." The shorter female brushed self-consciously at her untidy grey fur as though to flatten it, and I felt a twinge of sympathy – Shaya's immaculately-groomed coat and uncreased tunic always had that effect on me too. "We have just over three nineties of females and one-and-a-half nineties of younglings."

"I see. Well, it could have been worse." The breeze shifted for a moment, and Shaya coughed as smoke from the fire enveloped her. Brushing a fleck of ash from her brown fur, she went on: "What skills have we got, Milat?"

Ah, Milat! That was the name I'd been stretching for. Her whiskers twitched nervously as she made her report: "Three nines of artisans went with Colex, but we still have weavers, wood-shapers, builders, dyers and tunic-makers. There are eleven gatherers, who will be useful once the snow melts, plus of course six hunters including you, Shaya." She glanced around, scratching her snout, and added, "The fifteen healers are already proving their worth, attending to our broken wings. But there are over ninety traders, two cluster-cryers, and sixteen nest-nurses too – and none of them have skills we can use."

I could recognise an opening when I heard one, so I edged closer, ears dipped at a respectful angle. "Excuse me, Shaya, I came over to offer a suggestion. I hope you don't mind?"

She glared down her slender snout at me, and I tugged at the hem of my creased tunic, horribly aware that my fur looked uncombed, and hoped that I did not smell too strongly of the kestox I had used to dye it. "I don't think I know you?" It came out as an accusation, and I hunched over, all but dipping a bow as I answered.

"Thyla," I said, using the name Doran had suggested, "from the south-eastern cluster near the southern bay." I waited a moment, as though hoping she would remember me, then waved a dismissive paw. "But that doesn't matter now. None of it matters. This," I said, tugging at my tunic and holding out my paw to indicate those around me, "these colours don't matter here. We can be our own clusters with our own rules."

Shaya's ears and tail told me she was sceptical about what I was saying. A quick sniff of the breeze told me she was also getting bored, and I pressed on before she could dismiss me out of paw. "What I mean is – surely those of us who do not know how to hunt or gather or weave, or do anything else that might be useful out here, we can learn."

Milat snorted and opened her mouth to say something, but Shaya silenced her with a look. "Let's not drop the suggestion in the ocean just yet, Milat. It's a strange idea, I'll grant you, but if we are to survive I don't think six hunters, two fishers and eleven gatherers will be enough. Especially when we don't have a spear or an empty basket between us." She put her paws behind her back in a gesture that reminded me of Taral, the guardflight chief, and paced right round her campfire, head down, ears and whiskers twitching as she contemplated what I had said. When she was still a few paces away, she stopped and flicked an ear in acknowledgement. "I don't think that full-growns can learn how to hunt," she said, holding up a paw to forestall my protests, "but that doesn't mean you can't be trained to help." She turned to Milat. "Tell the other hunters to start showing the traders and the cluster-cryers how to dig up sandweavers – it's basic youngling-work, but we'll need bait and we can eat the things if we get desperate. Once we're on the move, everyone can watch for sideclaws, and when we come across seavines we have artisans who can demonstrate how to cut them into spears. As for the wingless…" She looked over to where a small knot of younglings were gathered round two half-buried black boulders that jutted from the shingle at the base of the ridge. The rocks, covered with slime and moss, were edged in white frost and dusted with snow. As we watched, Dru in his cream tunic, and an artisan's youngling in copper-and-white stripes, each jumped over a boulder, bending those long legs of theirs and leaping over the obstacles from a standing start. Others followed, their yips of glee carrying on the breeze and attracting the attention of other younglings.

"I couldn't begin to jump over one of those rocks like that," Milat put in. There was a note of pride in her voice, and I realised that her own youngling, Nixel, was one of those with Dru. "The tops of those boulders are almost as high as they are."

Shaya nodded and flicked an ear in agreement. "They're good climbers, too," she said. She glanced at me as she added, "Did you hear about Dru and Cavel climbing the Tusk?"

I'd been there. I had watched and worried with Doran as we'd tried to work out how to reach the younglings through the winds that swirled round the shard of sheer black rock known as the

Tusk. In the end, we had been able to do nothing but wait on top of the stack for the two wingless pups to finish their climb. But I could say none of that to Shaya. Instead, I dipped an ear and said, "I heard all about it from Doran. Almost turned her fur white, I should think!"

"My point," said Shaya, "is that these younglings can reach places that we cannot. There are cliffs north of here where they might be able to grub out some rockcrawlers to add to our stews. And they can shin up vinetrees far more easily than any winged drax I know. If they're anything like my Ravar, they are quick and eager to learn, and they're young enough to absorb any skill we can teach." She turned her head to gaze south across the bay, staring for a moment at the *Spirax* and the plateau it stood upon. They were close enough that I could see the two Elite guards flying around it on patrol and, if I sniffed hard, I could almost catch a whiff of the red moss that grew on the plateau. It had been two nights since I left. Would they be checking my dwelling yet, to sniff out where I might be? Likely not; I had told Kalis I might be several days in the Dream-cave. For me, it was still not too late to go back...

But I recalled the sign I'd received from the Spiral as I'd flown to the camp, the break in the clouds that had shown the Spiral's light streaming north to the Forest. Added to my Visions – of Dru triumphing over the Koth, and of my footsteps crossing the Ambit Estuary with the younglings – I knew I couldn't return to a life where my counsel was mocked and ignored. As I spiralled a paw over my tunic, Shaya sighed and said, "We've lingered here long enough. Time we were moving, if we're to reach the Forest before Kalis's patience runs out."

It was soon after dawn when she spoke those words. By the time everyone had been told, cajoled, or growled at to pack up and start walking, the day was halfway to zenith. Even then, the adults didn't begin to move till Shaya, Milat and the other hunters ushered the younglings ahead of them along the strip of sand that led north.

It was pitiful how slowly we moved. I had walked short distances with Dru on occasion, when I took him out to visit some of the clusters on the Expanse, but most of the females would not have walked further than the distance between a landing path and their dwelling door. While the younglings bounded along the sand in loping strides, collecting seafronds and exploring dunes, rocks, and pools, their dams struggled and straggled in their wake.

"My legs are aching," Doran grumbled, "and this carry-pouch is heavy. Can't we stop for a rest?"

I was walking ahead of her and half-turned, thinking that she was talking to me, but she was looking at Shaya who was over to our left, halfway up a snow-shrouded sand dune, urging us to move faster.

"We've hardly started," Shaya called. "Look at these dunes – you've walked past seven of them, Doran, and the adults at the back haven't even left the camp site. If we all stop, it will take another quarter-day to get moving again. Rest if you must, but don't linger."

"Are you saying we'll not be stopping to eat?" Limar, tucked in behind Doran's right wing, sounded affronted at the thought of not having a meal at zenith. She strutted over to the dune where Shaya stood. "Who put you in charge, anyway?"

Shaya bared her teeth. "Someone had to take charge, Limar. That first day was utter chaos. Too many drax were lighting fires, food was getting eaten regardless of how much of it we need to save for the journey, and everyone was squabbling and squealing. Sending my hunters to start organising things better has already cut our use of fuel and food. But if you think you have more experience than me of sleeping in the open or hunting for food, by all means speak up and give us all the benefit of your knowledge."

Her snarl and posture would have sent most drax whimpering for the nearest cover with their ears flattened in alarm, but Limar appeared undeterred, save for a slight swishing of her tail, which betrayed she did at least have some reservations about confronting Shaya. Ears set forward and snout raised, she would not take logic for an answer. "I just don't think it's fair that you assume we're all happy to take orders from you."

"No-one else appears to be questioning it." Not for the first time, I spoke before I thought, and backed away from Limar as she turned her head to snap her teeth at me.

"Who asked you?" She gave me a sniff and looked me up and down. "Who are you, anyway?"

What was my name now? Oh yes! "I'm Thyla. I just thought…"

I glanced back to see whether anyone else was about to join the conversation, but the other adults plodded on, heads and ears drooping, some panting with effort, others muttering in twos and threes, all concentrating on one thing: putting one foot in front of the other. The scent of despair carried on the breeze, along with the smell of salt spray and lying snow. The clouds that had parted so briefly the previous night were now bunched in an ominous grey blanket. I was sure there would be more snow before daylight faded. Some of the dams, I noticed, kept their younglings close. Rewsa held Ellet firmly by the paw, and I could hear Jonel's youngling, Manda, complaining that she wanted to go and play with her new friends. "They're chasing the waves," she whined, cuddling her toy egg with one paw and pointing with the other. "Why can't I?"

I had twisted an ear to listen for Jonel's reply, so I almost missed Shaya's response to Limar's question. "Thyla has made some constructive suggestions that we will start to implement over the next day or so."

Constructive suggestions! Shaya had never said anything that complimentary about me while I had been Zarda the Fate-seer. I rubbed a paw along my snout, preening just a little while I dipped an ear in acknowledgement.

Limar waved a paw, reducing me to an irrelevance. "The younglings need nourishment," she said. "We all do. None of us have ever walked this far – we need a rest."

"If we were airborne, Limar, we would have barely flown three wing beats." Shaya snapped out each word, her voice as harsh and cold as the breeze that chilled our noses and tugged at our tunics. "If you want to sit here on the dune and have a cud-chew, go ahead. But we are not going to stop to eat anything till we make camp this evening."

The sour odour of disdain poured from Limar, along with an edge of hostility, and for a couple of heartbeats it looked as though she was contemplating a physical attack on Shaya – in which case the only blood on the sand would have been Limar's.

22

A comfortable life in and around the *Spirax* was hardly the best preparation for taking on a hunter. Especially one who kept her teeth and claws in such good condition as Shaya did.

Fortunately for Limar, Dru bounded up the beach at that moment, calling for her to resolve a dispute with young Nixel. "He says that Tomax the Bold couldn't have fought the moon monster on his own," he cried. "Come and tell him, Limar." He pulled at her tunic as he spoke, then seized her paw and tugged her in the direction he wanted her to go.

Glaring over her shoulder at Shaya to make it clear the argument was not over, Limar allowed herself to be led down the beach to the damp sand above the slopping waves. As he passed me, Dru tilted his head and dipped an ear in a way that indicated he knew who I was. But it was not the time to wonder how he knew. Perhaps Doran had told him, or perhaps he had Seen it in a Vision. Just so long as he had not simply recognised me...

"Was there something you wanted, Thyla?"

A rest, a beaker of tea, a herb-encrusted fish, the opportunity to stretch my wings, a warm fire.

I said none of that. Trying not to cower beneath Shaya's haughty gaze, I waved a paw toward Limar's retreating back. "Not now." I looked for Doran's black-and-green tunic amid the shuffling groups, heard her call to Cavel who was running along the tide-line and, with an ear-flick in Shaya's direction, I ignored the ache in my legs and hurried to catch up with her.

Perhaps by now she had forgiven me for not arriving in Fate-seer black.

Three

"Shaya, we cannot physically walk any further today."

This time, when Limar spoke, there were several nines of other females gathered round her signalling their agreement. And this time, she had a point. My own feet and tail were numb with cold and effort, my shoulders and arms ached from supporting my carry-pouch, and my legs were howling with pain.

Hearing the argument, Doran and I exchanged glances, stood still, and put down our carry-pouches. Even if Shaya won the debate, the discussions were likely to take some time. We could at least have a rest while we waited for the argument to conclude.

Behind us, sighs and groans mingled with the thump and clatter of carry-pouches being lowered to the sand. I looked back to see a cascade of drax halting and sitting down. Those at the back probably did not even know why we had stopped – they would simply have been grateful for the opportunity to rest.

"We can't stay here all night." Though Shaya was answering Limar, she raised her head and her voice to ensure that her retort reached as many as possible. "The tide's coming in, so we can't stay on the beach for much longer, and the dunes just here are too high and steep for most of you to climb." She glanced over her shoulder at the massive mound of sand that rose from the beach to tower over our heads. From where I stood, I had to tilt my head back to see the snow on the top of it, and I tried to gauge whether it was as high as the *Spirax*. Likely not – half as high, perhaps – but regardless we would need to get past it before we could even think of making camp.

In response to the groans and complaints that followed her announcement, Shaya held up both paws and, when that did not bring the silence she wanted, she half-extended her unbroken wing. "I've sent Ravar and Nixel on ahead with some of the other younglings to look for a suitable site. Once they get back—"

"They're coming!"

"Here they are!"

The artisans in the group ahead of us called and pointed, anticipation in their voices though they could barely raise a tail-swish between them. I couldn't see much beyond the huddle of copper tunics, but a few beats later Ravar trotted over to his dam's side, his ears and tail signalling his pride in accomplishing the task she had set him. Even so, his steps had slowed from their usual brisk bounce. If the younglings who had to walk everywhere were tired, then it was little wonder that the adults were exhausted.

Shaya bent her head to listen to him, then raised it again to call to the rest of us: "Beyond this dune is a smaller one, and inland from there is a small mound of land which is higher than the Deadlands marsh beyond it. There's enough room there for us to make camp for the night."

Beside me, Doran sighed. "I don't think I can walk another step," she groaned. "My legs are so sore! And these extra foot-coverings haven't helped at all – they're all wet, and the sand's rubbing my toes raw. I'm sure they're bleeding."

The group surrounding Limar and Shaya were all making similar remarks, and the moaning spread back along the groups of seated drax.

"You go and make your new camp," Limar called, above the murmurs and mutterings of discontent. "I'm going to stay here."

I expected Shaya to argue, but instead the hunter simply flicked an ear to acknowledge the point and said, "If you want to stay here, I can't make you move. But once the tide comes in, the base of all these dunes will be covered with water. So your options are to move vertically and climb them, or move horizontally and follow Ravar to the camp site he's found." Without bothering to notice what anyone else did, she picked up her carry-pouch and followed her youngling as he led the way past the base of the giant dune.

A collective sigh gusted through the females as Shaya's words were relayed from group to group. And slowly, painfully, we began to move again, all of us trailing in Shaya's footprints.

Tired as I was, it was fascinating to watch how the hunters set out our camp. By the time Doran and I had staggered through the gap in the dunes to the small rise, where clumps of moss and fern showed through the snow, Milat had already put her carry-pouch in the approximate centre of the available ground and from her pack she'd pulled a spindle, which had twine wrapped round it. While she turned on the spot, Nixel took the end of the twine and paced around her, moving further and further away as the twine spun off the spindle. Every nine paces he stopped for a moment while Ravar marked the spot with a twig or a sea frond, which he pulled from small piles the other younglings had gathered as they had walked along the beach.

As each spot was marked, Shaya sent nine drax to set a fire there.

"This is different to how she sorted us out on that first beach," Doran said, as we followed two artisans, their younglings, plus Limar and Dru to a spot near the middle of the rapidly-forming spiral layout. "When we stepped out of the nets there, we tried to group ourselves by trade." She lowered her voice to a whisper and I twisted both my ears in her direction to hear her next words. "I don't know that I like this new arrangement."

I decided it was probably best not to mention my part in it – I still sensed that Doran was unhappy about my choice of tunic and my decision not to let anyone else know who I was. I would have to step carefully with her for a while, I felt, friendship or no friendship.

"Where's Varna-muz?" Dru asked, his whiskers quivering as he sniffed the air for his dam's scent. "She'll need to be looked after."

Limar pulled a blanket from her carry-pouch, sat on it with a sigh, and patted the space next to her. "She was right at the back, Dru. Galyn was with her – one of the healers. Sit down, it will be a while till they arrive."

The two artisans, who introduced themselves as Winan and Froma, had already managed to coax a smoulder from the pile of damp sea fronds we had been directed to. Calmly, they unrolled their blankets, separated their squabbling younglings, and sat down between Limar and Doran. "So this is Dru." Winan, a tall, hefty specimen with a russet coat that clashed with her copper tunic, dipped a respectful ear in Dru's direction as she spoke. "I've seen you bounding about, young Lord, and just want to say that I thought you did a splendid job on the Night of the Two Moons." She pointed to her own youngling, a bundle of russet fluff who was attempting to bite Froma's smaller pup behind her dam's back. "I'm sure my Chiva couldn't have done it nearly as well."

"He spent days practising," said Limar, stroking Dru's mane as she spoke, while he squirmed and flattened his ears. "Zarda spent a lot of time with him – and I helped too, of course."

I had no recollection of Limar helping at all, at least not while I had been in the nursery with Dru. I supposed it was possible she had helped him rehearse his chant while I was not there, but if she had then Dru would surely have mentioned it. I was close enough to hear his low growl of protest, but as Limar continued to paw at his mane, perhaps it was simply that he did not like being groomed by his half-sibling.

"I'm sure he did very well," said Froma, her voice and ears betraying her doubts. She was tiny, at least a head shorter than her friend, with fur the colour of dry mud. Turning her head, she gave her youngling a brief lick. "But it didn't prevent Kalis from—" She choked off her last words, and gestured at the encampment with a sweep of her arms, before going on, "From doing this to us."

"It was that Fazak," said Winan. She leaned down to her right, gave her offspring a firm nip, and moved her out of reach of the other youngling. "Couldn't you just smell the smugness coming off him when he came in to our shelter with those Elite Guard? It was him wanted us gone, no question about it."

"And it was Fazak who found the old record that said all drax had to be airborne for the ceremony." Was I supposed to know that? Zarda did – she had been in the audience chamber congratulating Dru when Fazak unleashed his thunderbolt – but Thyla…

"That's right," said Doran, her glance and ear-flick suggesting I should be more careful. "Zarda told us."

"Zarda told us a lot of things," said Froma, looking across the smouldering fire toward Dru. "That doesn't make them true." Glancing down at her youngling, she murmured, "Sheathe your claws, Sarys."

"But Chiva bit me!"

"You wouldn't share!" Chiva's tail was quivering with indignation and hostility. She looked up at her dam as she added, "She found a creature washed up on the sand, and she ate it all herself."

"Did not."

"Did so."

"Did not."

Dru chimed in. "Yes you did, Sarys, though I told you not to."

"And why should I take any notice of you?" Sarys snapped her teeth in Dru's direction, obviously annoyed at being found out.

"Because he is going to be Prime one day," said Limar. "Vizan Saw it as well as Zarda – he's going to defeat the Koth."

"That doesn't seem very likely from where I'm sitting," said Froma, her scepticism carrying on the breeze along with the smoke from the fire. "All the same…" She paused to give Sarys a firm nip on the snout. "You shouldn't eat things you've picked up from the beach, Sarys. It might have made you ill."

"Would have served her right," Cavel muttered from my right, though fortunately he spoke too quietly for Froma to hear.

"I was hungry." Sarys was whimpering and rubbing her snout as she spoke, and Froma gave her a comforting lick.

"We are all hungry," she said, "which is why we should share with each other."

Doran turned her carry-pouch around to untie her cooking pot from the front strap. "It won't be long till we get more warmth from this fire," she said. "Why don't we make a start now on sharing our food?"

We all had similar items – dried meat, pasties, branmeal, roots, meat patties, and an assortment of herbs.

"The pasties need eating. They won't keep much longer even in this cold," I said, pulling one from my carry-pouch and sniffing for another.

"I doubt any of us will." Limar adjusted the blanket she and Dru were sitting on, so that part of it draped over their shoulders, oblivious to the glares she received from the other adults.

"We can always rely on you, Limar, for a note of cheer," said Doran. She had peeled off her foot-covers and smeared poultice onto her toes. Her feet looked fine to me, and I thought her fussing was an unnecessary waste of precious resources, though I said nothing, not wanting to alienate my friend more than I already had. In any case, she was still talking to Limar. "You were telling us just now about how Dru is going to defeat the Koth, so presumably he at least has a future."

"Doesn't mean we all do. I was talking to Rewsa…"

A chorus of groans drowned the rest of her words, which was probably just as well. The younglings though had already heard their share of Rewsa's miserable predictions. "She says we'll all die," Chiva whimpered. She stood upright, ears flattened, tail rigid with fear, and howled her misery. A heartbeat later, Sarys joined in. Cavel and Dru exchanged glances, then added their howls to the din.

"What's going on?"

It was Shaya. She was holding a makeshift spear, which looked to have been fashioned from a short vinebranch, and had her water flask slung over her shoulder. Her tail and ears signalled her exasperation, and the howling stopped instantly. "I know this is not a good place to be," she said, shifting her gaze from youngling to youngling, "but if we are careful and learn from each other, we will all stay safe." She waited for each youngling to dip an ear of acknowledgement, then looked from adult to adult as she went on: "That goes for their dams too. Doran, I would like you to show the others here how to dress a wound. Winan, you are a tunic-maker?"

"Yes." I smelled Winan's agitation, and wondered why she was clutching her carry-pouch as though to shield herself from an anticipated blow. "But I swear I didn't know anything about those new maroon tunics the Elite Guard were wearing."

Shaya flicked the remark away with a wave of her paw. "Hapak would have dealt with that himself, or asked someone he could trust to get those made. I simply wanted to know if you can weave."

Winan gestured toward her friend. "Froma is the weaver. I know enough to make minor repairs to a tunic if I have to, but mainly I just cut and bind —"

"But you do know how to weave?"

"Yes, but —"

"Good, that's fine. Froma." The smaller female had almost curled herself into a ball, and as she peeked up at Shaya, she reeked of trepidation. Shaya seemed oblivious to her own intimidating stance. "Do you know how to weave nets?"

"I learned from my dam when I was a youngling," said Froma, uncurling slightly, "but I specialised in weaving warm season tunics once I was apprenticed out to Saran's cluster as a half-grown."

"We don't need more tunics," said Shaya, planting the blunt end of her spear on the ground and leaning on it like a staff. "At least, not yet. But we will need nets. We'll need them to help us fish once some of us get back in the air, and we'll need them to ferry the wingless over the Ambit when we get there."

I had seen and treated many of the females when they had had their wings broken by the Elite Guard. Even if we reached the Ambit by the next moon, ready to cross to the Crimson Forest, I doubted they would all be able to fly across. Even if they could, how many nets would be needed for the wingless and the grounded? Far more than could be woven in the time we had, I was sure. I opened my mouth to say so, noticed Doran's glare, and clamped my jaw shut. A trader would not know about such things, and anyway, it was important that the others had a sense of purpose.

Doran turned her attention to our supper, poking at the fire's feeble flames with the sharp end of a cauldron-hook before sticking it into the soft soil and hanging her pan from it. "Everyone is exhausted, Shaya, and most of us ache from the walking. We need to eat before anyone does anything else."

"Of course," said Shaya, standing straight and pulling her spear from the ground. "Froma, Winan, once you've eaten I'd like you to show these younglings how to weave nets. Doran, perhaps you can show Thyla and Limar some basic healing remedies while they do that?"

Doran flicked an ear in acknowledgement, and I saw her whiskers twitch in the merest hint of amusement at the idea of teaching a Fate-seer about healing. Froma, though, had some objections:

"But I've not done any net-weaving for cycles! That's Rewsa's speciality – and Cavel and young Dru are not Artisans…"

"We don't have the luxury of assigning younglings to individual trades and skills," said Shaya. "We'll need all of them to learn something of every skill if we're to survive. They'll all need to hunt, and they'll all need to know how to make spears, healing remedies and nets, at the very least."

"Doesn't seem right," Froma grumbled. She twisted her left leg up and began to massage her foot, sending little clumps of sand and mud to the ground as she did so.

"None of this is right," snapped Limar. "I haven't even had a wingless youngling. I'm here just because Varna is my dam, and I was nest-nurse to Dru."

"None of us deserve to be here, Limar," Doran chided, stirring the pot and giving it a sniff.

"But since we are," said Shaya, ignoring Limar's bristling fur, "we all need to be useful." She jabbed the blunt end of her spear at the seafronds that made up our fire. "We barely have enough of these to last the night. Tomorrow, we'll need everyone to pick up seafronds as they find them, wet or not, and any reeds and twigs they might see. Otherwise we may have to put eighteen round each fire, and no-one will be warm enough."

"Not warm enough now," Limar muttered.

Winan's voice was louder: "We already have our carry-pouches to manage. Why do we all have to collect fuel?"

"Because we all like to be warm and fed," said Shaya, "and those who don't contribute something to burn should not have the benefit of the heat. I think that's fair, don't you?"

Without waiting for a reply, she picked up her spear and swept off toward the next group to give them the same message.

Somewhere in the distance I could hear Varna howling in pain.

The next four days and nights passed in the same way: effort, cramps and aches by day as we struggled on to another makeshift camp, then a beaker of something hot as the sun dropped, followed by an evening of concentration while we tried to teach and learn. At least I had no trouble with Doran's healing lessons, being already well-versed in such matters, but my attempts to sharpen a vinebranch into a spear almost cost me a finger.

The younglings had no such trouble, and I watched with envy as they huddled round the weavers, wood-shapers, and gatherers, ears and tails a-twitch with interest before they made their own first attempts at producing the items we needed. It was also the younglings who had the energy to search ahead for suitable camp sites, who gathered reeds for the net-weaving from the edge of the marsh, and who collected the biggest and straightest branches from the storm-driven detritus that littered the shore.

But our day-to-day progress was pathetic.

"I can't believe we haven't even reached the Cleft Rocks yet," I said to Doran as we approached the camp site on our sixth day of walking. "It's hardly a half-day's flight from the *Spirax*, but at the rate we're moving, it will be at least another two days before we get there."

Doran had her winter fur fluffed against the harsh wind that blew from the south, and she kept her head down, eyes fixed on the scattered rocks that lay half-buried along this part of the beach. "I don't think any of us can walk any faster."

I ignored the snap in her tone and said, "I wasn't suggesting that we should start running, or bounding about like the younglings do. It's just…" I looked ahead to where the Cleft Rocks jutted across the shoreline, their distinctive stripes smudged by distance and the spray from the waves that washed around them. With an effort, I resisted the temptation to look back over my shoulder at the silhouette of the *Spirax*. I knew without looking that it would still dominate the view, still look as though I could reach out and touch it, still be an easy flight if I chose to spread my wings and take to the air. I sighed. "It's disheartening. Even when we get to the Rocks, we'll hardly be halfway to the Ambit."

"I can't think that far ahead, Zar – I mean, Thyla." Doran glanced about to make sure no-one had overheard her slip, then went on: "I just take one step at a time, and think about how nice it will be to sit next to a warm fire at the end of the day. Then I worry about what we are going to eat. Beyond that, I don't have the energy to think."

There was a stray seafrond in our path, which those up ahead had missed, and I bent to retrieve it. Draping the frond over my carry-pouch, I straightened with a grunt and trudged on. Overhead, the light was fading, but the Great Spiral was not visible through the cloud. That night, we could not even find the space for one large camp site. Instead our fires, such as they were, spiralled around the shoulders of three different dunes. Dru bounded over as I looked for a place to sit. "Come with me, we have room by our fire."

I was not keen on the idea of spending more time with Limar than I had to, but there was something about the set of Dru's ears that told me he had something important to say.

As I spread my blanket and rummaged through my carry-pouch to see what I might contribute to the evening's meal, Limar flicked an ear to acknowledge me, then turned straight back to the three artisans on the opposite side of the fire and resumed her usual 'it's not fair' moan. I didn't know them, but gave them a sympathetic ear-flick as I added some dried meat to the pot and sat down. I had scattered some of my other food and belongings over my blanket while I searched for the meat, and as I began to put them back, I asked Dru to help. "What is it?" I murmured. "Have you Seen something?"

"Yes." He spoke equally quietly, and I had to swivel both my ears to hear him over Limar's self-pitying monologue. His talent for Seeing had been triggered when I had taken him to the Dream-cave moons ago, and had been kept secret to prevent him being marked as any more different than he already was. I suspected he would have made a better Fate-seer than me, but I was not able to give him the training he needed. In any case, his destiny lay in a different direction. He picked up a twist of herbs from the corner of my blanket, sniffed at them, and identified them correctly as camyl. As he dropped them into my carry-pouch, he whispered, "The Guardflight will come tomorrow."

The chill that iced down my back from wings to tail had nothing to do with the freezing conditions or the steady breeze.

"Will they find me?" I asked, once I felt able to speak. "Did you See?"

He shook his head, and his ears drooped a little as though he felt he had let me down. "The Vision stopped when they landed on the dune. I'm sorry, I don't know what will happen after that."

I stuffed the last of my things into my pouch and closed the flap, opened it again to pull out a spoon. "I knew they'd be coming, Dru, but I didn't know when. At least now I'll be prepared for the morning."

I spoke with much more confidence than I felt. Would the Guardflight – would Taral – recognise me? Would Doran tell them who I really was?

And if I was returned to the *Spirax*...what would Kalis do to me?

Four

"Guardflight! Coming this way!" Milat's fur and ears stood on end as she howled and pointed, her cry of alarm accompanied by a twitching tail and a half-extended wing as she hopped from foot to foot.

Damp sand twisted under my feet as I turned to search the sky to the south-west. A uniform backcloth of high grey cloud made it easy to pick out the red tunics of the flyers heading toward us. Nine of them, all with bows slung across their chests, wings beating steadily in a perfect V formation.

A paw squeezed my arm as Doran arrived beside me. "You said they'd come."

"Seven days. I was beginning to hope Kalis had forgotten me." I spiralled a paw over my pale-blue tunic and tugged at my fur, examining the dyed strands for signs of my natural mid-brown colour.

"Don't worry about that." Doran pointed along the beach. Several nineties of wingless younglings and their dams were strung out behind us – the younglings bounding and capering and checking every footstep for useful items, the adult females in small plodding groups. "None of the others have guessed who you are – why should the guardflight?"

"Because the guardflight will be looking for me."

Kalis had stopped listening to me moons ago, but he would be furious that I had not returned to my dwelling after requesting his permission to fly to the Dream-cave. He'd ignored my counsel in favour of Fazak's, but without a Fate-seer there would be no-one to perform the rituals and incantations, no-one to maintain the ceremonial traditions. And tradition, as I had reminded Doran days before, was important to Kalis. So important he had exiled the wingless on the strength of a long-forgotten scratching on an ancient record.

The guardflight circled lower, wings and tails angled for a swift descent, and I saw they were splitting into three groups, with Taral and his wingflyers heading for the reed-tufted sand-dunes ahead of us.

Milat's baying alarm spread as the females alerted each other, looking upward to point and setting up a howl that passed along the beach till the whole straggling line had become a turmoil of panic.

"Ellet, where's Ellet?" Rewsa wrung her paws as she scurried about looking for her youngling. "I must tell her to hide. It can't be good that they're coming after us."

Her wings flapped uselessly, and I noticed others doing the same. It would take another nineday at least for broken struts to begin to heal; at the moment the females were no more capable of flight than their hatchlings were.

A few spans from me, Shaya kept her own wings folded and ears upright as she called for calm. "There are only nine of them, stop panicking. If Kalis had wanted us killed, he'd have had it done before we left the Expanse."

"Maybe he's changed his mind," Limar called, her voice a bleat of alarm. "Maybe he didn't want us killed so close to the *Spirax* and the Tusk."

"We'll die!" howled Rewsa. "We'll all die!"

The cry began to spread along the line, and the smell of terror was palpable. The pups had stopped bounding about. Some had sticks or reeds in their paws, a few had gathered armfuls of seafronds, most had sand stuck to their paws and tunics; all of them were sniffing the wind, their ears flicking nervously as they listened to their dams' whimpering.

"Be quiet, Rewsa, you'll scare the younglings." Doran extended a wing as Cavel rushed over to her, and he dropped his gathered seafronds to clutch the tip as he looked toward the flyers. Dru, who had been sniffing at the ice-rimed reeds on the dune to our left, bounded across to me, ignoring Limar and his dam.

"I don't think the Guardflight will recognise you."

"Hush, Dru." I looked around to see whether anyone else had heard him, but the breeze had snatched his words away from the gathering crowd and no-one but Doran turned an ear. "Remember, no-one knows I'm here, except you and Doran."

I had no time to say more before the guardflight landed. They alighted in groups of three: some on the dune just ahead of us, some on the shingle that patched the beach, the last group at the far end of the line of females. The halt in our progress had allowed the stragglers to close up, and there was a growing crowd at the foot of the dune where the Guardflight Chief, Taral, stood with his wingflyers, Jisco and Veret. At sight of Taral, my tail gave an involuntary twitch. Sidling nearer the others, I rubbed my snout, smoothed the fur at my neck, and ducked my head.

"Zarda, when you came over to me on that first morning, *I* didn't recognise you," said Doran, her voice pitched low. "Stop worrying."

"When I found you, everyone had their attention on Shaya and Colex, and that terrible argument."

"It won't make any difference—"

"What won't make any difference?" Limar took a step or two closer, ears twitching, and I sent up a prayer to the Spiral that she hadn't heard my name. Even if she kept it from the guardflight – and I was not entirely sure that she would – it was better for the moment that no-one else knew my true identity.

"It won't make any difference what we say," said Doran. "The guardflight will do whatever it is they've come for. And I don't need reminding it was the Elite Guard who broke our wings – I don't doubt for a heartbeat that the guardflight would have done it if Kalis had told them to."

Kalis *had* told them to. Taral had come to my dwelling after the Prime had given him the order and confided it to me. I knew that the command had sickened him, but I knew too that he would have carried it out. *"If I don't do as I'm bid, he'll name another of the guardflight as Chief, and have my wings removed,"* he'd said, when I'd asked if he would obey the instruction. In the event, he hadn't had to. The Elite Guard had been formed, in secret, at Fazak's urging, and they had carried out the wing-breaking with a relish that had tainted the air they flew through.

"I think that if Kalis had wanted us killed, he'd have sent the Elite Guard," I said, drawing murmurs of agreement from everyone within earshot.

In the distance, Varna howled alone. Limar made a show of flattening her ears and muttered, "Perhaps they've come to put Varna-muz out of our misery."

"For the Spiral's sake, Limar, she's your dam! You might at least show her a little sympathy."

"If she wasn't my dam, I wouldn't be here. I've got no offspring, winged or otherwise – all I did was hatch from Varna's proving-egg."

I suspected she would have said more, but everyone fell silent as Taral half-extended his wings and raised his ears. "Females," he roared, his voice carrying easily over the wash of the waves on the shingle, "Zarda, the Fate-seer, is missing. Kalis has ordered the guardflight to search for her."

Doran took a step toward him, Cavel at her wingtip. "You can see she's not here, Taral. We have not seen her since she bade us farewell."

"Why are you looking for her here? Maybe she's tending a sick drax on the Expanse? Or has gone to the Dream-cave?" Limar moved to stand at Doran's right wingtip.

"Kalis gave her permission to go to the Dream-cave," said Veret, the scar on his snout livid through the long black strands of his winter fur, "but she has not returned. Kalis is concerned about her."

"Guardflyers are searching the Expanse," said Taral, his head moving from side to side slightly as he spoke, as though searching the groups for a particular snout. I opened the flap of my carry-pouch and pretended to search for something, as he went on: "Fazak suggested that we should also check to see if she was with you, given her sympathetic attitude towards the groundlings."

So Fazak was still tilting wings at the *Spirax*. Well, that was unlikely to stop overnight, but I had hoped that Kalis had regrets about his decision, regrets that might one day turn on the ambitious drax at his wingtip.

"You can see she's not here." Shaya moved along the sand, putting herself between the guardflight chief and the exiles. She hefted her roughly-fashioned spear, and I hoped she was not about to make some foolish gesture with it. "You must have seen that, even before you landed. Now, are you going to stand there in our way, or are you going to go back to report what you've found?"

Turning my head a little, to avoid Taral's searching gaze, I saw that the six other guardflight were moving among the crowd, sniffing.

"Zarda's clever," said Taral. Hearing the note of admiration in his voice, I almost dropped my carry-pouch as I swung my head up in surprise. "She wouldn't need the Sight to know we'd be looking for a drax in a black tunic. I'm sure she's wearing a different colour now." He looked right at me as he went on: "Wherever she might be."

With that, he stalked down the dune, flanked by Jisco and Veret, sand shifting and sliding beneath their feet. As they moved toward our group, Cavel let go of Doran's wing and marched to meet them. "I'm hungry," he announced, his voice carrying clear and high above the wash of the waves. "Did you bring any food?"

Jisco and Veret had the grace to look ashamed, rubbing their snouts and twitching their ears like naughty nestlings caught licking the nut-syrup spoon. Taral made a show of looking around and sniffing at us, as though still searching for Zarda the Fate-seer. Perhaps he was.

"Come away, Cavel!" Doran hurried over to the youngling, nipped his snout, and hauled him away from the guardflyers, ignoring his whimpers. "You do not demand food from others – ever! How many times have I told you?"

Cavel began to howl, and several other younglings joined in, all protesting that they were hungry.

"Keep looking!" Taral was close enough to me that I could smell his own discomfort, but his snarl sounded genuine enough and Jisco and Veret hurried to comply. My fur stood on end, and I pawed at it in an effort to look less alarmed, willing my ears to an angle that didn't signal fear and distress. My unbroken wings trembled with the urge to take flight, but that would give me away in a wingbeat. I had to stay where I was. I had to trust that the blue tunic and dyed russet fur would be enough.

Taral stood right in front of me, his nose busy as he sniffed for my scent. "What is it I can smell?" he said. "Camyl?"

It was kestox – the leaves I'd pulped to rub on my fur – but I wasn't about to say so. "Camyl. Yes. The healers put a little on our wings each day to help them heal."

"I see." Taral rested a paw on the bow that was slung across his chest and moved alongside me. I thought he was satisfied with my answer and was strolling away, but to my horror, I realised he was sauntering around me. "The healers are doing a good job," he said, as he returned to stand snout to snout with me. "I can't even see where your wings are broken."

"I've been fortunate."

Or had I?

"I thought I knew all the Traders, but I don't recognise you at all." Taral scratched at his beard as he spoke, his ears twitching with curiosity.

"My name's Thyla," I ventured, "from the south-eastern Traders' cluster."

He looked around and over my head. "Where's your youngling?"

"His sire took him away when he hatched." I set my ears to a sorrowful droop and added a whimper for good measure. "I never saw him again. I help to look after Dru now – his dam can't even look to herself yet."

A howl drifted from the sand where Varna had slumped, reinforcing my point.

"So I can hear." Taral's whiskers twitched, and I saw him glance at my carry-pouch. My fur stuck up all over as I realised my mistake: it was the pouch I'd used when we took Vizan to his last nest. A pouch that still bore the faded stain of Vizan's blood.

A pouch that Taral couldn't fail to recognise as belonging to Zarda the Fate-seer.

Five

I hugged the pouch to my chest, as though it could protect me from my own foolishness. Idiot that I was! I'd brought it with me because it was the biggest pouch I possessed, but I should have thought, should have realised...

Taral stepped back. His physical demeanour had not changed – he still looked determined, imposing, a perfect example of a drax on a quest for his Prime, but I was close enough to notice that his scent did not match his appearance. Instead, I detected sorrow, sympathy – perhaps even friendship. And did I imagine that brief twitch of his whiskers? "Any sign of her?" he barked, as Jisco, Veret, and the rest moved through the knots of grumbling females.

"Nothing."

"None."

"I know the drax in this group. She's not here."

"Then Veret and Jisco will go back and report." Taral moved away from me as he spoke, leading his guardflyers back along the sand and halfway up the dune, where he stopped and turned to look back at us.

I put my carry-pouch down and sat on it, too astonished and relieved to stand. Taral had recognised me for who I was, I was sure of it. Yet he'd pretended to believe my story. More than that, he'd led the other guardflight away, and was sending his wingflyers to tell Kalis that I'd not been found.

As Jisco and Veret took off in a clatter of wingbeats, Taral raised his voice to issue another statement, his words loud enough to be heard by everyone clustered at the base of the dune he stood on. "We'll fly on along the coast as far as the Ambit Estuary. It's possible Zarda is up ahead somewhere. We'll also check to see if she's with the group crossing the Deadlands."

There were gasps from everyone within earshot, and a tumble of questions – "They're safe?" – "Maybe we should have gone with them?" – "How far have they got?"

I caught a whiff of Shaya's astonishment as she moved to the base of the dune and looked up at Taral. "They're still alive?"

Taral paused before replying, nose raised to sniff the wind that bore the unmistakeable odour of hope – and a certain amount of irritation, which I was sure came from those who thought Colex had had the right idea. He coughed, put his paws behind his back, and rocked on his heels. "Some of them are alive," he said, his voice loud enough to carry over Shaya's head, "but I can't say how much longer they'll last. They've lost half their numbers already." He waited while the whimpers and howls died away, spiralled a paw over his tunic, and went on: "They took a foolish course. I doubt Zarda would have travelled with them – but we will make sure." He spread his wings and paused again for a moment. "If she's still on the Expanse, we'll find her. There are guardflight in the air above the Manybend night and day, so if she tries to join you, we'll intercept her."

"Why would anyone want to join us?" Doran called. "Would *you*?"

For answer, Taral turned into the wind, flapped his wings and took off, his patrol following suit with not a backward glance between them.

I flattened my ears against the noise as females and younglings alike began to chatter. The overwhelming scent of relief mingled with sorrow washed along the beach like an onrushing wave, and I took a moment to smooth my fur and set my tail to a less alarmed angle.

Dru jumped up and down in front of me, and I dipped my head and swivelled my ears to catch his exultant whisper: "You fooled them, Zarda!"

"No. I didn't." I straightened, spiralling a paw across my tunic, and raised my head to watch the guardflight's steady progress north. They would be at the Ambit by sunset. Even allowing for a diversion over the Deadlands to check on Colex and her remaining group, they could be home on Guardflight Rock by moon zenith.

Home.

I thought again of my cosy dwelling, the fire in the hearth, the scent of the herbs that hung from the roof-stones, the comfortable nest. All I needed to do was stretch my wings and...

"Thyla? Are you quite well? Shall I call a healer?" I turned to find Shaya at my wingtip, ears twitching, nose busy, and I wondered how long she'd been standing there, and whether she had overheard Dru's use of my real name.

I waved a dismissive paw. "I was just thinking that those guardflight will be back in their own nests before dawn. I wish we could all do the same."

"Shaya-muz?" Ravar tugged at the hem of his dam's tunic, and Shaya lost interest in me, turning away to deal with her youngling.

Limar, unfortunately, had no such distraction, and her interest had clearly been aroused by Dru's actions in seeking me out. She'd followed him through the crowd, and even if she'd not overheard what he said, she could not have failed to hear Shaya questioning me. Her nose was busy, testing my scent, her ears twitching with curiosity. Or was it suspicion? "What are you doing over here with a trader, Dru?" Her voice was edged with contempt. "And why the excitement? Taral's just told us that drax have died in the Deadlands, but I can smell from here that you're pleased about something."

"Thyla was kind to me last night when we shared a fire," said Dru, ears set to full sincerity. "I thought she might have been scared when the Guardflight came."

"So you came to make sure she was alright?" Limar reeked of doubt, and her tail swished alarmingly as she turned to me. "Why did Taral single you out? He didn't question anyone else that thoroughly."

I managed to shrug a shoulder and flicked an ear to indicate that I had no idea. "You'd have to ask Taral." Lifting my carry-pouch, I fiddled with the straps, a hint that the conversation had ended. Perhaps it didn't matter whether Shaya or Limar discovered me; perhaps it wouldn't matter if they told everyone else. But I couldn't be sure that the guardflight would not come back, or that Kalis wouldn't send the Elite Guard next. If that happened, then the fewer drax who knew my identity, the safer I would be.

Shaya was still preoccupied with Ravar, who seemed to have found something in the sand which he wanted her to identify; but Limar was still staring at me, tail twitching, and it was clear she wasn't happy with the answers I'd given. Fortunately for me, Doran had spotted the danger and hurried over. "Ah, Shaya, Limar. Since we're stopped anyway, can we have a rest here and a cud-chew?"

"I don't want a cud-chew. I'm *hungry!*" Ravar, thank the Spiral, threw down whatever it was he had found and set up a wail that was taken up by the other younglings.

"I'm tired." Cavel kicked at the sea-fronds he had dropped and raised his snout in a high-pitched yowl. "I want to go *home!*"

As the howling spread through the groups of younglings – and some of their dams – I was grateful for the distraction, but had to flatten my ears against the racket. Clearly it was going to be a long, long day – and the most depressing aspect of it was that we had been walking for over six days, but the guardflight had caught up with us in less than a half-day's flight.

We had barely moved from where we started.

"I tell you, he recognised me."

Doran and I walked along damp sand, a little apart from the nearest group. The rattle of wave-washed shingle and the slap of wind-snapped tunics made it difficult for anyone to overhear us, but all the same I kept my voice low, and both Doran's ears swivelled my way as I spoke.

Her snuffle of amusement perplexed me and her next words turned the puzzlement to astonishment: "Well, I knew you liked the smell of him, but I hadn't realised it was mutual."

My tail twitched with embarrassment. "Don't be silly."

She waved a paw, dismissing my objection, and continued as though I hadn't spoken, "Let's hope for both your sakes that that's the last time Kalis sends guards after us." She dipped her head and waggled her ears in apology as she added, "I shouldn't have pressed you about putting on your black tunic. If you had, Taral wouldn't have been able to ignore it and you'd be halfway back to the *Spirax* by now." She paused, and then said, "Do you think they'll come back?"

"You mean, do I think it's safe to put my Fate-seer's tunic on?" I raised a paw to finger the badge of office I had pinned inside the top of my pale-blue tunic. "No, it's not safe. Not while we're within sight of the *Spirax*, and certainly not while they can reach us so quickly."

A small heap of green bubblefrond lay on the shingle where the waves had left it, and I hurried to pick it up before anyone else snatched it. It was as damp as our spirits and would make loud popping noises as it heated and burned, but we couldn't afford to be choosy. Wrinkling my snout against the smell, I added it to the single seafrond I had already collected that morning, and waited for Doran to catch up. "Kalis won't stop looking for me after a single search," I said. "If he sends the Elite next time, it might be a different story."

Doran looked around, eyes, ears, and nose all busy as she searched for one particular female. "Limar," she said, turning her attention back to me, satisfied that even Limar's twitching ears couldn't overhear. "You think she suspects?"

"I don't know. She and Shaya were both close by when Dru said my name, and they both asked questions."

She grunted. "Shaya's a hunter. It she sees a track or smells prey, she'll close in, but she won't fly to conclusions without evidence. Limar, on the other hand..." A snort. "We both know that one won't need facts to form an opinion."

We'd strayed too far down the beach, and both jumped sideways as icy water washed over our feet. "The tide's coming in." I eyed the high-water mark where it clung damply to the base of the dunes. "We'll need to get onto the dunes again soon."

"Or over them. If it's not too marshy on the other side."

"Let's go and see. The dunes aren't too high here, I think we can get to the top without too much trouble."

Our legs ached a little less each day as we began to grow accustomed to the walking, but even so it was an effort to climb the soft, yielding slopes of the dune.

At the top I turned, drawing in great gulps of air, and looked back along the beach. Behind us, the line straggled for the best part of ninety spans. The females waddled awkwardly with their heavy packs, some of them still dragging torn wings. They all had their heads down, winter fur puffed against the chill wind, which carried the scent of fatigue and worry.

The younglings had already recovered from their scare. A few of the youngest huddled close to their dams, but many of the older ones had somehow found the energy to leap on ahead again, looking for seafronds and twigs, and searching for a place for us to camp. Their bounding hops carried them further than I could jump with my wings folded, and they were constantly finding some new thing to be curious about, to stop and poke at with sticks, to point at, to show one another. Scarce wonder we were still so close to what had once been home.

"If we're going to make any progress, we'll have to move faster," I said to Doran, who had waited beside me. "We can't keep dawdling along like this, especially when there's a storm coming."

Doran had also scented the change in the wind. "It's coming in over the ocean," she said, indicating the darker clouds building on the south-eastern horizon.

"We'll need shelter."

"Yes, and it'll have to be more substantial than a makeshift nest and a blanket." Doran rubbed at the fur on her arms, doubtless remembering the past few nights, when winter fur and a fire had barely kept the chill at bay. "Could we make it to the Cleft Rocks, do you think? They'd keep the worst of the wind off, and we could use the blankets to cover our heads against the snow."

I endeavoured to call to mind the route we would take. In the air, it was a short, straight flight to the Cleft Rocks, and the sand beneath my wings had always appeared to me to follow the same easy line. But on foot, it was a different matter. The beach ran northward on a straight enough course, but there were dips, soft sand, the dunes, and half-buried rocks to negotiate – not to mention the tide. When the waves washed in, we had to climb onto the dunes or over them, and the soft sand and steep inclines slowed our progress almost to a halt. Immediately south of the Cleft Rocks, the dunes would give way to steep cliffs and shallow bays, which we would somehow need to negotiate. I had rarely flown beyond the Rocks, but I had a vague recollection of crags and rocky promontories lining the shoreline further north. "I doubt we'll reach the Rocks even by tomorrow's sunset, let alone today's." Where else might give us the shelter we needed? When I flew, I had never had to take much notice of the coast beneath me; I remembered there were stands of seavine here and there between the dunes, but otherwise I had no idea what might lie in our way.

"There's Shaya," said Doran, pointing. "If anyone knows what's ahead of us, the hunters will."

Even on foot, Shaya had a way of moving that spoke of searching alertness. She kept her makeshift spear ready, as all the hunters now did, but I had not yet seen any of them find anything to use them on. "Too many footsteps," Shaya had grumbled, when I'd asked her about it the previous day, "making far too much noise. And none of us can move fast enough to catch anything while we're stuck here on the ground."

As she climbed the dune toward us, Shaya used her spear to point at the gathering stormclouds. "That's going to be nasty. There's a stand of seavines a few dunes further on, but we'll need to hurry if we're all to get there before the storm reaches us."

Doran and I both dipped an ear in acknowledgement. "If the threat of getting caught in a blizzard doesn't get them all moving, nothing will."

Shaya extended her unbroken wing and raised her spear to summon the other hunters, then set them scurrying along the line, to encourage everyone to try to move just a little faster:

"Let's see how far we can get before the storm sets in."

"Do you want to be out in the open when it hits?"

"Come on, it's not far. We can shelter under seavines for the night if we hurry."

Dru, Cavel, and the younglings bounded on ahead, excited to be the first to find the vines. Doran hurried after them, anxious that they didn't damage themselves in their enthusiasm, while I went in the opposite direction to find Varna, who was right at the back of our band of exiles. Her ears drooped, she smelled miserable, and her head swayed from side to side in distress. I didn't need the Sight to sense her ongoing pain and misery.

"I'm sorry you're feeling so wretched, Varna," I said, matching my pace to hers. "Kalis was wrong to punish you as he did."

"Right or wrong is irrelevant." She snuffled, her ears limp against the sides of her head. "It's not just the physical pain. That will pass and I can bear it with the help of the salves that the healers put on. But every female who has produced a wingless offspring blames herself – you know that. Who knows, perhaps we *are* guilty of something the Spiral is punishing us for."

"I don't believe that. Why would the Spiral want your wings removed for catching a Sickness? Kalis—"

"Kalis needed a healthy heir and I failed him." She looked up from the tracks in the sand where nineties of clawed feet had trodden, and sniffed the air, which was now saturated with the odour of the oncoming storm. She pointed ahead to where Dru stood at the top of a dune, his outline blurred by distance and the dampness that now hung in the air. "I failed Dru, too. Look how he likes to lead, standing up there, encouraging everyone. He would have made a great Prime if only—"

"I'm sure Dru will prove his worth," I insisted. I almost spoke of 'my' Vision, but caught myself in time. "Remember what the Fate-seers said – that he'll lead the Drax to victory over the Koth." I picked my way round a weed-covered rock, and angled my ears and whiskers to indicate my uncertainty. "The Spiral alone knows how that will be accomplished, but I believe it will unfold as the Fate-seers said. It must."

Varna did not look up again. "If the Spiral wills it," she muttered.

To our right, grey waves heaved themselves into white-topped rollers that flung themselves onto the sand. They roared up the beach, throwing a fine spray over my head, and my fur prickled with anxiety as I realised the storm was almost upon us. Ahead of me, several nines of other stragglers shuffled on, their ears signalling alarm though their tails dragged in the sand, a sign of how exhausted they were. "Faster, everyone!" I called. "Let's get to shelter!" I held out a paw, an offer of assistance for Varna to take.

For a beat or two, she ignored me, and I feared that she was too far sunk in despair to take even my meagre offer of help. I watched as those ahead of us quickened their pace from a shuffle to a plod, and clambered up the dunes with grunts of determination.

"Come on, Varna. Don't let Kalis win."

An ice-cold raindrop splashed onto my nose, making me flinch and shake my head. Varna did the same as the storm's vanguard sent out a spatter of heavy droplets.

She shook herself again, though this time it had nothing to do with being wet, and after another beat, her ears nudged upward a little. They were far from upright, but the hopeless droop had gone.

"The storm's coming," she said, as though she'd just noticed. She reached for my paw...

Water. Tumbling, churning, choking. A glimpse of riverbank sandstone, reached for, lost as the current sweeps on...

Varna's paw was cold in mine. She stared down at me, where I'd dropped to my knees, and her free paw tugged at the strands of fur on my arm, which were standing on end. "You're Zarda."

It wasn't a question and there seemed little point in trying to deny it. I clambered to my feet, brushing damp sand from my legs. I checked to see if anyone else had noticed my collapse, but those ahead of us were intent on dragging weary feet past the dunes, making for the dip ahead where we could pass between them to the ground beyond. None were looking back. I breathed a silent prayer of thanks for that at least, and turned my attention to Varna. "Yes," I said, "I'm Zarda, but no-one knows except Doran and Dru."

"And now me."

I dipped an ear. Would she tell others? Or would my secret be safe?

"What did you See?"

"Water. The Ambit river, perhaps. Nothing helpful." I thought it best not to add that Varna had appeared to be drowning in it. She was depressed enough already.

She grunted and shrugged a shoulder to indicate that she didn't care. "We ought to just lie on the dunes and let the storm do its worst," she said. "The river, the Forest, the creatures that live in it – they'll kill us all anyway sooner or later. Why would you want to be part of this?"

A familiar voice called from the slopes of the dune we were struggling towards. "Varna-muz! Come on! Thyla, quick, we found the seavines."

"There's your answer." I extended a wing to let Dru know we'd heard him, and took a step, hoping Varna would follow. The rain was getting heavier and turning to sleet. "My Visions aren't always clear, Varna, but the one I shared with Vizan, the one that Saw Dru defeating the Koth, it hasn't changed. Your youngling is important. He needs guidance, he needs a Fate-seer – and he needs his dam. Are you coming?"

With a sigh and a roll of her wingless shoulders, Varna began to move, her pace a little quicker, a little more determined than before. "I'm coming – Thyla."

My legs were still unused to the amount of work the sand and the dunes gave them, and they shook with strain as Varna and I crested the last rise. After a final stagger down the western slope, the dunes gave way to low mounds of scrubby reeds, where the sand beneath our feet was dark with mud from the Deadland swamps. Varna stopped as her feet sank into the soft ground and gazed at the thicket of seavines up ahead. They reared skyward, their fronds writhing like torn tunics in the wind, several spans above the heads of the drax who were scurrying beneath them.

"Come on, Varna, we're nearly there. Another ninety steps and we can rest, get out of this snow."

The heavy drops that had announced the storm had given way to fat flakes, which were already beginning to settle. It wasn't falling heavily enough to penetrate our tunics or our winter fur, but a glance at the sky and a sniff of the breeze told me that there was worse to come.

The distance was more than double the steps I'd told Varna, but with a goal in sight we pushed throbbing limbs over squelching earth and staggered past the outlying vines.

I'd seen seavines from the air, and had assumed that their trunks were the same sturdy type as the orenvines, but as we reached the saplings at the edge of the grove, I saw that a few paw-widths above ground the trunks split into nines of twisting branches, twining around each other as they grew. Flexing and creaking as they swayed, they took the edge from the wind and snow, but any thought of finding a half-decent place to nest for the night was banished as soon as I saw the chaos ahead of me. Shaya was in the middle of the vines, barking advice that few seemed to be heeding. After the discipline of the last six days and nights, order had disintegrated as the storm swept in. Blankets were being snatched, younglings howled, pots clanked, females argued about who had claimed the best spots – and through it all threaded the constant snap of the fronds overhead and the deepening rumble of the wind that drove them.

Varna sighed, and squatted down with her back against the first substantial vine we reached. Her ears were drooping again, and she may have whimpered but it was impossible to be sure with all the noise going on. "I'll try to sort this out," I said, gesturing at the disorder, "then I'll get us something to eat."

Pushing my way through the squabbling females, closing ears and nostrils to the sounds and smells of fear and nervous irritation, I made my way towards Shaya. Twigs snapped under my feet, my tunic snagged on a twist of broken vinebranch that jutted awkwardly from a dead trunk, and I cursed as I stepped in a patch of sticky, malodorous mud. As I reached Shaya's side, I raised my voice over the noise of the wind and the protesting voices, and roared, "We should put the younglings in the middle!"

"That's what I keep trying to tell them!" Shaya's voice was impatient. "Milat and the other hunters are trying to put together some windbreaks with the weavers. See if you can make these idiots understand!"

Cursing to myself, I stomped toward the nearest group, and I recognised the tiny female, who looked as though she might blow away with the next gust, and the large russet-furred female she was barking at. "Froma, Winan, put the younglings in the middle where they'll be more sheltered."

Teeth snapped as both of them turned their hostility on me. "Go away, Thyla, you've no business interfering. This is between artisans."

"This concerns everybody!" Anger gave an edge to my voice, and heads turned as those nearby heard me. "Look at us." I was pointing and pacing as I roared, hoping that my words would carry through the vines. "Look at us, arguing between ourselves over a patch of damp leaves, arguing about who has the least-wet spot to shelter in. There are no clusters out here – we're all one cluster, thanks to Kalis – and one patch of leaf-mould is the same as the next. If we're to survive, we must start looking out for each other, as well as learning from each other. Above all, we have to keep the younglings safe. Now, put them in the centre of the grove, as Shaya has been telling you to do, where it's warmest."

I saw that Shaya had stepped away from the middle of the vines, leaving Ravar behind, bundled up in a blanket. Some of the healers, Doran among them, heard us at last, and took up the cry, herding their own younglings into the relative safety of the centre of the grove, and calling to others to do the same. As the message began to spread, I went to find Milat, interested to find out what Shaya had meant by 'windbreaks', and anxious to lend a paw if I was able. "*Never stop learning,*" Vizan had told me. Well, there would doubtless be much to discover on this journey!

I found two of the hunters, Milat and Azmit, with Rewsa and a nine of other artisans. The hunters were cutting finger-thin branches from the swaying vines, which the others were using to weave into rough squares. One glance told me that I could do nothing but get in the way of the artisans, who were pushing the cut stems back and forth, in and out of each other with a speed and skill I had no hope of matching.

"We've got one ready," Rewsa called, noticing my hesitation. "You can help Hariz tie it to the vinetrunks."

She pointed at a female with pale fur and black ears, whose black-and-green tunic indicated she was a Healer. Barking for help, she was trying to lift the first of the woven hurdles into place. I saw at once how tying the woven squares to the outermost vines might help to keep the worst of the wind's fury from blowing through the copse, but the one Hariz held seemed to take on a life of its own as it flapped and twisted in her paws. Grabbing a corner, I pressed it against the nearest trunk and leaned on it while Hariz secured it top and bottom with a length of twine.

"Look out!"

The wind plucked a half-finished hurdle from the paws of those working on it, and flung it into the air like a leaf. In moments it was over the vines and away, fortunately without hitting anyone on the way. I'd let go of the unsecured end of the hurdle and it tossed about wildly. I made a grab for it, tripping on a root and almost pulling the whole thing loose as I fell. My snout, my paws, and my feet were all numb, and it hurt to curl my fingers around the edge of the hurdle as I held it firm.

Snow blustered about us, making my eyes and ears sting. Clumped flakes swirled in stinging spatters, sticking to our fur, while the hurdle heaved and pulled beneath my paws like a live thing.

We managed to fix just three hurdles – 'windbreaks' – between the vines before Milat called a halt. "This wind is vicious," she called, "and the snow's getting worse. We'll all get icenipped fingers and toes if we don't get under the vines."

There wasn't much room left, and those who were already bundled in blankets grumbled as we tucked ourselves between them, keeping close together for warmth. By the time my numb fingers had unrolled my blanket, it was dark.

Sparks flew from a firestick somewhere to my left, and I heard Shaya bark, "No fires! Do you want to burn the grove down around us?"

There were no more sparks, though I doubted anything would catch light anyway. Sheltered though we were, flurries of snow still found their way through the fronds and trunks and hurdles, dampening fur, blankets, and spirits as it fell. Chewing on a cold and rather squashed pattie, which I shared with Varna, I tried to distract myself from the drips and the draughts by identifying the smells that carried from the Deadlands: decay, slime, a hint of wet moss – but they were overwhelmed by the salt smell the storm carried with it.

"It's getting worse." Doran, who I had thought was dozing nearby, tugged her blanket closer and wriggled about, presumably searching in vain for a dryer spot.

"There's nothing more we can do. We'll just have to wait it out."

Sleep became impossible. Ice-cold drips became runnels of water, wind-flung leaves and twigs became weapons to sting snouts and ears, and the wind…

The wind did not so much howl or roar as rumble, like trapped thunder. As though the noise was not enough, the constant anxiety kept me awake – waiting for the wind to triumph against our inadequate shelter, listening for the branches to groan and snap. I lay cowering under my blankets, wondering when the vines would stop bending and start falling – around us, on us? Would they be picked up and blown beyond the Deadlands? Once in a while there would be a lull in the storm's ferocity, a blessed moment of tranquility in which the entire grove seemed to sigh with relief, but then the rumble would begin again, signalling that our ordeal wasn't over. The rumble would become an angry growl, slamming against the vines as though in a fury that it was being thwarted. Something cracked overhead, and I covered my head with my paws, waiting for the smash and the howls, but the wind must have snatched the branch and flung it away. The crash, when it came, was muffled and distant, but none of us voiced what we were doubtless all thinking: that the next one might fall on our heads. Snow crept through shredded fronds and lashing branches, settling against sodden blankets and vinetrunks. The Great Spiral had never seemed so remote, so unreachable, but beneath my blanket my right paw spiralled endlessly across my tunic as I prayed for the wind to subside, while my left paw clenched in rage at the storm for making me feel so helpless.

And then, at last, the buffeting gradually decreased, the snow eased and the pauses between the worst of the gusts grew longer.

I began to doze, fitfully, my rest disturbed by the unfamiliar, uncomfortable ground, the noise of the wind, and the cries from some of the younglings. When I did finally manage to sleep, my dream was of Dru. He was clad in the heir's cream tunic, and this was a different Vision to any I'd Seen before. Instead of snow, I Saw zaxel-strewn black rock, and instead of a banner of triumph, he had wings in his hands.

Severed wings. Covered in blood.

Six

I came to with a start, my fur raised and lips drawn back in a
snarl. It took me a moment to remember where I was. Then
reality set in with the dawn light, and I pushed my soaked
blanket away and sat up, running a paw down the front of my
tunic in a vain effort to smooth the creases and remove the
smudges of mulch and mud.

The storm had subsided. Overhead, ragged vineleaves and torn
clouds allowed glimpses of the Great Spiral, its lights fading as
the sky lightened to the mauves and purples of sunrise. My
shoulder was cold and wet where it had been pressed against the
leaf-mould; my tunic and fur were damp. Water dripped from the
fronds and branches overhead, hitting the saturated ground with a
sound like a thousand distant wingbeats.

Here and there, snow patched the glade, some of it moving
slightly as the drax beneath it breathed steadily in the deep
unknowing grasp of exhausted sleep. The smell of wet blankets
and damp fur mingled with the odour of sodden leaves, sand, and

salt air. Somewhere beyond the vines a corvil screeched once and was silent, likely a victim of one of the myriad hazards that lay in the Deadlands. I thought of Colex and the others who had ventured that way, and wondered if any of them had survived the storm, knowing they were probably all lying dead in the swamp.

No-one else appeared to be awake, so I picked up my blanket and carry-pouch, making my way out of the grove and over the dunes to the beach. Soaking mulch, snow, and wet sand made it easy to move quietly, but meant that it would be impossible to find anything dry enough to start a fire.

The tide was retreating, revealing a line of rocks and boulders that marked the bottom of a steep rise. There was no beach beyond this point and no dunes, just cliffs and boulders, crags and stones, till we reached the Cleft Rocks. Beyond them lay a series of bays and promontories, which eventually curved eastward along the Ambit peninsula, but I'd rarely had the need to fly that way. Would we be better off moving inland from the Cleft Rocks? Heading along the Ambit peninsula would take us a long way from the estuary's northern shore, and far from anything else. But to strike inland and risk the Deadlands…it was an impossible choice, and not one any of us could make alone.

I looked for somewhere to dry my blanket, but the dunes were covered with caps of fresh snow, mountains in miniature, their lower slopes waterlogged and clinging underfoot. I draped my blanket over a rock, though I had no hope of it drying in the weak sunlight and still air, placed my pouch beside it, and walked down the beach to get a drink.

The sea was so cold as it washed over my feet that it made my legs cramp, but at least it was calm and there was nothing dripping down my neck. I slaked my thirst, filled my flask, and then moved back up the damp sand, still vainly hoping to find something to burn. Broken twigs and two or three large branches were scattered about, but they looked wetter than I did. Leaving my blanket and pouch where they lay, I made my way back to the grove. The new snow had found roots to settle and drift against, the white patches stark against the grey trunks and black leaf-mould. Perhaps there would be some dry fragments of twig beneath the mulch, or where we had slept? If there was anything dry at all, it would be underneath the spots where we had spent the night. After the relative brightness of the beach, I should have switched to night vision when I went back under the vines. I didn't, and paid for my foolishness when I tripped on a root and fell in an undignified heap.

"Are you alright?"

"Fine." I struggled to my feet, brushing bits of damp leaf from my tunic, and looked up to find Shaya moving through the vines toward me. Her steps were light, so quiet that any noise she made was drowned beneath the quiet wash of the waves beyond the dunes. "I didn't know you were there." I gave an exaggerated sniff. "Didn't even smell you."

She dipped an ear, pleased, and probably amused by my clumsiness, though she was too polite to snuffle about it. "When we hunt ground animals, we don't want to warn them they're being hunted – they can be swifter than you'd think. We learn to step softly, keep to cover, approach from upwind. Simple when you know how." She held out a paw, which clutched short stalks of zaxel. "So is learning to keep a little dry kindling in your pouch."

I flicked my ears in acknowledgement and relief. "I was about to start burrowing under the mulch."

This time she did snuffle. "So I saw." While I rubbed a paw over my whiskers and my tail twitched with embarrassment, Shaya kicked at the root I'd tripped over. It wasn't a root, I realised, it was another fallen branch. Half a span long and a little thicker than my fingers, its ragged end bore testimony to the strain that had snapped it from the vine last night. "Once it's dried out and shaped, that would make a perfect bow," she said, "and there are lots of smaller branches that would make good arrows. But we don't have any Guardflight with us to wield them, or to teach the rest of us how. All their females died of the Sickness or..." *or mysteriously disappeared overnight, along with their wingless pups, as Taral's nest-mate had done.* Shaya didn't finish the observation. She didn't need to. With a sigh, she moved past me and hopped carefully over the branch. "Would you collect up some of these small twigs? We can add them to the kindling. They'll burn readily enough once the zaxel catches."

Moving with a quiet grace that I knew would forever be beyond me, she stepped on to the sand, ears alert, snout raised to sniff, her head swivelling right to left to pick out the best spot to set her fire.

I bent to pick up the broken branch, and weighed it in my paw, then set it on its unbroken end against the nearest vinetrunk. Shaya was wrong. We did have someone with us who knew how to wield a bow and arrows, someone who had once been a member of the guardflight, till she had hatched her proving-egg and moved to the *Spirax*. But, after my conversation with her the previous day, seeing and sensing her pain and despair, could I – could anyone – persuade her to help us?

"I can't do it. Even if I weren't in agony, it's been cycles since I used a bow."

"But you must remember the basics, Varna, surely?"

Varna sat slumped on the damp sand, head down, her twitching tail a constant reminder of her pain and distress. I stood facing her, Dru at my side, my back to a fire that put out a lot of smoke and little heat, my blanket rescued from its rock and draped across my shoulders in an attempt to get it dry. Along the beach, at the foot of the dunes we had hurried past the previous day, nines of fires had been lit from the flames Shaya had started. Each one sputtered and smoked, and each one was surrounded by younglings nibbling cold food, their tunics dripping as they dried. Their dams stood behind them, many with damp bedding over their shoulders. There wasn't enough breeze even to stir the edges of the blankets, and though the early sunshine had disappeared behind a bank of pale cloud, there was no scent of oncoming rain or snow. Low-tide waves slopped lazily against the shingle further down the beach, as though exhausted from beating themselves against sand and rocks the previous night.

"You do remember how, Varna-muz." Dru dipped his ears respectfully as he quietly contradicted his dam, stepping closer to her to place a paw on her arm. He gave her snout a lick and murmured, "You taught me in the nursery chamber."

"It's something a Prime should know. Primes and guardflight."

So this wasn't about her pain or her inability to remember at all! It was about tradition. "We had to leave all that behind in the *Spirax* and on the Expanse, Varna." I raised an arm to gesture around and almost dropped my blanket on to the fire. I pulled it back round my shoulders, held it securely with one paw, and waved the other again. "Look around. Everyone has gathered twigs and seafronds for the fires, everyone is learning skills that will be useful on the journey. Rewsa and Froma over there are teaching others how to weave nets. The hunters are learning how to treat cuts and scrapes. The wood-shapers are showing us how to sharpen branches into spears, and all the younglings are learning how to use them. If we are going to survive, Varna, if you hope and believe that Dru will live to fulfil his destiny, then help us – help *him*."

She looked up, as though seeking guidance from the Spiral itself. Dru gave her another lick and her ears responded. They angled upwards no more than a finger-width, but at least they indicated that her mood had improved, even if it was so slight as to be almost imperceptible.

"Alright." Her voice was a growl, her tail still twitched with pain, and she ground the words out past clenched teeth that she doubtless wanted to clamp around my snout. "I don't like the idea, but then I don't like any of this – and you're right. There's a good chance we'll starve if we don't all learn to hunt and kill." She pulled a knife from her carry-pouch, handed it to Dru, and pointed at the vinegrove. "Cut as many branches as you can," she said. "They'll need to be no thicker than your arm and half the height of a full-grown female."

She watched him scamper up the sand, and we heard him call to Cavel and Ravar to help. As the three of them disappeared behind the shoulder of the dune, Varna stood up slowly and shook herself.

Limar, who had been standing by a neighbouring fire watching us, dropped her blanket on the sand and hurried over. "What's the problem? Where is Dru going with a knife in his paw?"

I was tempted to reply that if Limar was truly interested in the welfare of her half-sibling or her dam then she should share their fires more often, but fortunately Varna spoke first: "He's gone to cut branches for bows. I'm going to show some of you how to shoot arrows."

"I think that's an excellent idea." Limar spun on a claw and headed back the way she'd come. "I'll let Shaya know," she called over her shoulder as she scurried off to find the hunter, picking her way through the detritus that littered the beach.

Varna sighed. "And I'm sure she'll convey it as entirely her idea," she said, with an apologetic flick of her ear.

"It doesn't matter," I said, "so long as it's done."

"Can't we just stay here?" It was my trader friend Jonel who asked the question as she tucked Manda into a blanket under the seavines for a second night, but there were doubtless others who wondered the same thing. "The weavers could make shelters for everyone if we cut enough branches."

"And what would we do when the Guardflight come again?" I said, pitching my voice to carry further than Jonel's ears. "Or the Elite Guard?"

Young Manda, cuddling her toy egg as she wriggled under her blanket, wailed, "I want to go home!" and the cry spread through the entire group of younglings – and, unless my ears deceived me, some of the adults, too.

All except Dru. Unwrapping himself from the blanket Limar had folded round him, he got to his feet, spread his arms, and howled for attention.

"He wants a good nipping that one." Froma's voice, from the group to my left, was loud enough for me to overhear above the subsiding howls. "He's not a Lordling now, is he?"

I turned to remind her that Dru was the one whose destiny had been foreseen, but Winan got there first, flicking a dismissive ear in Froma's direction and telling her to "Hush and listen, Froma. He has a point."

"...can't go back," Dru was shouting, turning where he stood to make himself heard. "They don't want us."

"And we can't stay here." Shaya stepped into the middle of the whimpering younglings and looked around at the huddled groups, and the dark, enfolding branches of the seavines. The last whimpers and protests subsided, leaving behind the sound of waves on shingle and the pop of bubblefrond snapping as the fires on the beach died down. She lifted her snout and I knew she was not sniffing the onshore breeze or the aroma of smouldering seafronds. She was smelling the dejection of several nineties of damp, disheartened drax. It hung in the air like a Deadlands mist, and the edge of fear that accompanied it was easy to detect. Shaya set her ears to a resolute angle, gestured to Dru to sit down, and went on: "You know we can't stay here. We should have moved on already. I'm sure they are watching us from the *Spirax*. How many days do you think Kalis will let us rest in one place before he sends the Guardflight again?"

"Or the Elite Guard," Jonel called, from somewhere behind me.

Rewsa chimed in with a variation on her usual wail: "They want us to die."

"Then we must see to it that we don't." Doran stood up from the middle of the group of younglings, where she had been calming Cavel. Her voice was firm, her ears conveying determination. "Some of us will be healed well enough to fly soon. Think what a help that will be. We'll know what's ahead, and the flyers can take carry-pouches to set up camp and start cooking before those on foot arrive."

"We'll be able to hunt," said Shaya, brandishing her spear.

"And teach us all how," called Limar, brandishing a fresh-cut branch, crudely sharpened at one end.

"Only if you learn to hold it the other way round." Shaya's retort brought some much-needed laughter, and I looked across at Dru as he gathered his blanket around him to settle down again. Earlier that evening, he had sought me out at the water's edge as I filled my flask.

"Drax will die," he had said, quietly enough that I strained to hear over the wash of the tide.

"Not if we're careful. If we learn—"

"No. I've Seen."

I'd felt a stab of annoyance that he had again Seen where I had not, though I knew the feeling was irrational. The Spiral had seen fit to make a more powerful Seer than me and to awaken his ability early, but he had no more control over his Visions than I had. "Did you See how? Or who?"

He'd shaken his head and twitched his tail to signal regret. "Just the Forest, and tunics with blood on."

"Then perhaps the blood isn't drax," I said. "Perhaps you've Seen that we manage to kill something in the Forest for us all to eat."

He hadn't contradicted me, but I think we'd both known my words were untrue.

The next day, we left the beach behind, climbing a snow-crusted rise that took us steadily upward, away from the water's edge and onto the top of the towering cliffs that lined this part of the coast. If progress along the beach had been slow, this was painful. The younglings, using curious double-legged hops, bounded upward with hardly a pause, but for the rest of us it was like toiling endlessly up the *Spirax*'s main corridor, only without the knowledge that there would be a room and a rest at the top.

"Look how far down it is," I heard Manda say to Sarys, as they paused for breath and peered over the edge of the cliff.

"Come away from there!" Limar, ever anxious to prove that she knew best, hurried over to them and pulled them away from danger before their dams could reach them. "Stay back from the edge. If you fall, or if the ground gives way under your feet, your next stop will be those boulders down there. None of us could save you."

"And your head would explode and your brain would be spattered all over the rocks, and there'd be blood *everywhere*," Cavel chimed in as he darted up behind them. He picked up a stick and brought it down hard against a paw-sized stone that jutted from the frozen moss beneath our feet. "*Bam!*" he shouted triumphantly, as the stick shattered and Manda squealed, clutching her toy egg close.

"That's enough, Cavel," Doran growled. "I think everyone has got the message, thank you."

He waggled his tail cheekily and ran on ahead with the others. Doran scurried after him, wheezing threats, though she had no hope of catching him on foot and he knew it. I followed too, breathing hard, legs aching, claws scrabbling for purchase on the steep, slippery slope.

Looking ahead to see how much further it was to the top of the rise, I caught my breath in horror. Sea brambles! Young Sarys, eager as ever to find something to eat, was almost within reach of the stems, along with the two other younglings, and the feeding-pods began to click as they dipped groundward, sensing prey.

"Come away!" I didn't have the breath to bark loudly enough, so I quickened my pace toward them. So intent was I on reaching them before they got too close to the brambles that I failed to see the patch of ice under my own feet. Unbalanced, I twisted as I plunged over the cliff edge, flung out an arm in an effort to grasp the rock, and finally, instinctively, spread my wings.

I felt for rising air, found it, flapped clear of the cliff where eddies and swirls of wind might smash me against the rockface, and soared skyward. Doran told me later that there had been gasps and yips of shock from every drax on the slope, and the odour of astonishment had been palpable, but I couldn't hear or smell any of that. There was just the salt breeze that bore me aloft and the crash of wave on rock beneath me.

For a few beats, it was glorious. I glided and spun about on the updraught, enjoying the feel of the wind under my wings.

Then I saw the *Spirax*, and realised anew that we had made scarcely any progress at all. We were on the ninth day of our journey – but if it had been possible for me to approach the *Spirax* without hindrance from the Elite Guard, I could have been back on the plateau before zenith.

It would take even less time to fly to the Cleft Rocks, which were mere nines of spans or so beyond the brambles. But how long would it take to reach them on foot? From the air I could see that the brambles' thorny purple branches stretched inland for perhaps ninety wingspans, and lined the cliffs for at least five times that length. It would take another day at least before those on the ground would be within sight of the Rocks. Even then, we would be less than halfway to the Ambit estuary and its mudflats. How would we get across…?

I flicked my ears and shook my head. One problem at a time.

Below, winged and wingless alike were looking up and pointing. Females were extending their own wings, flapping them gently to test whether they'd healed. The younglings were jumping up and down, and I was relieved to notice that the ones near the sea bramble had moved away from the stems. Angling my wings, I glided to the clifftop, making sure to keep well clear of the feeding pods, and somehow managed to land without skidding nose-first into the snow.

"You can fly!"

"Your wing is healed!"

Nines of excited drax surrounded me as I folded my wings. Overwhelmed by the smell of encouragement and delight, I flattened my ears against the din of their cries and questions.

The knot of females in front of me parted and Doran pushed through. "Let me check that wing," she said, moving behind me. "I hope you haven't used it too soon."

While she busied herself examining my supposedly-healed wing, the crowd quietened. They had asked their questions and howled their joy; now it was my turn.

"Thank the Spiral," I said, raising my voice to bark over the heads of those nearest to me. "I can fly again. I'm sure it won't be long before you're all healed, too."

"Yes." There was an edge of suspicion in Limar's voice, reinforced as I took a quick sniff in her direction. "Wasn't it fortunate that it was you who fell off the cliff?"

"As I said, Limar," I said, spiralling a paw over the front of my tunic to reinforce my point, "thank the Spiral."

She smelled unconvinced, but Doran stepped toward her after giving my wings a gentle pat. "Why so sour, Limar? Someone had to be the first to fly again. It happens to be Thyla."

Shaya joined in. "It's wonderful. Now we have someone to scout ahead, check for danger, set up camp, light fires, start cooking. It will save time, perhaps save lives." She gestured at the brambles. "How far do these stretch, Thyla? Will it take us long to go round them?"

I set my ears to convey distress. "It's a big thicket," I said. "At the rate we've been moving, it will take till sunset at least to skirt around it."

"Skirt around? You mean, we'll have to go into the Deadlands?" Rewsa's ears and tail quivered with alarm. "We'll -"

"We're on high ground here," said Shaya, before Rewsa could finish her usual wail. "We'll be fine so long as we stay out of reach of the brambles. Dru!" He was leaning over the cliff edge, looking down at the waves washing against the rocks beneath. "Come away from there!"

He straightened up and walked over to us, dipping his ears in greeting. "If we wait for low tide and climb down the cliff to the beach, we could go past the brambles that way. It will be much quicker."

From where I stood, the possibility of the females descending the vertical rockface was as likely as Varna's wings growing back. The younglings might possibly find a way down – I had not forgotten Dru and Cavel's climb up the Tusk – but the adults would be stuck on the clifftop.

Still, it had been a long, tiring climb up the hill; there were nines of females still toiling up the slope toward us, and I saw no harm in taking a brief rest.

"What do you think, Shaya? Doran? I'm for a rest and a cud-chew myself."

Shaya nodded. "The tide is on the turn, we can wait a short while to see what's below."

But as the tide receded it became clear that the ground beneath the cliff was too treacherous to walk across, even if we'd been able to reach it. As the waves retreated, razor-sharp rocks and fallen boulders appeared, along with loose scree and deep, dangerous crevices.

Again, I was struck by how little of our coastline I had noticed when I was flying over it. Brambles, dunes, rocks, none of it had been of any interest when I flew to the Dream-cave. Now it might mean the difference between life and death.

"Perhaps we can cut through the brambles?" said Dru, his voice hopeful but his ears drooping with disappointment.

Shaya shook her head, her ears set to signal the danger in such a move. "The brambles would fight back," she said. "Even if some made it through, a lot of us would be pod-fodder. No, no. We have no choice. We must go around."

The grumbling started up immediately, with several females demanding that we pursue Dru's idea and cut through the brambles.

"I've seen what these things can do." With a couple of bounds, Shaya placed herself between the younglings and the feeding-pods. "They're like the brambletrap in the Deadlands – but worse. Much worse."

"I suppose if we *must* go around…" muttered Rewsa, bending to pick up her carry-pouch.

"Nonsense!" Limar pulled a long-handled knife from the straps of her own pack, and started towards the nearest stem. As she headed for the thicket, she disturbed a small groundrunner that had been feeding on the scrubby ferns that poked through the snow here and there along the clifftop. The creature squeaked, pounded its hind legs to warn others of its kind of the 'danger', and finding itself between us and the brambles, chose the latter. As it plunged into the thicket, it squealed again, this time with an unmistakable edge of pain that made my hackles rise. The brambles moved, swaying against the wind and creating a vortex of branches with the squealing in the middle.

The squeals stopped and the brambles stilled. "It isn't dead, it's stunned," said Shaya. "The sea brambles like to feed on live prey."

Vizan had said the same thing to me, and I opened my mouth to reinforce Shaya's message, then remembered just in time that I wasn't supposed to know such details.

Limar had halted in mid-stride, her knife half-raised. With her ears and fur raised in alarm, she turned back to face us, lowered the blade, and said, "Well, if no-one's coming with me, I might as well keep with the group, I suppose."

As Limar returned the knife to her carry-pouch, Shaya raised her voice again: "Let's not hear any more talk of heading through the brambles. Unless you want to end up like that 'runner." She turned to me. "Thyla, do you think your wings are strong enough for another flight?"

I glanced at Doran, as though I needed confirmation from a Healer that all was well. Only when she had dipped an ear and nodded, did I say, "I'm sure they are, Shaya. It felt good to be flying again."

"Good. Perhaps you'd scout overhead, make sure we're not walking into another problem?"

I dipped an ear. "Gladly. And I'll check for a good place to make camp, too."

The clifftop beyond the brambles provided plenty of space for a camp, though it was clear that the gentle slope would provide no cover from any sort of storm. In the lee of the brambles, moss mottled the ground with dots of crimson where it pushed through the snow.

I sniffed the wind as I glided down and glanced up at the pale clouds, though it was too early in the day to guess what weather the night would bring. Perhaps the Dream-cave...?

I dismissed the thought almost as it formed. The Cleft Rocks were just a few spans away, but the Dream-cave was too important to use for Seeing the weather. Besides, what would happen if I lost track of time, as I had on my last visit there, and was noticed by the others as I came out? The cave would be discovered, and no doubt I would be too.

No. We would trust to the Spiral, and our winter fur.

I spent the rest of the day flying to and fro, collecting carry-pouches from those who were struggling to keep up, gathering broken vinebranches and kindling from the seavines that were such a short flight behind us, keeping Shaya informed about the safest and quickest route, and collecting water from the ocean. I flew over the waves to see if I might catch a fish or two, but the water was murky beneath the clouds, and I could see nothing moving beneath the surface.

As the sun dropped toward the western mountains, I lit the campfires. I had permission from Doran and some of the other females to open the carry-pouches I'd taken from them, and by the time the first of the walking groups arrived at the camp, pots of stew had been set over the fires to cook.

"There's barely enough here for half a bowl each." Limar – who had earlier refused to give me her carry-pouch – stooped over a pot, stirring and sniffing, and peering at the contents as though she expected a sawfish to surface and bite her nose.

"I didn't have all the carry-pouches," I said. "Even if I had, Shaya has told us to be careful about how much we're eating. At the rate we're moving, it will take moons to get to the Forest, and we've no guarantee of getting anything to eat when we get there."

Behind Limar, Rewsa slumped on her blanket, plucking the fur from her tail. There were just a few odd clumps left on the tip now, but I could do nothing to ease her worries. She would need to do something about keeping her tail warm, though; if she pulled all the fur out, she might lose some of it to icenip. If that happened, she'd never fly properly again.

"Did you check the ocean?" There was a note of disdain in Limar's voice and her ears were flicking, dismissively. "I'm sure there are plenty of fish."

"I'm sure there are." My fur bristled at the implied insult, but I set my ears to signal resolve and made sure my voice carried on the breeze. "Unfortunately, none of them are in the shallows, and I didn't have time to fly further out. I had rather a lot to do."

Shaya, who was rolling out her blanket beyond the next campfire, had already swivelled her ears in our direction, but it was Dru who bounded up to stand between Limar and I. Despite his small size – still no higher than my tunic belt – I was reminded of Kalis, standing between Fazak and myself on the *Spirax* balcony moons ago when I had first been summoned in Vizan's place. But fortunately, Dru spoke more wisely than his sire ever had. "You're full-growns," he said. "Stop arguing."

Shaya stepped across and rested an approving paw on Dru's head. "He's right. It's been a long day and we're all tired. I suggest we concentrate on getting some sleep, and work out what we'll do about supplementing our food supplies in the morning. Perhaps more of us will be flying by then."

"I doubt that." Limar extended her damaged wing, displaying the still-healing tear. "The Healers say it'll be a nine-day at least before I'll be airborne. Rewsa's the same. So is everyone I've spoken with today." She paused, spinning in a slow circle to make sure everyone within earshot was listening, while I wondered how many drax she'd managed to talk with during their journey. Turning back to face me, she half-raised her other wing, displaying a challenge, and pointed right at me. "I want to know why you can fly, when no-one else here is close to healing yet. Did the Elite Guard even break your wings? And what did Taral say to you when the Guardflight came? I've spoken to the traders here, and none of them know who you are."

I looked around. Others were nodding and murmuring, and there was a scent of curiosity on the breeze. Limar had made her case, and she might have pushed it far enough for me to pull my black tunic from my pouch and admit my true identity if her suspicions hadn't got the better of her. Instead, she strode forward, jabbed a finger against my chest, and snarled, "I think you're spying for Kalis, and you'll fly back to the *Spirax* one day to tell him everything that's been happening."

The idea was so absurd I didn't know where to start – Kalis was rid of the wingless, rid of their dams, why would he care what any of them said or did? I snorted with laughter, Doran did likewise, and Shaya began to snuffle. Within a few beats, half the clifftop was barking with laughter, and the danger of discovery had passed – for the moment at least.

Limar's ears were rigid with anger and humiliation, and her teeth clenched as she pressed her snout close to mine and growled, "You're hiding something, Thyla, or whoever you are. I know it, and I'll find out what it is. I promise."

Seven

"**P**erhaps you should just tell her who you really are."

Doran made the suggestion the next day, as we rolled up our blankets and repacked our carry-pouches. Beyond the smouldering ashes of the next fire, Limar was already at work gossiping to a couple of Traders and an Artisan, who all had their ears turned to listen while she talked and nodded and pointed in my direction.

"If I tell Limar, I might as well put my black tunic on and let everyone know," I said, "and if the guardflight come back – or Kalis sends the Elite Guard – I can wave goodbye to my wings." My shoulders cramped at the mere thought, and my shudder had nothing to do with the knifing wind that swept across the Deadlands from the Western Mountains.

"You can't be sure of that."

"No. But I can't be sure that everyone would keep silent either." There seemed to be less room in my carry-pouch now than there had been when I first packed it. Pulling the top flap open, I peered inside, giving the wrapped patties and jars of herbs a bit of a reshuffle. The whole thing really needed unpacking and repacking properly, but if I did that someone might notice the rare herbs that Fate-seers used, or a corner of the black tunic might unroll from the bottom of the pouch and flap in the breeze. I pushed my licked bowl and spoon in, stuffed my blanket on top, and tugged the straps shut just as Shaya appeared beside me.

She stretched her wings. "It will probably be at least three or four ninedays before I can join you in the air," she said, as Doran scurried behind her to check the broken strut, "but some of the others were less badly hurt. Milat and Jonel may be able to fly in a few days, and Hariz and Galyn are not far behind."

I ran my paw over the front of my tunic. "Thank the Spiral."

She flicked an ear in rather half-hearted acknowledgement. "We made better progress yesterday, without so many carry-pouches to burden the slower females. Will you be able to do the same again today? How sore are your wings?"

"There's a little stiffness," I said, truthfully for my wings had been folded for too many days, "but nothing a day's flying won't cure."

"Good. We can keep to the coast for a while once we're past the Cleft Rocks, but when we get to the Ambit peninsula, we'll have to cross the hills there, otherwise we'll be heading the wrong way."

I hoisted my carry-pouch and strapped it on. "It'll be days before we get to the peninsula," I said. "From what I could see yesterday, the ground immediately ahead looks fairly level, but it's not easy to tell what's underneath the snow."

For another nineday, I flew back and forth, collecting pouches, building fires, and calling directions and guidance as the others straggled and struggled along the shoreline. Beyond the Cleft Rocks there were sandy bays, rocky promontories, and headlands that were washed by the sea even at low tide. Meanwhile, a knot of gossip and suspicion formed around Limar, and every time I landed she would turn to this growing group – Rewsa, Froma, Hariz the healer, a pawful of traders, and Norba the cluster-cryer – and mutter something while pointing in my direction. I prayed through snow, sleet, clouds, and sunshine that someone – anyone

– else would regain the use of their wings before the hostility and suspicion spread further.

Azmit, a hunter with a lean, sinewy look beneath her grey winter fur, killed a groundrunner, and though there was scarce enough meat on it to feed three drax, it was put into nine large pots and the resulting stew was ladled out to everyone. There were glowshells to be found in rockpools, their tiny occupants adding flavour to our meals, while their shells were slipped into carry-pouches – ready for use on the dead, though no-one said so. Doran found a sideclaw stranded spans above the high-tide line, probably deposited there during the storm, and that same day a group of younglings under Milat's supervision dug up a potful of sandweavers. Varna, helped and encouraged by Dru, began to demonstrate how to use a bow, while the wood-shapers, who knew how to make arrows, started teaching the skill to nines of eager younglings. Progress on the nets was slow, hampered by clumsy fingers, bored younglings who wanted to be making arrows, and a scarcity of zaxel juice to help bind the fibres, but at least most of us were trying to learn something useful.

Then, on the morning of the nineteenth day of our exile, I was woken by the sound of excited cries. When I realised that the calls were coming from overhead, I scrambled from my blanket, heedless of the pots, carry-pouches, and warm bodies nearby, and looked skyward. In the dim grey of another sleet-laden morning, Doran circled around the clifftop camp, her wings tilting and flapping in the onshore breeze.

"My wings are healed!" she called. "We'll all be flying soon!"

"Not all of us."

I glanced down to see Varna roll herself tighter into her blanket, turning her back to the sky, and felt a twinge of sympathy. No-one else seemed to have heard her though. Just as they had done when I took my inadvertent tumble off the cliff, every other female in the group stretched their wings and flapped them tentatively.

"Be careful, all of you!" I called. "Remember what the Healers say – if you try to fly too soon, you might set back the healing."

Limar, heedless as ever of any advice and instruction, ran along the undulating ground anyway, flapping her wings furiously in an effort to take off. At the crest of a small rise, she left the ground, and for a beat or two began to climb. Then her right wing gave way, the left fluttered in a futile attempt to keep her aloft, and she crash-landed in a tumble of fur and muffled curses.

"Limar!"

I spread my own wings and skimmed across to the prone form in the slushy hollow. Doran landed beside me, and I read concern in the set of her ears, but as we reached down to help, Limar pushed our paws away and sat up. "I'm not hurt, leave me be. Don't fuss, for Lights' sake!"

She climbed to her feet and brushed at the mud on her pink tunic, managing to do little more than smear it right across her front.

"Do you have a clean one?" I said. "I'm sure one of the other nest-nurses will lend you a spare—"

"I said don't fuss!" Limar's teeth snapped at my outstretched paw and I jerked back, stepping on Doran's foot in my haste.

"I'll check your wings, Limar," Doran said. Her hackles were still raised from the scare Limar had given us, but she smoothed her healer's tunic, as though to remind herself that her skills were needed, and shook out her fur. "As I feared," she said, after she'd examined Limar's wings, "the struts are healing but the tears in the membrane have ripped open again. You'll be grounded for at least another nineday."

"I'm sorry, Limar," I said. "I did try to warn you."

"Well, you should have said it louder," she said, her ears flicking viciously back and forth between pain and anger. "I didn't hear you."

I felt it best not to argue. Her teeth looked awfully sharp.

Slowly, with grumbles and complaints and petty arguments along the way, we began to settle into a routine, of sorts. Milat the hunter was next to regain the use of her wings, and she took turns with Doran and myself to scout ahead each morning, reporting back on obstacles and difficult ground. From the air, it seemed a short stretch from the Cleft Rocks to the shoulder of land that marked the turn of the coast from north to east, a stretch that was mainly snow-lined dips and ice-rimed hills that rose above rocky coves in colour-banded cliffs. But to those on foot, every slope was a challenge, every stone hidden under the snow was a bruised toe, every step was a torment for aching legs and cold, weary feet.

Still, with some of us able to fly, it was possible for the wingless and grounded to spend more time moving, and more of the adults began to look around, sniff out possible sources of food, and take an interest in where they were, rather than where they had once been.

By the twenty-third day of our journey, the groundlings were approaching the turn in the shoreline at last, and I landed to let Shaya know that if they hurried it would be possible to make camp that night within sight of the Ambit. She was pulling Froma's youngling, Sarys, away from a scrawny rotberry bush that bore sharp thorns and green berries, and shooed the youngling's friends back too as she spoke: "We can't eat those. They taste disgusting, they're poisonous, and when the weather starts to warm they will be riddled with rotorfly grubs. You certainly wouldn't want a mouthful of *those!*"

Sarys pulled a face and twisted her ears to indicate her disgust, while the younglings with her made spitting noises, and one or two clutched their stomachs and rolled their eyes, moaning as though in pain.

"Stop making those stupid noises!" It was Varna, bow in hand, walking ahead of the other females for once but looking and smelling as miserable as ever.

"Leave them be, Varna, they're learning, and it's good to hear them behaving like normal younglings," I said.

"If they were normal younglings, we wouldn't be stumbling about out here, would we?"

I couldn't think of an answer, and in any case she did not appear to be in any mood to listen, so I turned to Shaya instead. "The peninsula—" I began, breaking off when I heard Milat calling from the sky overhead.

"There's something washed up on the beach to the east," she called as she circled. "Looks like a seatach." She glided down to land next to Shaya, folded her wings and flicked an ear in deference and greeting. "I know it's not the direction we want to go, but it'll feed us for moons."

Casting a brief prayer of thanks to the Spiral for deliverance from hunger, I turned at once to call to the younglings. "A seatach! A huge creature that lives in the ocean – we don't see them unless they come ashore to die. Would you like to see?"

With squeals of excitement, and cries of "I'll race you!" they bounced off along the clifftop, heedless of snow and ice, and I took to the air to scout a way down to the beach for everyone.

Milat and Doran had already landed on top of the massive carcass by the time I dropped onto the sand beside it. I had seen seataches before, but never so recently dead as this one. Always before, the Fishers and Butchers had been there already, leaving nothing behind but the skull, tail, and a few scant bones. This one must have beached itself the previous night. Its head was as high as three drax if they stood on each other's shoulders, its body a black scaly cone with flippers, and its fluked tail was under water, though the tide was well out. Blood in the water told its own story – something was feeding on the submerged part of the creature. We would need to move fast if we were to take the carcass for ourselves. Its two sets of eyes were closed in death and I was fascinated to see that it had hairs edging its lids, just as we did. If only I'd had a blank scroll-leaf, I could have made some useful notes on the creature. As it was, I had to content myself with looking, sniffing, and touching, hoping I would remember the details when next I was able to scratch down my observations. The scales, each the size of an extended claw, were already drying, and felt rough, like unworked vinebark. In the half-hearted sunlight that sparred with the pale clouds racing overhead, I saw that they were not an even black – they shaded, from a night-dark black to dark purples and blues, appearing to glisten with a life of their own. My nose told me that the thing was dead, and that flisks and mitches would have been all over it if not for the icy conditions.

Dru and Cavel led the first group of younglings down a slope of loose pebbles and onto the sand. At sight of the seatach, they halted for a moment, ears signalling alarm. Then, cautiously, they approached its flanks, noses busy as they sniffed the air, tails a-twitch with curiosity.

"Remember the shelters we used for the Night of the Two Moons? This is where the hides come from," I explained, placing a paw on the creature's black scales to indicate it was safe to approach. "We can take the skin off this one, clean it, dry it, and make shelters for ourselves."

"And the flesh is good to eat," Doran called from her perch on top of the beast's head. "We can make patties and dry it to take with us – so long as the Fishers don't come and claim it."

"They won't," I said. "We're well beyond the Cleft Rocks now. But all that meat will be heavy to carry, even it's dried or pattied."

Doran scratched her chin and flicked an ear. "There are nineties of us," she said. "We'll manage between us. In any case, we've still not seen any fish – unless you count whatever's eating this thing's tail. The patties we've got won't last much longer, and everyone's hungry. We've got the peninsula to cross, the mudflats, the river…" She eyed the younglings crowding round the base of the seatach and closed her mouth on her thoughts. I could guess what they were, though – I'd been worrying about the same things. It was all so easy from the air – fly over the land, glide across the mudflats, soar above the river. But with so many who could not…

"Can we touch?" Dru's question jolted me back to the beach and the Spiral's gift of the dead seatach. The youngling took a timid step as he spoke, though with his ears flattened and teeth bared he looked as though his fear might get the better of his curiosity at any moment.

"Certainly. It's dead, it can't hurt you," I said. Then, gesturing to the other younglings, I said, "Come, all of you! This is a rare thing, and you should take a good look before we make use of it. Come closer, Nixel – see how it has fins like a fish?"

"But bigger," he said, staring up at the huge wall of flesh.

"Much bigger," said Milat, gliding from the head of the creature to land next to her pup. "And do you see the way the scales show patterns of purple and blue?"

Nixel nodded. "They're pretty."

"Yes. The fishers say no two are the same. Perhaps it's how the seataches tell each other apart."

Dru and Cavel had already made their way to the head of the beast, and were exclaiming over the size of the creature's teeth. I left Milat to look after Nixel, and hopped across to caution the other younglings about getting too close to the open jaw. "There's a story that a Fisher once lost an arm when a seatach's mouth dropped shut."

"We're just looking," said Cavel.

"We don't want to get too close anyway," said Dru, backing away. "It smells horrible!"

"It would smell worse if the weather was warmer," I said, "but you're right, the thing is already beginning to rot. If we're to make use of it, we have to work quickly. You may help if you like, but there'll be lots of blood, and I expect its insides will smell even worse than its outsides."

"At least there's room for a proper encampment while we work." Doran indicated the stretch of sand to the east of the seatach, which was flat and wide, with enough dry sand above the tideline to accommodate all of us at the foot of the weathered slabs of rock that loomed above the beach. Lichens and mosses had been stuffed into crevices all the way up the cliff face, indicating that rockcrawlers slithered up there to nest during the warm season.

"They make a tasty meal," said Milat, noticing the direction of my gaze, "but the racket they make with that incessant clicking and snorting is unbearable. Good thing they've gone into hibernation for the cold season."

"Speaking of tasty meals," I said, ignoring the grumble from my main stomach as I turned to point at the seatach, "the tide will be well in before the others get here. The seatach will be half-eaten by tomorrow."

Milat's gaze swept from the remains of the creature's tail, which floated in a spume of blood and bone, along its flanks and up to the top of its head. "We must fly to get the nets," she said. "Let's hope we have enough of them."

"Nets?"

But she had already flapped up to stand beside Doran on the beast's head. "Dru, Nixel, Cavel – all of you!" she called to the younglings clustered around the seatach three or four deep. Those at the back pushed and clamoured to get closer, while the ones at the front were reluctant to yield their spot. "Quiet!" Milat spread her wings, demanding attention, and the noise of yips and squeals fell away. "We need to protect the seatach from the sawfish that want to eat it. So we must anchor our nets all along both sides and over its back near the tail. I'm going to get the nets with Thyla; Doran will stay nearby. While we're gone, I need you all to collect rocks and stones." She pointed to the cliff and the pebble-strewn route they had taken down from the hillside. "The biggest ones you can carry, please, and lots of them."

As the younglings bounded away, tails twitching with excitement, Milat glided to the sand again, to stand in front of the creature's gaping mouth, and a moment later Doran followed. Milat walked to the left of the creature's head, then retraced her steps and went the other way. Her ears twitched nervously as she tilted her head from side to side, making a study of the saw-edged teeth and purpling gums. I glanced over at Doran, flicking a query with an ear, but she merely shrugged a shoulder – it was clear she had no more idea than I about what Milat was looking for. Time was wasting if we were to fly to fetch the nets...

"Milat?"

"Here! This one." She pointed at a front tooth in the lower jaw which looked a little crooked. "These things lose their teeth one by one and grow new ones. This one's ready to come out – I hope."

Milat hopped up the beach to our discarded carry-pouches, flipped open the flap on hers, and pulled out a spare ochre tunic. "We shouldn't actually be doing this without propping the jaw open," she said as she stood between us, her tone conversational, though her tail gave the lie to her casual air. "But we can't prop it open without a vinetrunk. And to get one of those we need a good, sharp seatach tooth. So..." She turned her head to look at me, then at Doran, then at the task confronting her. "I'm going to lean in and wrap this tunic round the back edge of that tooth," she said. "Then we can pull on the hem and the straps. It should come free, Spiral willing."

Still she hesitated, glancing up at the mighty upper jaw that cast its shadow over us, a curve of sharp, white death waiting to fall. Milat took a breath and sighed it out. "If..." Another glance upward. "At least it'll be quick."

80

Without further ado, she stepped up to the creature's bottom lip and leaned over the line of jagged incisors, grunting and coughing as she strove to push the tunic into place. "Gah! You wouldn't believe the stench in here!"

Her attempt at lightening the mood was wasted on us. Doran's fur, like mine, stood up in alarm, and our tails swished uncontrollably. "I need to regurgitate," Doran gasped, "and not in a good way."

I knew what she meant. Personally, I had a sudden urgent need for a waste-pit, but as Milat stood up and backed away from danger, the ends of the tunic in her paws, I let out a breath and decided I could wait after all.

"Now we pull," she said, her own relief evident in her voice as we all shook ourselves and rubbed at our fur to flatten it.

Milat and Doran took a strap each, and I pulled at the hem of the tunic, feeling the give and movement in the tooth it was wrapped around. Did I imagine it, or was the business end of the tooth now a little higher than its neighbours, a little further forward?

"Keep pulling!" Milat barked, and I kept up the traction, though my shoulders ached and my paws were cramping. "It's -"

The great mouth slammed shut without a sniff of warning, cutting the tunic into pieces and sending us tumbling backward onto the sand. A ripple of laughter from the younglings told me they had all been watching and found the undignified tumble of their elders hilarious. I wondered how they would have reacted if the jaw had severed Milat rather than her tunic. How would *I* have reacted?

Milat seemed unfazed by her near miss. While Doran and I were still gaining our feet and brushing ourselves off, she had already scrambled back to push at the fleshy mouth that had closed over our prize. Turning side-on to it, she squeezed her right arm between the lips, right up to her shoulder, and pulled it back out after a few beats, clutching the loose tooth and the tattered remains of her tunic in a slimy paw. "Got it!"

Throwing her prize onto the sand, she headed for the water and paddled in far enough to wash her arms. Doran shooed the younglings back to their rock-gathering, and I took a closer look at the tooth we'd dislodged. The upper section was as long as my arm, a thin triangle with a serrated inner edge, and a point that looked as sharp as a claw. I tapped it. Smooth. Hard. Hollow? It had been anchored to the seatach's jaw by two hooked roots composed of the same white enamel.

"So." Milat waded out of the surf, and Doran trotted past me proferring a drying cloth for her. "We have a saw." Dried and fluffed, she took the tooth from me and showed it to Doran. "You see how the roots make perfect handles?"

Doran flicked an ear. "Yes. But why do we need it? And why the hurry to pull it out? Couldn't it have waited till the others get here?"

Milat shook her head, and dug the tooth point-first into the sand, freeing her paws to point up at the cliffs. "There's a stand of tanglevines up there, a little further east."

I hadn't noticed, and chided myself for still being too unobservant. Doran was also signalling surprise, so at least I was not the only one who flew about with her eyes half-shut. Thank the Spiral we had the hunters, with their trained eyes, ears, and noses.

"What of it?" said Doran. "Are we going to shelter under it, like we did with the seavine grove?"

"No." Milat tugged the tooth free and handed it to Doran. "You're going to cut down some of the vines."

"But—"

"It's easy. Start with the outermost vines, set the serrated edge against the straightest trunk you can find, a couple of paw-widths from the ground, and saw through it. Make sure you cut so that the trunk falls away from the other vines, and make sure there aren't any younglings underneath it."

Doran hefted the tooth that had become a tool and waggled her ears, her scent confirming her uncertainty. "Alright. I think I can do that. But why?"

Milat glanced at me. I had an inkling of what she was striving towards, but was it Vizan who had told me the tale, or Swalo the fable-spinner? The hunter must have read my uncertainty as ignorance; she flicked an ear in apology and said, "I'm sorry, I'm still not used to explaining things to grown females." She knelt, extended a claw, and scratched a neat row of circles in the damp sand. "These are the rocks the younglings are fetching." Lines above the circles, running horizontally and vertically. "The rocks anchor the bottom of the nets." Finally, a thin rectangle along the top of the lines. "And the logs are attached to the top. The logs float and the net expands as the tide comes in." She looked back at the slopping waves, which were beginning to claw their way back up the sand and along the sides of our precious seatach. "And we'll need them soon if we're to save this thing from the sawfish."

The three of us moved fast, Doran flying over the groups of younglings before she headed off to the vinegrove, Milat and I flying against the breeze to find the other females. They were closer than I'd anticipated, the idea of meat to spare having spurred them on. Unfortunately, there were only four finished nets – not enough to protect the entire seatach, but sufficient at least to save most of it, Spiral willing. As the tide lapped in, paw-width by paw-width, we laid out the nets, two on each side of the beast, and left the younglings to cover the bottom edges with rocks and stones while Milat and I flew to and fro from the vinegrove, using ropes to carry the trunks Doran had felled. By the time we had dropped the third log onto the sand, Shaya and the first group of flightless females had arrived, and they set about tying the logs to the nets' top edges.

As the final log was rolled into place, the water was already nudging at the edges of the nets nearest the tail. "Once the logs are properly afloat, we'll stretch a rope across the back of this thing," Shaya said, as she straightened up from checking knots and placed a hand on the flank of the seatach just below its front flipper. "It'll help draw the top corners of the net together. I'll post some of my hunters on its back too – most of it'll be above the water-line I think, so they can try to fend off any hungry fish. Might even spear one or two if we're lucky."

By a quarter after zenith, we had done what we could to protect our prize. The nets were in place, the logs already rising on the incoming tide, and Shaya and her fellow-hunter Azmit had been lifted onto the creature's back by Doran and Milat. Everyone else made camp and dared to eat well for once, anticipating that our meat supplies would be replenished by the next sunset.

Tired from my morning's exertions, I dozed for a while on the soft sand at the base of the cliffs, till I was woken by raised voices. Winan and Froma stood a few spans away, next to a smouldering fire, arguing about the best way to butcher the seatach.

"My dam's sire was a farmer," Winan said, straightening to her full height and scowling down at the smaller female, "and I know he always took the head off first when he cut up a groxen."

"That'll just waste time," Froma insisted. She sat down to rummage in her carry-pouch, ignoring her friend's glare. "I tell you, my sire saw it done, cycles ago. We should cut along the spine, then slice downward every span or so. The blubber will unpeel and we can get at the meat and the heart. Aha!" She pulled a drawstring bag from the depth of her pouch. "I knew I had another pinch of kestox powder somewhere. It should go well with a bowl of seatach stew."

"Nonsense." Winan knelt to open her own carry-pouch. "That's far too bland. We need chalkmoss, and plenty of it."

Their talk of meat and herbs made my stomachs gurgle. As I sat up and brushed sand from my fur, I saw that the tide was still on the rise. Raising my snout, I sniffed for blood in the water, but the nets, it seemed, had held so far. I was about to rummage in my carry-pouch for another pattie when Shaya stepped across to our fire. I doubted she would approve of anyone eating any more than they had to, seatach or no seatach, and I froze awkwardly, paw on pouch, looking up at the hunter like prey on the end of her spear.

"We'll start cutting as soon as the tide turns," she said. "The fishers know how it's done." Winan and Froma leaned in, ears pricked, eager to discover which of them had been right. "Apparently, we have to slice down behind the head and then along the spine," Shaya went on, pleasing both – or neither – of the artisans, "then cut along just above the flippers and peel back the skin from neck to tail. We'll use the skin to make shelters, so we'll need to be careful with it and get it up the beach above the high-tide line as quickly as possible. Once that's out of the way, we can cut away the blubber and get at the meat."

"Spiral be praised," I said, spinning a paw over my tunic and raising my eyes to the sky where the sun had already slipped behind the mountains and the Spiral's lights shone clear in a cloudless evening, accompanied by a swollen moon. Others nearby echoed my words and actions, though I noticed that Varna looked away and made no sign. Well, I supposed she had even less to be grateful for than the rest of the females.

"Who's going to do all this?" Limar, sitting at a different fire from her dam, spoke from the shadows. "The fishers? Most of them went with Colex."

"We'll all do it." Shaya's voice had an edge as sharp as her spear. "The fishers and some of the artisans will cut up the carcass. Everyone else will carry what's been cut straight up the beach and put it on top of the skins. We'll be working against time and tide, so let's not worry about treating it, cooking it, or eating it till it's out of the way of the fishes. Meanwhile," she said, her whiskers twitching with amusement as her gaze rested on the paw I'd set on my carry-pouch, "get something to eat."

As everyone moved down the beach, Milat flew to the head of the carcass to make the first cut, while two fishers in deep blue tunics called instructions from the sand beneath. I waited beneath the cliff, cloaked in shadow, and quietly murmured a heartfelt prayer of thanks to the Spiral for providing such bounty. As the night wore on and everyone grew sticky with blood and ooze, the stench of raw meat and blubber clinging to every hair, I felt less inclined to be grateful. Wading knee-deep in seatach guts to collect another armful of dripping flesh, I had to remind myself that the meat would feed us for moons, the skin would shelter us from bad weather, and the teeth would make excellent knives and saws.

Dru, as ever, was a furball of energy and enthusiasm, asking questions, fetching, carrying, learning the right way to cut up a carcass, and wrinkling his snout along with everyone else as the creature's stomach contents spilled onto the sand, reeking of rot and death.

"Urgh! Lights!" Froma used her knife to poke at the half-digested remains of the seatach's last meal. "It's got wings. I think it was drax."

Several females and a clutch of younglings rushed down the sand to retch in the water. Rewsa howled, Limar stalked away up the beach, barking that she would not go near 'that thing' again. The sour smell of disgust and alarm spread from drax to drax, and fur stood on end all along the beach.

I forced myself to look at the disgusting mess, and thought of all the females who had gone to the ocean with their wingless hatchlings in the dark days before Dru's hatching made such offspring less contemptible. How far had this one flown? How long had she drifted with the current before the seatach claimed her? Any tunic the remains might have worn had long since dissolved; there was nothing to give us a clue as to who it might have been.

Probably just as well.

"What should we do with it – her?"

"She ought to be put in the Deadlands, whoever she was."

"We can't do that. We don't have a Fate-seer to chant the rites."

I turned away, intending to carry the slab of meat I held up the beach, and found Doran at my wingtip. "Don't glare at me like that," I muttered. "You know why I can't put the black tunic on."

I moved past her, but she fell into step beside me. "I know why you didn't wear it when you first joined us," she said, "but it's nearly two ninedays since Kalis sent the guardflight to look for you." She half-turned to look back at the crumpled remains on the sand. "Look how distressed everyone is. If they know we have a Fate-seer, if they're able to give that poor female a last nest, it'll ease the upset."

I placed the meat on the seatach skin, noting that we would soon need to start adding a second layer. The skins lay like open wounds beneath the cliffs, blood oozing from the chunks of flesh they held and streaming onto the sand. My paws dripped with it and I resisted the urge to wipe them on my tunic. Beside me, a line of other females placed their own bloody slabs next to mine and turned to head back for more. I followed them, taking the opportunity to wash my paws in the waves. Doran trotted close behind me and hissed in my ear, "Come on – we're over a half-day's flight from the *Spirax*." She pointed to Milat and Azmit who had the sorry task of carrying the dead female's remains up the beach in a net. "Think of all those missing females." Doran's voice was urgent. "She could be any of them, or all of them."

I glanced skyward. The clouds had closed in while we worked, and the sky was a uniform grey, misting in the dawn light to a haze that dissolved the landscape. I would get no help from the Spiral.

But I knew what Vizan would expect me to do.

The sea was numbingly cold, and after I'd washed I stepped out of the water to find Dru waiting, as though he sensed what I was about to do. "Dru, fetch my carry-pouch, would you please?" He touched my paw for a beat, then turned to dodge away through the crowd. With my stomachs fluttering like a glittermoth in a jar, I smoothed my blue tunic with a damp paw and flew up to perch on the beast's head. Raised my arms. Raised my wings. Raised my voice. "We can take that unfortunate female to the Deadlands."

Knives stopped scraping, as drax of all sizes stopped what they were doing and turned toward me. Those too far away to hear began to move nearer the moment they realised something was happening.

"Whoever she was, we can send her to her last nest. Because we do have a Fate-seer." I was fighting nausea. I saw ears twitch with puzzlement, caught a whiff of hope, and heard the uncertainty wash through the crowd. Raising my voice so that it carried over the crash of the surf against the shore, and the puzzled murmurings that rumbled through the throng, I announced, "I'm the Fate-seer. I'm Zarda."

Eight

The overwhelming smell of astonishment rippled from female to female, youngling to youngling, as word spread from those within earshot to those at the back of the crowd. My name – my real name – was hissed and murmured, growing in strength like an incoming tide till…

"Zarda! You're Zarda?" Limar had been nowhere in sight when I'd flown up to the seatach's head to take my perch; now, she was at the front of the crowd, her voice edged with the same disbelief she'd displayed back on the clifftop when she'd last confronted me. She stared up at me, sniffing, ears quivering with suspicion and disbelief. "You don't look or smell anything like her. You're just saying that so that you don't have to tell us your real name, or what you're actually doing here." Behind her, Shaya sheathed her knife, wiped bloodied paws on a cloth, and stepped closer. Limar, confident that she had captured everyone's attention, stood back a little and half-extended her undamaged wing in a clear challenge. "If you're Zarda, where's your Fate-seer's tunic?"

"It's here." Dru's voice carried high and clear from somewhere near the cliffs. A moment later, females were drawing aside to form a path as he scampered down the beach. Every few steps he turned to tug at the straps of my carry-pouch, which Doran was carrying as she hurried close behind him. "I couldn't lift it," he said, as I glided groundward to meet them. "It was too heavy."

"What have you got in here – rocks?" Doran grumbled as she set the pouch at my feet, but her ears and whiskers told me that she was pleased I'd listened to her at last.

The tunic was, of course, right at the bottom of the pack. I pulled out my spare Trader's tunic, the food I'd wrapped, bags of herbs, and jars of ointments, piling them on the sand. My paw closed on the bag of spirelles...but no, I'd spilled enough secrets for one day. There were still more jars and wrappers and bits and pieces in the pouch, but now there was enough room to move them about and push my paw to the bottom. I felt soft cloth between my fingers, grasped it, and pulled. Jars rattled as they clattered around the pouch, and I knew I would have to check later for cracked lids and spilled herbs, but there was no time for that now.

Standing, I lifted the Fate-seer's black tunic above my shoulder, and turned in a slow circle to allow as many to see it as possible. With my free paw, I turned back the top of the blue tunic I was wearing to show the Badge of Office I had pinned to its lining.

"Now you all know," I called. "If the Guardflight come again to look for me or, Spiral forbid, the Elite Guard, you will all have to choose: lie to them, or tell them where they can find me."

"Why would we tell them?" Limar had folded her wings and was a picture of contrite friendliness, ears set to convey her sincerity. "They've not helped us, have they?"

I flicked my ears to acknowledge the assurances being called by everyone round about me – "we'll be safer with a Fate-seer"– "Spiral be praised" – "Lights bless you Zarda for helping us."

I looked around at all the hopeful faces, wondering how I could be worthy of such faith, wondering whether my own trust in them was misplaced. There were so many. It needed just one of them to say the wrong thing at the wrong time...

Still, as Doran had repeatedly pointed out, the Guardflight had been and gone. Taral, may the Spiral bless his curly black mane, had kept my secret, and there was no-one else to tell it to so far from home. Surely I would be safe enough, so long as Kalis didn't send anyone else after me.

I lowered the black tunic, brushed futilely at the creases, and turned my attention to Shaya. "Set the body aside, further along the beach," I said. "We must finish work on the seatach first."

Fires were stirred and pots were filled with fresh-cut meat. As the first skin was freed of meat, the younglings helped to peg it to the ground, inside up, and started to scrape it clean under supervision from the fishers. Milat and Doran flew inland to fetch ice, and everyone else searched through carry-pouches for herbs, knives, spoons, and bowls.

Meanwhile Varna, who had been no help at all, found an old vine stump to sit upon and complained loudly about the waste of time – "We can't possibly carry it all" – and how we had done it wrong anyway – "My grandsire cut up many a seatach, and he never started at the head!"

As nightfall approached once more, we feasted on thick, meaty stew that filled our bellies properly for the first time in days. The seatach hides that would provide shelter for us over the coming moons had been cut into nine pieces and were drying above the high-tide line; the creature's intestines had been pegged out along the damp sand for the tide to wash clean. Strips of flesh had been cut and distributed through the camp to be salted or dried; and five more females had regained the use of their wings. I'd kept my trader's tunic on all day, but as the time for the ceremony approached, I entered the creature's skull. Emptied of flesh and brain, still above the high-tide line, it provided a perfect chamber for changing tunics – if you didn't mind the smell. The remains we were to take to a last nest smelled worse, and even though I was not one of those carrying it, I was grateful long ropes would keep the net well below arm's length. We sent up a death-howl to prepare the way. Then, with an escort of every airborne female, we headed south and west to the Deadlands.

"Any brambletrap will do," I called, as we left the coast behind and flew over the black mud and low mounds that marked the boundary of the Deadlands marsh, "so long as they're not designated for a particular cluster or trade."

The clouds, which had lowered overhead all day, kept the Spiral's lights from us as we performed the ceremony, but I added an extra prayer to help the poor dead female's light find its way. With no heart to share it didn't take long, and we lowered her remains into the brambletrap just as the clouds parted overhead and we glimpsed the Spiral as well as a bright, fat moon.

The next day, with our bounty still drying beneath a feeble sun, we buried one of the seatach's hearts just below the high-tide mark as an offering of thanks to the Spiral, then feasted on the other – even with so many of us, there was plenty to spare for all. That night, exhausted from days and nights of physical toil and emotional stress, warmed by the fire and with a belly full of rich meat, I fell asleep content for the first time since our journey began.

I should have known better.

I was woken soon after sunrise by a stinging blow on my snout. It was followed by another, on my foot, accompanied by a rush of noise that sounded like pebbles cascading down a slope. Drax, I realised. Drax in flight.

"It's the Elite Guard!" Shaya shouted, pointing upward. "Nine of them. They're dropping sticks on us!"

They were calling insults too, though fortunately the wind whipped away many of the words they were barking. I started to sit up, but was pressed back by Doran's firm hand on my shoulder. "Stay under your blanket, Zarda, you're still wearing the black tunic." She had the grace to look apologetic, and I caught a whiff of shame as she dipped her ears and hung her head. "I shouldn't have pressed you to put it on. Now everyone knows. It only needs one of them to shout…"

Her words tracked my own thoughts, but I flicked an ear to dismiss them. The decision to reveal my real self had, after all, been mine and had, after all, been the right thing to do.

"The sticks," I said, jerking my snout at the one that had hit my nose. "There are message-leaves wrapped around them."

Above, maroon-clad half-growns were barking with laughter as they pulled more sticks from their carry-pouches and threw them down. Swooping and gliding, they were scattering the messages right along the beach, and females were flapping wings in vain attempts to take off and chase them away.

"I wish we were better shots with those arrows." Shaya made do with shaking her makeshift spear up at Murgo, who responded by throwing another stick directly at her. She stepped aside and the stick buried itself end-on in the soft sand, the leaf around it unfurling and waving in the breeze like a small red banner.

"What does it say?"

Doran snatched it up, read it, and threw it aside in disgust. "Fazak's scratchings," she spat.

"But what does it *say*?" I was thoroughly alarmed by now. Was this a warning that the Elite had orders to follow us? Take more wings? Kill us? I squirmed under my blanket, wanting to sit up and snatch the leaf for myself, but a glance upward told me that the Elite Guard still lingered overhead. "Doran?"

She ground the leaf under her foot, growling. "It says that if any female sees you and tells Kalis where you are, she'll be pardoned, and allowed to live in a cluster again."

I let my head drop back to rest on the blanket, oblivious to the sand that had crept over it while I wriggled about. "Perfect timing. No sooner do I drop my disguise and let everyone here know who I am—"

"No-one here will give you up." Shaya spoke loudly enough for those surrounding us to overhear, her ears set to reinforce the warning that the growl in her voice implied. "It was brave of you to choose to join us, even if I don't see much advantage in having a half-trained apprentice with us. No-one here will repay your courage by giving you up to those…those *fwerkian* half-growns." As she swore, she tore up the leaf she was holding and released the pieces to float away on the breeze. Others were doing the same, cursing Kalis and Fazak as they did so, and calling insults at the Guards who still swooped over our heads – though none of them flew low enough, I noticed, for the leaping wingless to pull them to the ground. Murgo had learned his lesson, moons past, when Dru had dragged him groundward and damaged his wing.

"I'm going to chase them off. Arrogant young pups. Shaya, may I borrow this?" Without waiting for answer, Doran snatched up Shaya's spear and picked her way across the encampment to get a clear run along the shore. Wings flapping hard, she took off, brandishing the spear as she circled about and flew toward the jeering knot of Elite.

"Too slow, too slow!" they chanted, as they swooped and dived. I recognised Murgo's thin snout as he glided past, barking, "You are *all* too slow! Be over the Ambit by moon-end." He shook the bow he carried in an unmistakeable threat. "Moon-end. We'll be checking."

"Doran, be careful, they're armed!" Rewsa's whine was lost beneath the sound of wingbeats and pounding feet as others ran along the beach to try to take off in Doran's wake. Milat led the way, waving her spear; Azmit ran behind with Winan and Froma. I recognised Carma, the artisan welcomer, and Hariz and Galyn the healers, all beating their wings furiously as they ran. Some were still unable to take off, their anger and frustration carrying them far along the beach as their wings tired and their flapping slowed, but Hariz, Carma, and two nest-nurses lifted off to cheers from the nineties who were still grounded, and circled about to join forces with Doran.

The Elite Guard, it seemed, had no teeth – or orders – for a fight, even with unarmed nest-nurses. No sooner had the females circled about to converge on them than Murgo barked a command and his entire troop set course for the *Spirax*.

"Cowards, the lot of them," said Doran, as she glided down beside me and handed Shaya her spear.

"Perhaps." Shaya drove the spear's pointed end into the sand, and bent to pick up another message-leaf. "But they've done what they needed to do." The leaf fluttered in her paw as she gazed across the camp at the nineties of cold, angry females. Some of them were piling the leaves onto their fires; others had trampled them into the sand, or crumpled them in clenched fists, but all knew what the message said.

I didn't need the Sight to know that the likelihood of betrayal had just increased a ninety-fold.

Nine

I returned to the skull to change back into my Trader's tunic, berating myself for ever having changed out of it, but knowing I could not have done otherwise. The smell of death clung to the bones over my head, a high-pitched moan assailed my ears as the wind blew coldly through the eye-sockets. I prayed for a Vision. None came, but I reminded myself that I had Seen myself standing next to Dru at his moment of triumph. I would – I must – survive to fulfil that Vision.

Of course, just because I would be alongside Dru did not mean I would still have my wings when I got there...

I shook my head to clear it of such morbid speculation and concentrated instead on climbing out through the back of the skull, being careful to avoid slipping on the oozing remnants of flesh, which still clung to the lower jaw. Outside, above the tide-line, several nines of younglings were pressing strips of tongue between flat stones, some of them standing on top of the upper rock and jumping up and down. More younglings were climbing the cliffs behind the beach, poking sticks into the crevices to try to dislodge a hibernating rockcrawler or two. Strips of meat, soaked in salt water and left to dry, were curing in the weak sun, which was warm enough to soften the edges of the ice on the crags. Several females were dragging their packs and blankets from the shelter of the cliffs and I turned an ear to catch their cries: they were getting wet as the snow and ice above melted and dripped on them.

"Well, at least Murgo and his cronies have done us one favour." Doran's voice was brisk, louder than it needed to be as she bounded over to meet me. "All those sticks and leaves burn beautifully."

Limar stood nearby watching the younglings climb, but her ears had twisted our way the moment Doran spoke. "They've also told us we've only got till the end of the moon," she called. "We should be moving on, not sitting here curing meat and cooking patties." A gust of wind tugged at our tunics and ruffled our fur, carrying a hint of further snow to our noses. "It's too cold to linger here, anyway."

"Perhaps if you actually did some work, instead of standing there 'supervising'..." Doran muttered.

"What was that?" Limar bared her teeth, sure that she had somehow been insulted.

"I said there's still plenty of work to be done." Doran flicked a conciliatory ear. "Besides, it might be possible to cross to the Forest from here. Shaya's sent Milat to scout for somewhere to land and camp on the far side of the estuary."

Limar gingerly stretched her wings, turning where she stood to indicate the encampment and the ground-bound females that trudged about the beach. "There's about a nine of you can fly right now. And we've still only got four nets. How many trips across the estuary will you each need to make? How many drax can you carry before your arms get tired and you drop someone in the water?"

More ears were turning our way, and I noticed Rewsa a few paces away, clutching her tail and whimpering.

"We've got time, Limar," I said, a snap in my voice I'd not intended. "We still have half a moon to get to the Forest. There'll be more females flying by then – and even if there aren't, it gives us time for plenty of trips across the river. I'm sure we can net everyone over by moon-end."

And I'd have been right – if there had been somewhere on the Ambit's northern bank to land.

Daylight was fading when Milat returned from her mission. She staggered a little as she landed, and Shaya guided her to the fire where I sat with Doran, Froma, Winan, and their pups. Dru bounded over too, his ears erect with anticipation of what Milat might say.

"Sit down and eat something," said Shaya, pressing a beaker of stew into Milat's paws, "then tell us."

It was clear from the set of Milat's ears, and the scent of her disappointment, that the news was not good, but we tried not to fidget while she gobbled down a second helping and emptied an entire flask of water. When she finally set the beaker aside and licked her whiskers, we all leaned toward her, ears turned to listen.

"We can't cross from here," she said, confirming my worst fears. "If we fly straight across the estuary, there's nowhere to land. The Forest runs right to the edge of sheer cliffs, and it's a mass of tanglevine and knotvine for nineties of spans."

"Did you check north along the coast as well as west along the river?"

In response to Shaya's question, Milat nodded and knelt to scratch in the sand. This time, her claw produced an outline of the river and estuary. "Here's the Ambit," she said, sketching a wavy line. She added a great curve, rounded like a groxen's rump, to represent the headland on the far shore, and a second line beneath the river to represent the ribbon of low hills that squatted between the Deadlands and the Ambit. Below and to the right of the other lines, she scratched the curve of the peninsula where we camped. "I flew north for a quarter-day and couldn't see anywhere to land – not even for myself, let alone nineties of us. Then I turned and headed back to where I'd started, and flew upriver as far as the Abandoned Cluster." She dug the tip of her claw into the sand, marking the ruins on the Ambit's southern bank, then looked up and dropped her ears in apology. "I'm sorry Shaya, Zarda – there's nowhere on the north bank that's clear enough to land so many drax and make an encampment. Not this side of the Abandoned Cluster."

Shaya sighed and dragged a foot across the sketch to erase it. "No need to apologise, Milat, it's hardly your fault. I already had an idea of what you'd find, but at least now we know for sure."

She glanced at me, as though hoping for some wisdom or insight, but all I could think to say was: "We have to make for the Eye, then?"

Shaya sighed again. "I can't see any other way."

"You mean we have to cross the mudflats?" Froma clutched the shoulders of a wriggling Sarys. "And walk all that way upriver? Through the snow?"

"I know it's a long way," said Shaya, "but we have meat to spare now – and we don't even need to carry it all."

"We don't?"

I was glad that Doran had spoken first. It saved me from sounding like the 'half-trained apprentice' Shaya still regarded me as, and allowed me to set my ears to a less quizzical angle as the hunter explained: "So long as the cold weather lasts, we can leave caches of food buried in the snow." She looked to each of us in turn as she added, "It will be hard work for those who can fly, carrying nets of the stuff up ahead, but it will be worth the effort, I think?"

We started next morning, piling meat, patties, and anything else that would freeze into the nets that had protected the seatach from seaborne scavengers. There were two nines of us now airborne, and more regaining the use of their wings each day, but we were hampered by the number of nets. While we flew back and forth to the cache sites the hunters identified, handing empty nets to another pair of flyers on our return, the weavers and those who showed any aptitude for the skill busied themselves producing more from the sea-reeds the younglings gathered.

Others continued to scavenge the seatach, using the creature's own teeth to saw at its bones, producing sharp tips for our spears and arrows, as well as the glue to bind them firm. But with every cut of meat and guts, and every flight along the river and back, we were conscious of the deadline Murgo had passed on to us: moon-end, when there would be but a sliver of moonlight above us in the evening sky. It had taken us over twenty days to get to the Ambit peninsula, and we had taken four days so far to cut up the seatach. We still had to cross the peninsula, find a way over the estuary mudflats to get to hills on the river's southern bank, then somehow get across the Ambit to the Forest. And we had to do it in less than three ninedays.

Pots and bowls were busy day and night, preparing meat, drying meat, making patties, and cooking stew; the hides were dried and scraped, and rubbed with the creature's own blubber to keep them supple and waterproof; the last of the teeth were pulled and shaped to make knives, axes and saws. Hunters and Artisans worked alongide Varna to make strong, flexible bows from the ribs, while the weavers experimented with the intestines, and found they made excellent nets and flexible bindings.

I kept my blue tunic on, in case Kalis sent another flight from the *Spirax* to look for me. I didn't think it was likely – he had made his offer clear enough – but it would be better to be cautious than caught. When I wasn't flying supplies upriver, I helped with the cooking, and added some of my special balms to wings that had been slow to heal.

And every time someone took to the sky I watched to see where they flew.

As Dru and Cavel bounded down the slope from the clifftop on our fifth day there, with more armfuls of reeds, I made for the bluff overlooking the beach. Ignoring the stab of pain that told me I had stepped on a broken pot, I took off into the wind. Below me, the seatach carcass was now little more than a giant skull and a few scattered bones, though enough meat and marrow still clung to what was left that I had no difficulty catching the stench, even as I gained height.

From the beast's remains, lines of females and younglings stretched along the beach, leading to and from each campfire. The tunic colours were less distinct than they had once been – dirtied with sand and mud, stained with seatach blood that would not come out in the saltwater washes – but it was clear that the traditional groupings were beginning to break down. Traders sat with artisans; gatherers and farmers stood with the hunters and fishers, some of them wielding spears or bows.

Purple. Purple tunics on a crowd of drax.

I'd jerked my head and tail as the Sight struck me, having to flap my wings and correct my flight path while I thought on what I'd Seen. Everyone in the same colour – a colour that no-one currently wore because the dyers had long ago concluded that there was no way to produce such a deep, rich colour from the plants and materials on and around the Expanse. Clearly the boundaries between trades and skills would continue to be eroded as our journey went on. Perhaps eventually everyone would be capable of weaving a net, wielding a spear, or applying a healing balm. It was not the way things were ordered back on the Expanse, but in the Forest we would all need to learn new skills or die.

I flew higher after a glance upward to check the cloudbase. It was too cold for floaters, but it didn't hurt to maintain the habit, even during the freeze. A nine or so others were airborne too, including one or two who had still been grounded the previous day. They swooped and dived, clearly enjoying the feel of the wind under their wings once again, but I couldn't help but look back toward the *Spirax*. Its outline had been softened by damp and distance, but its dark bulk on the southern horizon still provided an intimidating reminder of how close we still were to the Expanse – and Kalis.

I turned north to glide over the peninsula, noting the clumps of sea bramble that those on foot would need to avoid as they made their way over the hump of land. With plenty of flyers to guide the wingless and the walking wounded, that part of the journey would be straightforward. The problems would start on the northern shore of the peninsula, where the land dipped to meet the tongue of Deadlands Marsh that lay between the peninsula, the sea, and the river's southern hills.

I flew on, to the place where sea, river, and Deadlands met. I'd flown over it before once, when Vizan took me back to the Forest after my misadventure with Doran, but on that occasion my attention had been fixed on the terrors that awaited us beneath the crimson-leaved vines on the far bank of the Ambit. I'd not even noticed the vast stretch of thick black mud that stretched beneath us at low tide. Now, as the smell hit me, I took a better look and almost whimpered out loud at the difficulties the groundlings would face.

Rivulets of water carved channels through the mud toward the receding tide. A bevy of scallets honked to each other as they frolicked across the black, glistening surface. As clumsy as they looked, with their rounded bodies and squashed snouts, they made easy work of skipping over the mud, their strong fore-flippers leaving distinctive curved marks which their hind-flippers twisted and flattened. Every few leaps, they would stop to sniff at the mud, and I watched as they formed a circle to dig something out from the sludge. The spherical grey blob they pulled to the surface was fringed with tentacles, and I saw why the burrowers had formed a circle: it made it easy for each of them to bite a tentacle and render the thing helpless. With a squelch, the thing was pulled apart, blood mixing with the mud and turning the ripples blue as the scallets scurried back to their burrows, each bearing its prize.

Here and there, glistening suckerworms clung to the slime-strewn rocks that protruded from the morass, their thin, transparent bodies writhing as they searched for moisture. I remembered that Vizan had warned about the dangers that lurked beneath the surface of the mud, but I couldn't recall what they all were. Adult suckerworms, I remembered, were harmless, though you wouldn't want to touch one, but their young…yes, there was something about their young…

I shook my head. I'd have to consult my notes, if I could find them in the depths of my pouch. Perhaps I'd scratched something down at the time. In any case, that sucking, stinking mud had to be avoided. But how? It stretched for spans, chasing the river estuary westward till it morphed into the hillocks and dank pools of the Deadlands. The hills that lined the Ambit's southern bank would provide a refuge, and safe ground to walk on, but how to reach them?

I flew west and a little south, to glide over the Deadlands. The black pools were glazed with ice, the low mounds and brambles covered with snow. I checked the entire distance, from the high tide mark to the eastern boundary of the Deadlands. Perhaps there was a way – if the ice was solid enough…

As I turned into the wind to return to the beach where the seatach lay, I caught sight of something writhing in the mud and flew lower to see what it was. A dead scallet lay on a mudbank, its skin dry and mottled, eyes reduced to empty sockets. Its body was a mass of wriggling young suckerworms, and I remembered with a jolt to my stomachs what it was that Vizan had said about them. Flapping hard to regain some height, as though the things could reach me where I flew, I made my way back to the others to report what I'd seen.

"Suckerworms? But they just feed on mud and seawater don't they? Horrible things to look at, but harmless enough." Doran spooned some seatach stew into bowls for us both, handed the ladle to Shaya, and waddled across the few spans of sand to the rocks where I was sitting.

"Thank you." I gave the stew a sniff and a stir, detecting hints of chalkmoss and salt as well as the rich, dark meat. I waited till Shaya had joined us before I answered Doran's questions. "The adults are harmless," I said, "but the young lie beneath the mud in groups and attack anything that disturbs them. They burrow under the skin, feed, grow, and suck their victim dry – very slowly."

There were squeals and whimpers from the younglings within earshot, and from Winan who was sitting a few spans away beside the fire to our left. "That's horrible," she snapped. "You shouldn't be saying such things in front of the young ones."

"They need to know." I waved my spoon to indicate the wider group, many of whom hadn't heard me. Blobs of stew dripped from it and spattered the hem of my tunic, and I dropped the spoon into my bowl to brush at them while I made my point. "Everyone needs to know. They all need to understand what's at stake if they don't keep exactly to the route."

"But you said yourself, you don't know where the route is – or even if there is one!" Limar, warming her tail and wings beside the fire to our right, chimed in. "I say that you fly if you can, and carry those who can't."

I chewed on a mouthful of meaty stew and looked about, at the nines of fires and the nineties of females and younglings. Even the youngest of the wingless was six moons old, and most of them were now too big and heavy to carry in a harness, even if we had the time to fashion them. "It would need two flyers for each one who can't take off," I said, "and there's what, a couple of nines who've got our wings back at the moment?"

I ignored Limar's snort and her muttered *Never lost yours*, and looked instead to Shaya and Doran for some sensible advice. "Is it practical, do you think? Carrying everyone who can't fly?"

Shaya, who had sat down on a blanket beside me, licked her bowl clean while she considered it. "It's a long stretch to get to those hills, even on the wing – nothing but brambles and hillocks and mudbanks for beats on end. To walk will take a half-day at least. And there's the tide to consider."

"But there's ice, too," I said. "The mudflats are frozen over above the high-tide line."

Froma ladled a second helping of stew for Sarys, handed her the bowl, and came over to join us. "Isn't that what Colex said, Shaya. That the ground was frozen?"

She smelled of alarm. I saw those nearby react to it, ears pricked, fur on end, tails waving, and could think of no immediate retort. All those who were back on the wing had looked to the Deadlands for signs of life, for distant splashes of colour, for some movement that indicated the other group was still alive. There had been nothing there but the crackle of ice, the smothering stillness of snow, and the odour of frozen sludge.

I'd never seen Shaya undecided before, but her ears flicked back and forth as she considered the options. She licked a paw, smoothed the immaculate fur on her neck, and finally set her ears to show cautious agreement. "If we hadn't been given that deadline, I'd say we should wait till we had more flyers and net the rest across. But we don't have time for that." She pulled a cloth from her tunic pocket to wipe her paws. "I don't like it, but unless anyone has a better idea, we have to risk the mudflats and hope that the ice is firm enough to hold us. If we can trace the shortest route from hillock to hillock, it will keep us above the mud for as long as possible."

"Let's get to the other side of this peninsula first." Doran licked her bowl clean and put it aside to dry. "We can camp on the northern sands tomorrow night, and work out the best way to cross the mudflats from there."

The younglings had named the curve of shoreline 'Seatach Beach', and the creature's great skull seemed to watch from all four of its eye sockets as we packed our belongings and set off up the steep slope that led to the neck of the peninsula.

The morning had dawned cold but clear, and as two of the hunters led the way up the rise, water dripped from the cliffs as the weak sunshine warmed the edges of the snowline.

"This won't help us cross the mud," said Doran, indicating the clear skies and melting ice. She adjusted the straps on Cavel's new seatach-hide carry-pouch, tied his beaker to it, and gave him a lick.

"But if it stays clear, it will freeze solid tonight," I said, spreading my wings to test the breeze. "In fact..." I paused, thinking about the practicalities of moving over unknown territory with only the monochrome assistance of night-vision. "Perhaps that would be the best time for us to travel across it." The more I thought about it, the more I was sure it would work. "The Spiral will light our way."

"But we've already been travelling all day."

"And most of us had to walk. It's all very well for you flyers, but the rest of us are tired."

"The tide's in."

"It's too dangerous to cross at night."

I knew my ears were betraying my annoyance at the number of objections to my plan and made an effort to set them to a more placatory angle. The sun had almost vanished behind the mountains and the sky to the west was a wash of red and purple. Over the ocean, the blackness was broken by a moon that had already slipped a sliver past the full, a reminder that time was running out: we had twenty-four days left to cross the Ambit and leave Drax territory for good.

Looking up, I spiralled a paw over my tunic as the lights of the Great Spiral began to glimmer in the dimming sky. "The Spiral has blessed us with this crisp, clear night," I called, raising my voice so that it would carry across the scrubby, snow-covered slope where we camped. "The tide will turn again soon. The ground we cross will be frozen, the mud and the marsh will ice over, the Spiral will light our way. Even the mitches will leave us alone on a freezing night. By morning we'll be on the hills overlooking the Ambit, and we can rest."

"Well, I'm not going." Limar squatted beside her carry-pouch and made a display of unfastening it. "I'm not taking Dru or any other youngling across that...that death-trap while I'm tired and they're hungry."

"I didn't say we shouldn't eat." I waved a paw at the flat, dank land beyond the campfires, where ice glistened and crackled as the temperature fell. The wind had dropped, but we were close enough to the Forest now to hear occasional shrieks and chilling screams that sounded like death-cries, though I thought they might be hunting calls or some creature seeking its young. "We can sleep for a short while," I said, trying to ignore the harsh rattling noise that clattered across mud and water. "The tide will be on its way out soon, and the ground will freeze. We'll have to be sure it's firm enough to hold us, but we must set out before moon-zenith if we're to have a hope of crossing by morning."

Shaya and Doran lent their arguments to mine – there was no guarantee the weather would hold, the mudflats would soften if the day was fine, the tide would turn – and what if the morning brought fog – or even rain? But Limar, Froma, Rewsa, and several nines of others were adamant: they would wait for the daylight.

"It's their choice," said Shaya, holding up a paw to stop me as I opened my mouth to continue the argument. She said it loudly enough for them all to hear as they unrolled their blankets and settled their younglings. "We could pick them up and carry them, I suppose, but the night will be busy enough without saving fools from themselves. Get something to eat, Zarda."

We ate quickly and repacked our carry-pouches. Flyers were designated to scout the shortest route to the hills on the Ambit's southern shore, and to set up camp on the nearest safe slope. I placed my carry-pouch on the pile to be flown across. "I'll walk," I said, when Shaya suggested that I join the other flyers. "This was my idea. I don't think I should leave the flightless and the wingless to cross on their own."

Shaya dipped an ear in acknowledgement and handed me an unlit torch. "Then, when the tide turns, perhaps you would lead the way?"

Ice crunched under my feet as I stepped cautiously onto the mud. I waited for a moment, holding the torch aloft to check the ground ahead and beneath me. My feet were chilled, but the way was firm and I took a step, then another. "It's frozen solid," I called. "Come along, everyone – but take care to stay above the tide-line. Let's get the younglings over – quickly now."

The distant hiss-and-wash off to my right confirmed that the tide was receding, but it would turn again before dawn. The part of the estuary I'd flown over the previous day would be awash by sun-up; the mudflats we were stepping across would still be frozen – but for how long? Perhaps, if Limar, Rewsa, and the others saw that we were crossing safely, they would set off before the morning brought new challenges.

Ahead of me, a light sparked in the darkness and darted right and left before steadying at what seemed to be snout-level. A torch, in Doran's paws, indicating the nearest bramble-strewn hillock at the edge of the Deadlands. I adjusted my path slightly to head toward it.

"Is that where we're going?" Dru's voice piped from the darkness behind my left wing. I didn't ask whether Limar knew where he was. "It's a long way."

"That's the nearest dry mound," I said. "We'll need to go along the edge of it because it's covered in brambletrap. Where's Cavel?"

"I'm here." On my right wing.

"Your dam has flown ahead to put the torch there to help us walk in the right direction," I said, extending a wingtip for him to grasp. "When we get there, we'll see another torch on the next mound, and another one after that. By then, we should be able to see the campfires on the hillside by the river and we'll be nearly there."

"But that's spans and spans! And I'm *tired*." Cavel's paw tightened around my wingtip as he spoke.

Another youngling called, "Can't we wait with Limar and the others?"

"No. The mud is firm now," I said. "If we wait till the morning, it might not be."

"Does that mean they'll die?" The voice was a wail, which others took up, and I hastily cast about for something to distract them all.

"No, no, of course not. It just means their journey will be more difficult. Would you want to walk all that way with the tide coming in and mud sticking to your feet?" I looked down to see where I was treading and realised I had Seen this moment: my feet, the younglings' scampering limbs, the mud...it was the fulfilment of the Vision I had had in the Council chamber, the Vision that had made me realise I should travel with the exiles.

Dru must have noticed some reaction on my part – my hackles rising, or a hesitation in my step, perhaps. I felt his paw in mine and he whispered, "Did you See something?"

I shook my head, then my entire body, shedding the strange sensation that always came with a Vision fulfilled. "I Saw this; now it's real. But somehow it always seems a little *unreal*, when something you've Seen actually happens. You'll find that out for yourself soon enough." The other younglings were still whimpering and I raised my voice so they could all hear: "Now – who can tell me the Legend of the Spiral that is helping to light our way?"

"Me, I can! Before the Spiral..." Dru let go of my paw and scampered about, ice crunching beneath his feet. I sucked in a breath, fur on end, as I grabbed his shoulder and pulled him back.

"Stay behind me, Dru!" I placed a paw on his head to reassure him – I couldn't see or smell any break in the ice where he'd bounced on it – and deflected attention back to the story. "I know that you know the legend. What about somebody else? Cavel, perhaps?"

I glanced round as I spoke. Cavel looked less sure than Dru did, but he peeked up at the Spiral for a moment as though for inspiration, let go of my wing to clasp his paws together, and began: "Before the Spiral, there was the sun and the moon. And they had two eggs. And one of the eggs had lots of little younglings – and that's us. And the other egg just had one big youngling – and that was the Spiral. And the Spiral grew and grew and grew." At this, Cavel extended his arms, almost swiping Ravar on the nose in the process, and I held up a hand.

"That's very good, Cavel, and very well told. Manda, do you know what happened next?"

Manda moved a little closer to me, cradling her toy egg and rocking it slightly from side to side as she continued the tale. "The Spiral grew so big that it was more biggerer than anything," she piped. I made a mental note that her phrasing needed help, but allowed her to continue. "And the sun and the moon said that it had to leave because there wasn't room in the sky for all of them. But the Spiral was unhappy and didn't want to go."

"Thank you, Manda. Would someone else like to finish the story?"

Chiva, Winan's pup, spoke up. "The Spiral saw that it was taking the light from the sun and the moon, and hurting the little younglings. So it agreed to go further away. But it didn't go too far. It stayed close enough so that we could see it and remember; and it could always look after us."

"That was well told, all of you. Your dams have obviously taught you well." The torch up ahead looked a little closer, a little brighter. If I could manage to keep their thoughts occupied a while longer... "Now, the Spiral sends us gifts to help us remember that it is looking after us. How many of them can you think of?"

They did well, listing *spirorns*, the *Spirax*, slimecrawlers, the strange shell-shapes in the rocks of the Copper Hills, and several different crawling creatures that lived in tiny spiral cases.

A small paw tugged at my tunic and I looked round to find Chiva tucked ahead of Cavel. "If the Spiral is looking after us, why are we out here in the dark and the cold?"

Why indeed? I stepped on a sheet of ice, claws scrabbling for purchase, and picked my way through frosted runnels of mud. My breath misted, my legs ached, my left foot kept reminding me that I'd bruised it, and my nostrils were numb. Frozen water reeds shattered when I stepped on them, their broken stems sharp enough to scratch as they were trampled on; the scent of rotting weeds, mud, and salt hung on the light inshore breeze. Chiva was scurrying beside me, waiting for an answer, and I gave her the only one I had: "Vizan and I both Saw that Dru will one day defeat the Koth. When Dru hatched without wings, the Spiral was not punishing Dru – not punishing any of you – it was testing Kalis' belief. And Kalis' belief was not strong enough. Now he is without an heir and without a Fate-seer. He is the one alone in the dark. We have the Spiral to guide us, and we must believe that its lights will help us find our way."

Chiva pulled on her ears for a moment and scratched her snout as she thought this over. She turned her head to look back along the line of females and wingless younglings that straggled back into the darkness, then looked ahead to the glow of the torch that was now mere spans away. "Find our way to where?" she asked.

And for that, I had no answer.

Ten

"I keep underestimating how long something like this will take." I sat by a smouldering campfire on the hill beside the Ambit, Shaya and Doran on either side of me, their exhausted younglings already dozing beneath their blankets. All of us had our fur fluffed for warmth and nursed a beaker of avalox tea. We didn't have much avalox left, but after the long night we'd had, I thought that everyone who had made the crossing with us deserved a decent drink. The last of them were still straggling across the last few spans of frozen mud, while in the east the sky was shading from black to deep blue in the first hint of sunrise. I sighed. "I thought everyone would be here by now."

"It doesn't matter." Doran sipped her tea, her gaze fixed on the hump of land to the south. "We have to wait for the others anyway."

"Let's hope they set out soon," said Shaya. She pointed left toward the estuary, where the tide had already covered the rocks

I'd flown over at low tide the previous day. "With the tide washing in and the sun coming up, it will get a lot muddier down there."

Below us, Galyn and Hariz were checking the feet of all the new arrivals, sluicing them with river water if necessary, and making some sit down and lift their feet higher for a closer inspection of toes and claws. "It's getting worse already, by the look of it," I said. "Galyn and Hariz have made the last few nines wash their feet thoroughly."

Shaya grunted assent. "Everyone who wasn't airborne came by the same route," she said. "It was bound to get a bit worn." She sighed. "If it gets worse out there, we'll have to start netting them over. We can't risk anyone getting wormrot."

I glanced skyward at the fading lights of the Spiral and the vast moon that was falling towards the mountains. "It'll take a lot of time we don't have."

"I know – but what choice do we have?" Shaya gestured at the campsite and the hillside it lay on. The hill, and those that lay beyond it to the west, were not much higher than some of the sand-dunes we had negotiated in the early part of our journey. Swathed in snow, they looked innocuous enough, a smooth, undulating route along the southern bank of the river – but I already knew enough about walking to know that the path would not be as easy as it looked. There would be pockets of deep snow in the dips and hollows that would have to be dug through, while sharp stones and hidden thorns could damage unwary feet.

Further west, where the river meandered in huge lazy bends, we would need the flyers to direct those on foot along the shortest route, otherwise they might spend half a day following the river in a great loop while moving a bare few spans west.

"Perhaps that's what they wanted." Doran's voice interrupted my thoughts and gave me something new to ponder.

"What?" Shaya looked as though she had found a flisk in her tea, and she turned her head to stare across the mudflats. In the distance, the long shadows of those still on the peninsula moved and merged as the nines over there began to make ready. The hunter's ears were set back, and her whiskers quivered with disapproval.

Doran waved her beaker to indicate the distant figures. "There aren't many of them over there now – just a few nines. Perhaps they thought, if they waited, we'd send nets back for them."

"Let them wait, then," Shaya growled. She drained her own beaker and licked it clean. "I'm going to get some sleep while they work out that they'll have to make their own way across. I suggest you do the same." She leaned down to give Ravar a sniff and a lick, before unrolling her blanket.

"Perhaps..." Doran unrolled her own blanket and lay down next to Cavel, feet toward the fire. "Perhaps we can net some of the younglings over, at least?"

Shaya grunted and rolled over, giving me a good view of her damaged right wing. "Perhaps."

I followed their lead, smoothing creases from my crumpled blanket and using my carry-pouch to rest my head, but tired as I was after the night's exertions, I couldn't sleep. The wash of tide and river, the smell of salt and mud reminded me of the danger the others still faced; a danger that would be increased by the faint warmth of the sun as it rose, unclouded, over the sea.

"Zarda? Zarda!" Dru was beside me, shaking my shoulder, his fingers tugging painfully at my fur. "I Saw! We have to stop them!"

"Stop who? What did you See?" I sat up, wondered what the stale smell was, realised it was me. To either side of me, Shaya and Doran slumbered, though Shaya turned an ear toward me as I spoke, listening for threats even in sleep.

"He says the others are in danger." I twisted around to find Varna behind me, and realised she had followed Dru across the camp. "Limar is out there," she added, her tail signalling concern. "Can you get a net? Can you help them?"

"Doran?" I shook her shoulder. "Shaya? We need nets." I unpeeled myself from my blanket and stood up, shading my eyes with a paw as the low sun bounced off the ice and water lining the mudflats. A line of drax – so far away that they looked no bigger than flisks – moved along the route we'd taken overnight, a thread of colour against the black.

"There's over two nines out there," Shaya said, already at my shoulder, "and we have six complete nets."

I stretched my wings, glancing down at Dru. "We'll have to fetch as many as we can. They're in trouble."

"We told them it would be more dangerous to cross in daylight." Shaya did not seem inclined to move. "But it's still early – the ice should hold firm for a while yet, if they hurry."

"No." I gripped her arm – too tight, as she made clear with a snap of her teeth – and pointed with my free paw. "We have to start netting them over now."

"A Vision?" It sounded almost like an accusation. Shaya shook herself free of my grip as Doran sat up, grumbling, and several others rolled over under their blankets and demanded to know what the barking was about.

I dipped an ear to confirm the answer to Shaya's question. "A Vision, yes." I didn't tell her it wasn't mine.

"Very well. I don't like having to rescue others from their own stupidity and stubbornness, but we'll do what we can. Milat? Fetch the nets."

I flew with Doran, a net flapping in the breeze as it dangled between us. Milat and Winan led the way, with four other pairs at our tails. Limar and those with her were almost a third of the way across the flats, approaching the first of the low mounds where a torch guttered, its dying flames feeble in the sunlight. It was obvious where we had stepped during the night – the snow had been swept into uneven piles by nineties of swishing tails, the ice beneath clawed and roughened where we had fought for grip. Doran pointed to several worn patches ahead of the drax on the ground. "Look how thin the ice is there, you can see the mud showing through."

Beneath us, the groundlings' steps were slow and laboured, tails dragged in the mud, those who had wings were flapping them in an effort to lift off. Some of the younglings were straying from the path we'd made, looking for something to eat, perhaps, or attempting to find a less muddy route. When I saw Sarys, Ellet, and a couple of others scampering about on the ice near the high-tide line, my fur stood on end.

Waves from river and sea met and sloshed just a few spans from where they jumped and slid. The ice there would already be softening in the sun; the water would hasten its disappearance.

I tugged on the net to get Doran's attention. "We need to fetch those younglings first. Looks like Sarys' curiosity is putting her in harm's way again."

She flicked an ear in agreement and we called to the others as we angled our wings to turn and descend.

In the estuary below, squeals and shouts turned to howls of alarm. Dru's Vision was becoming a reality.

Eleven

"There's nothing I can do. Nothing anyone can do."

The morning had vanished in a flurry of panic, flight, and frantic efforts to free Sarys, Ellet, and the other younglings from the mud before the suckerworms found them. Ellet had been fortunate, as had three of those with her; they had been freed from the clinging, sucking muck in time. But Sarys had stepped into a patch of quickmud. She'd been hip-deep in the stuff within a few beats. We didn't dare land beside her for fear of being sucked in ourselves, but hovering over her to pull on her arms made the youngling howl with pain without moving her at all. Milat had spread a blanket over the mud and lay on it as she tried to scoop the sludge away from the squealing youngling, but for every beaker-full she scooped, water slopped in to replace it, and the muck grew stickier.

Froma had scurried straight across the ice as soon as she heard Sarys's howls, sliding, slipping, and wings outstretched for balance, heedless of the danger to herself. We had to hold her back from rushing straight into the mud as she tried to reach her youngling.

"We'll get her out, Froma." It took all my strength to hold on to her flailing left arm, and I jerked my head aside as her teeth snapped where my snout had been. "If you go to her, we'll have to pull you out too."

"Calm down." Winan, despite her size, had to use both paws to wrestle with the tiny Froma's right arm. "You're upsetting Sarys, Froma. You smell terrified and your fur's on end. Don't let her see that you're scared."

Another snap, this time in Winan's direction, but the struggling stopped and I'd eased my hold on her a little.

"Of course I'm scared!" Her voice was a whimper. "The tide's coming in, the mud's sucking her under..." Ragged breaths, a whisper: "She'll die."

I'd patted her arm, trying to smooth her fur though I realised it was hopeless – Froma couldn't mask her terror, though she did stop trying to push against us and she set her ears to a more confident angle as she spoke to Sarys. "They'll get you out, little one, don't worry."

"What we need," I said, as I watched Milat's futile efforts to scoop away the mud, "is a harness. Something like I used to carry Dru."

"Well we don't have any," Milat snapped, "and we don't have time to make one."

Away to the west, there were howls and cries on the wind as the other flyers began to net younglings to safety. Limar and the rest of her group had halted on a low mound, huddled together as they watched and waited, their inaudible murmurs punctuated by occasional howls of sympathy and whimpers of sorrow.

"What about a half-finished net?" Winan looked at me as she spoke. "There's one in my carry-pouch, shall I fetch it?"

Milat knelt up and stretched her arms and shoulders. "Yes. It might be worth a try."

With a glance at Doran, who moved across to take her place beside Froma, Winan took off. Her wingbeats were almost inaudible beneath the crash of waves as the waters heaved and mingled, rising inexorably toward us. Scallets honked as they rolled with the waves, and the adult suckerworms, their single foot clinging to the rocks, stretched themselves thin as they reached for the water, writhing with the wind.

And Sarys began to thrash about, howling, "Something bit me! It hurts – it hurts!"

Milat stood up and stepped back, the lay of her ears and scent of her alarm confirming what I already knew: we were too late. The young worms had burrowed under Sarys' skin and were beginning to feed on her.

My stomachs roiled and Froma began to howl again. It took all my strength, and Doran's, to hold her back till Winan returned. The big female was panting with effort as she held out the knotted strands in her paws. "It's a full width," she gasped, "but half the length it should be."

Milat took one end and held it out to examine it. "It should be strong enough if we roll it up from the edge to edge."

The oncoming tide had reached Sarys by the time Milat knelt to push the makeshift harness around the youngling's chest beneath her arms. Winan and Milat took off and hovered low, while Doran passed the ends of the net to them. Pulling upward and flapping hard, they heaved the youngling free, the mud giving her up with a lingering suck.

"Get a net," Milat called, as they turned to fly to the hillside, Sarys dangling between them. "Bring Froma."

I left Doran to wait with Froma, and flew with Winan and Milat as they whisked Sarys back to the camp. I called for someone to bring a net, but when Azmit brought one, Shaya handed it to Milat instead. "The Fate-seer should be with Sarys," she said.

I knew I couldn't help the youngling – her legs were bloodied as well as muddied, already swollen below the knees, smelling of rot – but I could ease her pain at least. As Milat took off again, Galyn hurried over, bearing pots of warm water to sluice the mud from Sarys's fur. The healer stretched out a paw to rub the youngling's legs, and I grasped her arm to prevent her coming into contact with the punctured flesh. "Don't touch."

Sarys was shivering, her fur on end, and she began to rock where she sat as Galyn slipped a blanket over her shoulders. "Where's Froma-muz?" she whimpered.

"Milat and Doran are fetching her in a net," I said. "She'll be here any moment now."

"Could you rub your legs for me, Sarys, as I pour the water over them?" Galyn tipped a little more water over the matted fur, and handed Sarys a cloth. "That's it. Looking cleaner already."

"Well done, Sarys." I put a comforting paw on her head as I stood; it was safe enough to do that for the moment, but it wouldn't be long before... *Pain. Sleep. Death.* The brief Vision didn't tell me anything I didn't already know, but it was a shock to See it all the same. "You were very brave." I turned and took a few steps away. My stomachs were empty, but they churned now as if they had something to regurgitate. Shadows on the ground heralded the arrival of Froma in the net, and I moved to intercept her before she could rush to Sarys. Best that the youngling didn't hear what I had to say.

"Froma..."

Seeing the relief, the hope in the artisan's eyes, I choked on what I was about to tell her. But she must have smelled my despair, seen the set of my ears, for she halted in her tracks and her demeanour changed in a beat from anticipation to alarm, her hackles rising, ears upright, and tail twitching. Around us, the babble of conversation had dropped to a murmur: I knew without looking that the entire camp was watching and wondering. "It took too long," I said. "I'm sorry, Froma. There's nothing I can do. Nothing anyone can do."

"No." Froma's teeth snapped together as she barked her denial. "No. She was just exploring. Having some fun. Just..." With an angry slap of her tail, she pushed past me and hurried up the slope toward Sarys.

"Be careful," I called after her. "Don't touch her where the mud clings."

I wasn't sure she'd heard me – or whether she would take any notice even if she had – but when I made my way back to Sarys's side, I found Froma holding the youngling's paw and licking her snout. Sarys's legs were stiffening, the swelling already spreading above her knees, but I set my ears to a neutral angle as I crouched next to her. "I'll brew some zenox tea for you," I said. "It will help with the pain and make you sleep."

As I got to my feet and made my way wearily to my campfire to find my carry-pouch, I heard Sarys's voice behind me, weak and thready as she spoke to her dam. "Will I be alright, Froma-muz? I'm not going to die am I? It hurts…"

"It's much worse than when we found that dead drax in the seatach," Winan said as we flew back from the Deadlands, where Sarys's body had been lowered to her last nest. "One of our own. A youngling…" She choked to a halt for several beats. "My Chiva's so upset. They quarrelled all the time but…" This time, she couldn't continue.

"I'm afraid Sarys won't be the last." Milat, flying ahead of us, flicked her ears in apology at her harsh words, though I knew she was right.

Behind me, Froma was still howling, and a glance over my shoulder confirmed that Rewsa was one of those carrying her net. "That'll be a help," I muttered. Rewsa's wings had healed only that morning, and despite the harm she'd done with her tail-plucking she'd been able to take to the air. She had spent the flight opining that Sarys was 'better off with the Spiral', and that the rest of us 'would be joining her soon'. I wondered whether I should drop back a little and attempt to say something myself, or at least tell Rewsa to shut her teeth for a while, but it didn't take much thought to know that that would probably make things worse. Before we had taken off, Limar had joined Froma in throwing blame at everyone except themselves, and at me in particular; no sense making myself a bigger target than I was already. If Froma didn't want to listen to Rewsa's gloom and doom, she could snap at her herself.

"What's that?" Milat pointed to our right and banked that way.

As Winan, Doran, and I followed in her slipstream, I saw what had attracted her attention. On the Ambit peninsula, where everyone had waited to cross the mud, a pawful of campfires still burned.

"Don't tell me they haven't all crossed," said Doran. "We're running out of time, we can't keep waiting for people."

119

There were nine or so females and younglings huddled round the flames as we landed on the slope above them. Most looked to be asleep, but as we folded our wings one of the figures sat up, silhouetted against the fire as she unrolled herself from her blanket and picked her way through the slushy snow toward us. She wrung her hands as she welcomed us, and I realised it was Carma, the female who had greeted Taral and me cycles ago when we had visited Rewsa on our way to check the river ice.

"What are you all doing?" Milat barked the query loudly enough for her voice to carry beyond Carma to the apparently-sleeping forms beside the fire. "We can't wait another day and night, we have to get moving or we'll still be on this side of the river by moon-end."

As though to reinforce her point, a cloud slipped across the moon, deepening the shadows and blotting out a section of the Spiral's light.

"You don't need to wait." Carma gestured behind her at her companions. "We've discussed it, all of us, and we're staying here."

"But...you *can't* stay here." Doran's voice was brittle with anxiety, though, like Milat and Carma, it was little more than a harsh whisper.

"The Elite Guard will be back," I pointed out. "They've given us a deadline. At moon-end, they'll come and check that we've all crossed the Ambit. If you and your younglings are still here..." I trailed off, not wishing to spell it out.

Milat had no such qualms. "You'll lose your wings at best," she hissed. "At worst, they'll kill you. Do you really want to risk—"

"We've decided." Carma's paws were still locked together, but her voice was firm. With her ears set forward, and the scent of determination pouring from every hair, she was more resolute than I had ever seen her. "If we go to the Forest, chances are we'll all die anyway. No—" She held up a paw as Milat took a breath to speak again, then went on: "Don't bother giving us the speeches or the arguments again. Any of you." Her glare took in Doran and Winan, and flicked over me to Milat. "We're staying here. On the peninsula. There's shelter in that seatach skull on the other beach, there are scallets and rockcrawlers to catch and eat.

We've food enough between us for a moon or so, and by then the fish will be back in shallower waters."

I looked at Doran, then at Milat, who shook her head. They smelled of anger and frustration, mingled with sorrow, and I knew my own demeanour reflected the same. After a beat or two, Milat flicked her ears and set them to an angle that indicated she respected Carma's decision, but didn't agree with it. "If you change your minds," she said, "I expect our trail will be easy enough to follow. Unless there's another snowstorm."

In which case, I thought, *Lights help us all.*

We all touched snouts with Carma and trudged up the nearest rise to catch a breeze. "What will we tell the others?" said Doran, as we took off and set course back toward the bank of the Ambit.

"The truth," said Milat, shortly, "but not till morning. For now, I suggest we all get some rest."

It had been a long and tiring day and night, and I drifted off as soon as I'd rolled into my blanket...

And woke to full light, and cries of alarm.

Twelve

When I opened my eyes, Doran was a mere step away, and as I sat up and pushed the blanket aside, she held out a paw to help me to my feet. "It's Limar, Zarda. I was just about to wake you."

"Limar?" I tweaked my whiskers to banish the last fuddlement of sleep, but the confusion remained. Limar had been as angry as anyone the previous day. Had she returned to join Carma on the peninsula? Had she realised she should have crossed the mudflats earlier, and set out towards the Deadlands as penance?

"She's there, look!" Doran pointed south and swore under her breath. Her other paw squeezed my shoulder. "She tested her wings this morning and took off. She's heading for the *Spirax*."

I saw Limar then, her distinctive pink tunic bright against the high clouds that were scudding in from the south-west. She must have left soon after dawn, I guessed, to be so far south already. "I must go." I still clutched a corner of the blanket in my paws, and I began to roll it up, made a mess of it, and flapped it straighter. I concentrated on the fabric, trying not to think about what Kalis might do. "I'll have to see Kalis myself, try to explain—"

"No." Doran's voice was firm, as was the paw that pressed my arm and made me hand over the blanket. In a moment she had rolled it tidily, ready to go back in my carry-pouch. "You're not to go anywhere, Shaya said. She's sent Milat to take care of it." She set the blanket on the ground and pointed again. "Don't you see them? There look. A hunter, a fisher, and two artisans."

There were four of them. They were flying slightly higher than Limar, probably feeling for a favourable wind, and their wings were a blur. But… "They won't catch her. She has too much of a head start."

"Her wings have just healed. She'll get tired."

"She might even need to land for a rest." Varna's voice. I looked around to find her standing a few spans off, one paw resting on Dru's shoulder as he gazed into the distance to follow the pursuit. "I saw something similar happen once," she added, glancing across at me and flicking an ear, "when I was still Guardflight."

I flicked my own ear to acknowledge her comment, before returning my attention to the sky. Was it my imagination, or were the pursuers a few spans closer now?

Dru confirmed my observation with a cry of, "They're catching up!", and Cavel bounced up and down, calling, "Go on, Milat! Faster!"

"Limar's getting lower," said Doran, her voice matter-of-fact though her fur was on end and her ears upright. Blue vinesmoke curled from our campfire, masking other smells for a moment as it was blown toward us by a contrary gust of wind. Then, as the hunting group closed in on Limar the breeze blew the smoke away from me to drift toward Varna, and I caught the scent of others nearby: anxiety, excitement, distress, disappointment, betrayal. I looked around to find every snout turned skyward. There was no way of telling who felt what, or whether the disappointment was because Limar had fled – or because she was being chased.

"If she gets close enough to the Expanse, the Guardflight will help her." Azmit the hunter reeked of frustration, doubtless wishing she could join Milat in the air. Her observation voiced my own thoughts. It was one thing for Taral to pretend he didn't know me when he was distanced from the *Spirax* and able to take charge; it would be another thing for him to ignore a drax who would no doubt be calling for help. Even if he didn't send Guardflight to intercept...

"The Elite Guard will be watching too," I said. "They're the ones who brought the message."

"Don't fret so. Milat and the others will catch her long before she gets anywhere near the Expanse. There – see how she's starting to glide more and flap less?"

Shaya was at my shoulder, her matter-of-fact report shifting my attention back to what was actually happening. She was right: Limar's flight pattern had changed. She would glide a little, flap a little, glide a little more. Her wingbeats were sluggish, their sweep and angle straining as she fought to make progress. I remembered how my own wings had ached after days of disuse – and mine had not even been injured.

Limar swerved and dipped as the pursuers closed in, though what she hoped to gain by such dodging I couldn't imagine. All she was doing was tiring herself and making their task easier.

The final manoeuvre, when it came, was executed with the sort of care and precision Milat would have learned when netting floaters. A net was extended between the four pursuers as they flew below and behind Limar. The non-hunters, new to the manoeuvre, took a few beats to adjust to the flight-pattern, but when the four of them accelerated upward – two above, two below Limar – she was scooped into the middle of the net. Each flyer crossed with her diagonal opposite and the catch was complete, the net closed. Within a few beats, the four flyers had turned and set course back toward us, the net – writhing and jerking with Limar's no-doubt-frantic struggles – dangling between them. A sigh ran through the watching crowd and I scented relief, admiration for the manoeuvre – and, again, a hint of disappointment. Varna was growling, Dru was leaping about, shouting curses I didn't know he knew at Limar.

Beside me, Doran shook her fur straight and set her ears to signal relief. "It will take them a while to get back here," she said, as she stooped to pick up her cooking pot. "Let's have something to eat, shall we? And a beaker of tea."

At Shaya's direction, Limar was set down in the dip between the hill where we'd made our encampment and the next rise. After they'd untangled the net, her captors stepped back – far enough to isolate Limar, but close enough that she knew there was no point even trying to take off.

Those who were able to fly to the further hillside had done so, ensuring that Limar was surrounded, while the younglings had been given simple tasks to keep them out of the way – stir this pot, re-pack that pouch, see if you can find some seed-pods for the fires. But as I stood at the base of the slope, a little apart from the crowd, I noticed that many of the younglings had managed to find vantage points. With everyone gathered on the slopes where they could look down on Limar, the moss and snow had vanished beneath a mass of colourful tunics, cramped and crowded together. Even now, the colours were not completely intermingled. Here and there a healer's tunic or a cluster-cryer in orange dotted a nine in pale blue or a group of artisans in their copper tunics, but mostly, like had gathered with like. I supposed it would take more than half a moon of travelling together, and a few days of seatach-butchering, to overcome the traditions of generations. At least the smell was consistent: meat patties, avalox tea, unwashed fur, muddy tunics, all overlaid with an overwhelming scent of anticipation. The air buzzed with speculation, and I heard Rewsa's bleat behind me, answered by Shaya's hard-edged bark. It was an effort to keep from turning my ears to hear what they were saying, but a moment later Limar untangled herself from the net and stood up, and the tongues stopped wagging.

She looked dreadful. Her fur was matted with mud. Her pink tunic was torn and filthy, her ears drooped. The smell of defeat and despair wafted from her on the breeze, taking my anger with it. She had lost her home through no fault of her own; her stubbornness had contributed to the death of young Sarys. Now she had lost her one chance to regain a warm dwelling and a place on the Expanse.

The crowd shifted, and I realised everyone was waiting for me to speak. "Limar," I began. I'd rehearsed in my mind what I would say when I confronted her, but saying it to myself had been easier than saying it aloud. I coughed, as though clearing my throat, and began again. "Limar. You were going to the *Spirax*. You were going to betray me – betray a Fate-seer – and therefore betray everyone who has helped to keep me from Kalis." As I spoke, my anger sparked again, my voice growing more certain as I took a step forward and went on: "I chose to ally myself with the exiles and the wingless – with you. All of you. I chose to become Fate-seer for Dru, not Kalis. To travel with you, eat with you, sleep in the cold and the storms and the wet with you." I was speaking to Limar, but my words were for everyone; my nose told me Limar was not the sole malcontent looking for a way to get back to an easier life. She just happened to be the first of them to regain the use of her wings. "I am *your* Fate-seer." This time I turned as I spoke, making it clear that I was addressing them all. I faced Limar again, setting my ears to indicate regret. "Your guilt is clear. The question is: what do we do about it?"

The question had been rhetorical. I had already discussed the options with Shaya and Doran, and we had decided that the best course would be to bind Limar's wings till we were far enough from Drax territory that she could be allowed to fly again. But there were plenty of angry shouts and vengeful suggestions from the crowd in answer to it – "Break her wings" – "Drop her in the ocean" – "Leave her in the mud" – "Take her back to that sea-bramble, see how she likes walking through it."

I held up my paws for silence, spreading my wings when it was not immediately forthcoming. "We'll do none of those things," I barked. "They're what Kalis would consider to be justice, and that's not an air current I want to ride."

"My Sarys died! She wouldn't have been in the mud if Limar hadn't insisted we should wait."

"That was your own choice, Froma." I turned and dipped my ears to acknowledge Froma's terrible loss, but couldn't allow her anger – or mine – to dictate what should happen. I pulled a roll of supple seatach-gut binding from my pocket and held it up. "For now, we will –"

126

"That's not enough!" The snarl, a few spans away to my left, came from Varna. She pushed through the crowd and I moved to meet her – but it wasn't me she wanted to confront. She took a few paces toward me, and then, faster than a striking serpent, she pulled a knife from her tunic belt and leaped toward Limar.

"Varna, no!" I flapped after her, Milat brought up her spear, but neither of us was fast enough. In a heartbeat, Varna spun Limar around and brought the knife down. It sliced through membrane and muscle, drawing howls from Limar and gasps of shock from the watching crowd. Two hunters pulled Varna away and I saw the knife drop to the ground, blood dripping from its serrated edge. Limar was on her knees, howling, and I bent to see how much damage Varna had done.

The strut of Limar's right wing had been sliced nearly through. The wing itself drooped at an unnatural angle that told its own tale: Limar would never fly again.

I looked round to find Doran and Galyn already hurrying toward us with pots of salve and leaves of precious camyl. Milat and Azmit were pulling Varna away up the hillside, but she had accomplished what she'd wanted to do.

I checked the wound again, flattening my ears against Limar's howls. Deep, clean, effective. One efficient move. One blow.

Varna had either been extremely lucky.

Or she'd done that before.

Thirteen

"Well, at least there's no danger of Limar taking one of Varna's wings in revenge."

My attempt at a joke was a poor one, and in bad taste, but it brought a faint twitch from Doran's whiskers. "No, but she could try ripping her throat out."

We were breaking camp. Limar's flight and capture had robbed us of the entire morning, and there were grumbles about moving on in the short amount of daylight that remained, but we had taken too long already to cross the mudflats. We needed to start moving upstream along the Ambit if we were to have a hope of finding a way across it before moon-end. After dealing with Limar, I had put my blue Trader's tunic back on, and was pushing my black tunic to the bottom of my carry-pouch, pulling jars and bags and bundles of herbs out of the way as I did so. Piling them back in, I stuffed the blanket on top to keep everything from rattling together, shoved in my spoon, and fastened my beaker to the straps. Limar's whimpering carried to my ears from where she sat alone at the bottom of the hill, and I reminded myself that I should not feel sorry for her. If she'd not been caught, my own flying days would have been numbered. "I don't think Limar will be ripping anyone's throat out," I said. I'd missed my bowl in the rush and unfastened the carry-pouch again to push it in. "Certainly not her own dam's." I checked quickly to make sure no-one was listening before I added, "She's dangerous, that one."

"Varna?" Doran picked up her own neatly-packed carry-pouch and adjusted the straps on her shoulders. "Well, I suppose Limar wouldn't argue with you, but—"

"She was Guardflight," I reminded her, as I hoisted my own carry-pouch into place, "before she was Kalis' nest-mate." I thought of something else. "She said she'd seen a chase like that before, but when? Where? I don't remember hearing anyone else talk of it, not even the fable-spinners. Why not? If she'd helped to chase down a Koth…"

"You're reading too much into it," said Doran. "Now, where have those younglings got to? Cavel! Dru! Come and fetch your carry-pouches, or you won't have a blanket between you when we stop tonight."

The two of them were a few spans away, taking it in turns to leap sideways and slash down with a quick right paw. They were barking with glee as they mimicked the move Varna had made, and I opened my mouth to chide them, then stopped. Dru had discovered his dam had capabilities that none of us had suspected; perhaps I shouldn't discourage him from admiring that.

Still, I glanced up the hill to where Varna stood, bow in hand, demonstrating to Shaya the correct way of nocking an arrow. Her ears no longer drooped and her nose was busy scenting the wind. It seemed she had rediscovered her old vigour and found a strength that had been buried under her pain and anger.

Should it worry me that, in order to do that, she had had to hurt her own offspring?

For four days we straggled inland along the riverbank, our progress slowed by the snow underfoot, which grew deeper as we headed west. Those who had the use of their wings flew as much as they could, and wings were healing by the nine each day, but with the younglings so heavy now, and the nets few, it wasn't possible to pick them up and carry them, which would have been the easiest option. Instead, we had to circle and glide, looking ahead for possible places to pitch camp, trying to gauge how far the wingless and the grounded might walk, worrying that we had over-estimated their stamina. The river was a little narrower now that we were away from the estuary, but the water still roiled with an imposing force that discouraged the thought of carrying anyone across it.

Even so, Shaya sent flyers to scout over the Forest, to check for possible campsites and see if they could find anything worth eating.

"There's nothing stirring in the canopy at all," Milat said, as she landed beside Shaya, a few spans from where Doran and I were getting a fire started. "And no gaps in the vines big enough for a camp. Not till we get to the Eye."

I'd seen that for myself the previous day when I'd flown to the Eye, but I'd hoped the keen eyes and nose of a hunter might find something I'd missed. All I'd seen were the ice-laden vine-branches of the Forest, the spiky tops of river reeds poking through the snow on the river banks, and the vines on the Eye laden with ice-spikes which, in places, almost hung to the water. It had taken me a half-day to fly there; it would take less than that to fly back to the ocean. "At the rate we're moving, the Eye must be a nineday away at least."

"We have time." Doran rummaged in her carry-pouch as she spoke, finally pulling a small blue jar from its depths with a triumphant, "Aha! Knew I'd got a pinch of chalkmoss left somewhere." She shook the contents into the pot of seatach meat she was readying. "Moon-end is two ninedays away. If we can get to the Eye in less than that, we have a chance. The river's narrower up beyond there, we might be able to carry the younglings over."

Shaya flicked her ears in agreement. "I think it's our best option," she said. "We just have to hope there are no more delays."

As if in answer to her words, the wind gusted, lifting powdered snow and whipping the particles into another needle-sharp attack on eyes, ears, and snouts. The toxic smell of the Deadlands to our left was edged with a faint whiff of salt and damp. A glance at the sky to the south added to the sorry picture: purple clouds shrouded the mountains, bearing the promise of more storms, more snow.

Shaya tilted her snout left and right, testing the air and gauging the threat. "We'll be alright under the seatach-hides tonight, but we'll have to find decent shelter tomorrow or there'll be more deaths."

"We can build bigger fires." I'd not seen much of Flori since I'd met her at Doran's campfire on the first morning I joined the exiles. She was still finger-thin, and was showing early signs of fur-clump, but her voice was clear enough as she spoke up. "We've got the hides for shelter. We can huddle closer together. We have our winter fur and—"

"It won't be enough. If the storm's bad enough, we'll never keep the fires going. The seatach-hides will blow away if the wind gets under them – and in any case, the younglings' coats aren't as thick as ours. They'll be vulnerable to the cold out in the open if it gets really nasty." Shaya was beginning to pace about, her ears twitching as she thought and planned. "We could try to get to the Forest, I suppose, or..." Her head came up and she looked upriver for a moment before turning to us. "How far is the Abandoned Cluster?"

I shivered. "There's nowhere else?" I thought of Shaya's other suggestion, the Forest, just a short flight over the river – for those of us with functional wings. I eyed the water again, calculating how long it would take to fly back and forth across it to take every wingless – or flightless – drax to the shelter of the vines on the far shore. The answer was the same as it had been when we crossed the mudflats: too long. Besides, where would we set them down? The vines grew thick on the far bank, and while they would give shelter from the storm, they would also harbour all manner of other threats.

But the Abandoned Cluster…

As a youngling I had listened with my fur on end as Swalo the fable-spinner had told the tale. The way he repeated it, monsters had come to the cluster after nightfall, devouring drax of every hue and every size. The few drax left in the morning had packed their belongings and left their nests, babbling tales of terror all over the Expanse. The Prime had despatched armed guardflight to investigate, but they too returned with stories of creatures in the night, and refused, even when threatened with de-winging, to return to the cluster.

Vizan had given me a less colourful version of the story when I asked him about it. *"Groundeels,"* he had said, firmly, *"that's all it was. The cluster was only ever meant to be occupied seasonally by the hunters anyway, but it was built over a groundeel colony, and they couldn't get anything to grow there. Damn eels kept feasting on the roots and everything died. No orenvines meant no vlydh to do the heavy carrying, so the cluster was abandoned."*

He had shaken his head at the wild stories of drax being eaten, and barked with laughter at the idea of the guardflight being sent in.

But for me, the horror story that Swalo had told still held sway in my imagination, and I was sure that that would be the case for most of the exiles. We had all listened to his stories, all been held in thrall by the battles and the monsters.

Now I was going to have to confront my own fears and ask everyone else to do the same. But… "You're right, Shaya. We don't have a choice."

The cluster had been built on a tongue of land that pushed the river into a long northerly meander. There was familiarity in the spiral-built stones and the arrangement of the dwellings, but the blocky entrances and the absence of see-shells seemed strange, and I wondered how long ago the place had been constructed – and left derelict. Dirty snow had drifted from the Deadlands to lie against the stones, sculpting the conical shapes into strange, soft waves. It was fortunate that the entrances had all been built to face away from the prevailing wind, or we might have had to dig our way in – and I was not sure I would have been able to summon the nerve to dig where I knew there was a groundeel colony.

Eighteen of us had flown ahead at first light, battling gusty winds and dashes of sleet. The clouds that had been over the mountains the previous evening were now advancing across the Deadlands, and the smell of fresh snow blew from the south with every gust.

"I don't like the look of those dwellings." Milat indicated the worst of the structures, which had crumbled and sagged, their stones giving way beneath the twin assaults of wind and water. "They look like they'll fall in at any moment."

"There are nines here that won't keep the snow out," said Doran, after she'd poked her snout into the dwellings on the outer rim of the cluster, "but there'll be enough still intact to house all of us, so long as no-one minds a bit of overcrowding."

"What will we do about the floors?" This from Milat. "They're just beaten earth, not the usual flat stones. They'll warm up once we're in there and the groundeels will come looking."

I shuddered, imagining the howls and chaos that would ensue if a single eel surfaced in a crowded dwelling. They wouldn't bite anything that might bite back, but the fables we had all heard would crush any assurance or calls for calm. "What about the seatach-hides?" I suggested. "We won't need them over our heads while we're here. If we spread them on the ground inside the dwellings, the groundeels may not sense the warmth. Even if they do, they won't get through seatach skin."

Milat nodded. She had one of the hides neatly rolled on top of her carry-pouch, and began to unstrap it. "Wait," I said. "Let's check all the dwellings first and find the ones that are fit to shelter in. We can't use more than nine anyway, that's all the hides we have."

Snow was beginning to fall in chunky flakes as we made our way to the centre of the cluster. The Welcome Place was covered with moss and smelled musty inside. "We can get nines in here," said Doran, sniffing thoroughly, and pressing her paw against the wall stones. She halted beside the hearth, where cold ashes spilled onto the hearthstone, and picked up a pawful of vinesticks that had been stacked beside it. "There's even kindling for a fire—"

"No." I set my ears to an apologetic angle to remove the sting from my retort. "No fires, Doran. The groundeels will be attracted to the heat."

Milat ducked into the entrance behind me. "We'll be warm enough," she said. "With so many of us in each dwelling, we won't need fires. And there's a cache of seatach meat under a drift by the outermost dwelling. But we will have to make do with cold food, I'm afraid. Unless you *want* the eels to come?"

Doran shuddered, flattening her ears at the thought. "Let's get those hides on the floor," she said.

It was almost zenith – so far as anyone could tell – by the time the first of the wingless arrived at the cluster. Snow clung to their snouts and tunics, their fur was sodden, and I felt Dru and Cavel shiver as I ushered them into the Welcome Place.

"It's nice being in a proper dwelling again," Dru said, looking around and sniffing. Three torches had been lit and placed in sconces near the apex of the roof. They didn't provide much in the way of heat, but their glow at least gave an illusion of warmth.

Cavel was already being rubbed down by his dam, who had a dry tunic ready for him, and blankets unrolled and set at the back of the dwelling, away from the door. "Can we stay here?" he said, wriggling with impatience as Doran's cloth moved vigorously across his shoulders and along his arms.

"Only while the storm lasts," I said, "unless you want groundeels for company."

"The cold will have driven them deeper underground, won't it?"

I was startled that such a sensible remark should come from Varna, more startled still that she had kept up with the younglings, but there she was, ducking into the entrance right behind them.

"Let's hope so." I left her to find a place to settle and went back outside. I would need to make sure that Limar was directed to a different dwelling, and see to it that a healer went with her. The snow was coming thick and fast now, the figures struggling toward us barely discernable through the flakes. I hoped that this time, for once, everyone had kept up with the pace. Anyone left behind in this might never find their way – and with the weather too bad to even take off, there was no way to look for anyone who got lost.

If they weren't at the Abandoned Cluster by nightfall, they would die.

Fourteen

"How many unaccounted for?" I raised my voice over the howl of the wind. It sliced between the dwellings like a sharpened claw, hurling the falling snow sideways. It stuck to my tunic, stung my ears and nose, and had soaked enough of my fur that icy trickles penetrated to the skin at my neck and below the hem of my tunic. It was dark enough that I had switched to night-vision, though I was sure it could not be more than a half-day after zenith.

"Fifteen." Shaya's reply was snatched away by the wind, and she leaned closer to make sure I could hear her next words. "All grown females – including Froma. The younglings are all here, but..." She looked over her shoulder, as though the missing females might appear around the curve of the hillside. Shaya had been the last to complete the journey, mere beats ago, but already her footprints were becoming soft, smudged by the driving snow. In a short while they would be lost completely – just like our missing group.

I shivered, and sent up a prayer to the Spiral that perhaps the stragglers had found shelter elsewhere – though I knew there was none – and that they would survive the night. With their winter coats… But another trickle of ice-water under my collar reminded me that even winter fur might be penetrated if the weather was bad enough.

"We can't stay out here." Though they were no more than a few spans away, the swirling snow made it difficult to see Winan who, along with Azmit the hunter, had been directing each arrival to the dwellings we had occupied. Two of the seatach hides would go unused, as we had found only seven intact dwellings, but they would have to be enough. Azmit and Winan had been standing outside for at least as long as I had, and were no doubt feeling equally as cold and miserable. But what to do? We couldn't light a signal fire – even if it was possible in such weather; it would bring the groundeels, and any pathway through the snow would be masked by the storm within a few breaths. "A tunic," I called, as Shaya bent her ears to my shouts, "a bright one. Perhaps if we can fix it to a spear, it will guide the lost females to us?"

Shaya's ears indicated her scepticism, but aloud she said, "It's better than doing nothing. Norba's in the Welcome Place. Perhaps she'll lend us one of her orange tunics."

Norba, one of the exiled cluster-cryers, kept her spare tunic at the bottom of her carry-pouch, and there was a deal of grumbling and muttering as she rummaged for it, an odour of discomfort and resentment spreading through the crowded space. The Welcome Place was bigger than a normal dwelling, but there were ninety drax inside, sitting side-by-side in tight circles – one group of adults lining the outside walls, another at their feet, and the younglings huddled in the middle. Something as simple as pulling a tunic from a carry-pouch meant that several drax had to stand up and try to keep out of the way, and the tunic itself had to be passed from paw to paw before I could grasp it and whisk it outside. But the fabric was bright, and as I helped Shaya tie it to a spear beside the cluster's end-most dwelling, I almost believed that our signal would work.

If it would just stop snowing.

I had not expected to sleep – half-sitting for lack of room, damp from the snow, and above all wondering and worrying. It was not just our missing females that concerned me; the groundeels loomed large in my thoughts. I didn't care that Vizan had told me they were harmless, there was still a part of my mind that recoiled from the idea of sharing groundspace with something as repellent as a span-long, slithering, eyeless creature with two rows of sharp teeth.

But sleep came, and with it a Sight-dream – a kind of Vision – of flying over the river we were travelling along so slowly. *On the far bank, I hovered above the Forest, seeing nothing but creeper-nests and serpents in the vines below. I flew on. North and north I went, with nothing but tangled vines beneath me for span after span. How were we to get through it? Kalis had banished us 'beyond' the Crimson Forest, but it didn't seem to have a 'beyond' to be banished to.*

At last, I flew over a northern shore. The Forest was behind me, the vines stretching along the shore east and west as far as I could see. Ahead of me, the sea stretched to the horizon.

I woke to darkness, cramped and cold, my blanket tangled round my feet. I drew it up around my shoulders, but it had little effect on the chill I felt. I knew that what I had Dreamed was true: there was nothing beyond the Crimson Forest but ocean.

There was nowhere for us to go.

Too disturbed by my Dream to go back to sleep, I sat and watched the torch-flames throw shadows and smoke against the stones. Did Kalis know, I wondered, that we would not be able to travel beyond the Forest as he had decreed? Had anyone ever flown to the northern edge of it to find out? I had not heard of anyone doing so, nor had Vizan ever mentioned it. Perhaps the Dream was mistaken…

But no. I had not had this kind of Vision before – a dream that told me the way of things, rather than something that had happened, or that would happen. But Vizan had warned me about them, and I was sure that what it told me was true.

I had been worried about travelling through the Forest, with its inherent dangers and wild creatures. Now, it seemed that we would remain there, trapped between hostility and a distant shoreline; trapped in a place that was more dangerous than any other I knew. I remembered the vine-serpent, and my encounter with the mouldworm, and shuddered. How could we possibly live in such a place?

I shook my head, trying to clear it of such morbid thoughts, and reminding myself that there were more immediate things to worry about: we had fifteen missing females, the snow was getting deeper, and when we could eventually resume our trek upriver, we still needed to find a way to cross it. The storm howled outside like a creature denied its prey, but at least the temperature in the shelter had risen, thanks to so many drax being squashed so closely together. I put a paw on the seatach hide beneath me. It was warm where I'd been sitting, but would that warmth have transferred through to the earth beneath? And, if it had, how long before the groundeels came calling?

I was jerked from my reverie by howls and cries outside. I banged my head on the low lintel as I rushed to get out of the dwelling, and was still rubbing at the ache as I stumbled outside.

In a grey dawn, vicious with driving snow and a whistling gale, two younglings were cowering against the wall of the dwelling opposite. Manda was hugging her toy egg as though to protect it, while Ravar was howling as he threw stones at the groundeel confronting them.

It was a hideous-looking thing. Its scales were a mottled green and it had a way of moving that made it appear to shimmer across the soft snow. Like the younglings it had frightened, this was also not fully grown, being no more than a half-span in length and still bearing the vestiges of a tiny beak above its mouth, which would disappear once it reached maturity.

"Leave it!" I called, as I hurried along the path, my hackles rising at the knowledge that I'd have to pick the thing up and move it if it didn't slither away. I saw that other adults, including the younglings' dams, were stumbling out of the dwellings, drawn by the howls, so I waved a paw, signalling for most of them to go back inside. "It's just a small groundeel," I called, trying to sound as though the sight of it didn't sicken me. "Go back inside, it's bitter out here. Stay warm!"

To my relief, the groundeel was already moving away, sliding over a drift of snow toward some of the unoccupied dwellings, and I shook out my wings with relief. The younglings were getting a scolding from their dams for venturing outside without a spear between them, and Manda was howling. She had dropped her toy egg in the ruckus, and it lay in pieces at her feet.

For three days and nights we stayed in the Abandoned Cluster, passing the time with stories and learning games for the younglings. Each morning I opened the door to check whether the storm had blown over. Twice a day, we ventured outside in small groups to use hastily-scraped waste-pits – little more than hollows in the snow.

The smell of unwashed fur and nearby waste climbed, while our tempers shortened. It was uncomfortable, but we were warm enough with our fur fluffed, though the cold food was boring and chewy. But at least we were safe from the weather and for that I gave thanks to the Spiral.

On the fourth morning, I woke to a strange silence, and realised that the constant whistle and thrum of the wind had ceased. Putting my snout outside, I found that my whiskers were not in danger of being scoured off, and a cautious sniff produced a distinct smell of riverweed, borne on the remaining breeze.

I pulled the door open, stepped outside, and stretched my wings, then roused the other dwellings. "I think we might risk a cooked breakfast this morning." Despite the difficulties of the past few days, we had at least had roofs over our heads, and I suspected there would be some reluctance to move on. I hoped that the prospect of hot food would help with morale and looked about for a way to make that possible. "If we use some of the loose stones from the ruined dwellings to build platforms, and light the fires on top of them, they will help keep the heat from the ground for a while. With luck we'll be gone before the groundeels come to investigate. We must hurry, though!"

Glad of an excuse to run about again, the younglings wasted no time in digging through the snow to find the stones we needed. In places, the blizzard had formed drifts that towered over our heads, but the dwellings had sheltered the old spiralling path well enough for us to build our cooking platforms – nine of them, each a paw's-width high and a half-span in diameter. With the dry kindling from the Welcome Place, and food from the nearby cache, it didn't take long before we were able to enjoy the feel of warm flames and the smell of hot food.

I had spooned down the last of my broth and was in the process of licking the bowl clean when Dru wandered across and sat next to me.

"Why do we keep travelling," he said, quietly, "when there is nowhere to go?"

So he had Seen it too. I suppose I should not have been surprised, but I had hoped that, if he had Dreamed, he would not have understood its significance.

"We travel because we must," I said, pushing my bowl back into my carry-pouch. "No-one on the Expanse will know if we don't continue on through the Forest. Even the hunters venture no further than a half-day's flight over the vines, and that's only if they are on a creeper hunt. If we make sure we are beyond their range…"

"A half-day's flight?" Dru waved a paw at the cluster we had spent over four ninedays reaching. "Didn't you once tell me it took you and Doran a half-day to fly to the river? To get somewhere near here?"

"It took all the hours of warm-season daylight," I said, "and we were a little further upriver, on the high ground where the Ambit cuts through the foothills from the mountains. But yes, we're less than a full day's flight from the Expanse."

Dru looked from me to the drax grouped around the fires, eating, stretching wings, licking bowls, and comforting younglings whose dams had vanished in the storm. "But it's taken us most of a moon to get here, hasn't it?"

I dipped an ear to acknowledge that he was correct. Even after so many hard days of travel, we were still within easy reach of the *Spirax*. I scarcely dared think about how many more days of travel we had ahead of us. Or how difficult and dangerous they would be.

Fifteen

I t seemed that the storm had been the freeze's last major assault for the cycle. As we pushed our way through the snow, probing with spears for ruts and rocks, the breeze shifted to the east and the sun glowed behind pale clouds. Progress was painfully slow. From the air it seemed that the line of fur and fabric barely moved: on the first day's travel from the Abandoned Cluster, we got no further than the next riverbend. But the next day was a little warmer and the clouds that moved in brought a drizzle of rain that softened the snow and began to slough it away. It was also clear to those who were airborne that the river was beginning to loop and meander; we would waste time and energy if we continued to follow the bank.

"We're running out of time," said Shaya, as we made camp on the fifth day out from the Abandoned Cluster. "We'll not get to the Eye before moon-end. Not at the rate we're travelling."

We still hadn't worked out a way to get everyone over the river even when we reached the Eye, but I clamped my jaw shut on saying so. It wouldn't help.

For the first time since the snow storm, the sky was clear enough to see the Spiral and a waning moon. "It'll be cold tonight," Doran observed. "Everyone will be jostling for a place near the fires." She'd already set out her own blanket, and Cavel's, within a few spans of the flames she'd kindled. I unrolled mine next to them, and was about to start looking through my carry-pouch for a seatach pattie when Shaya spoke again. "Doran, that's brilliant."

"Me? Why? What did I say?" Doran, a pot in one paw and spoon in another, twitched her ears uncertainly.

Shaya had a bounce to her step as she moved nearer. "It will be cold tonight. Even under the seatach hides no-one will sleep well. Everyone will want to move about to keep warm." She spread her arms. "Well, let's all move!" Her gesture had drawn the attention of those nearby, and she raised her voice as she went on: "Once we've eaten and rested, we'll move on. We can travel by the lights of the moon and the Spiral as easily as we can by daylight."

"Shaya. Everyone's exhausted." Doran spoke quietly as she stood, but her words were echoed in the murmurs that rippled back through the crowd. "Slogging through all that snow—"

"Which is starting to melt."

"—carrying everything—"

"In pouches that the flyers can take ahead." Shaya spread her wings and set her ears upright. It wasn't a challenge exactly, but it was close enough that all the murmurs stopped. For a moment, all I could hear were crackling flames, the splash of the river, and the mating call of an optimistic glump in the Deadlands to the south. Then eerie screams from the Forest sounded a dreadful testimony to what lay in wait for us across the river, and the muttering started again till Shaya reminded us of what would happen if we didn't cross: "Kalis will send the Guardflight to check that we've crossed the river. Who knows what will happen to us if we haven't?"

I pretended not to notice Doran glancing my way at the mention of the Guardflight. Perhaps she hoped that Taral would refuse to carry out Kalis' orders – whatever they might be – but I remembered his reaction when he thought he'd have to break the wings of the females. He'd have carried out the orders rather than risk losing his own wings. I had no wish to test his loyalty by not reaching the Forest by moon-end.

"Perhaps we should just wait here, and ask the Guardflight to net us over." Doran's ears indicated it was a joke, but I was not in the mood to hear it.

"Or perhaps we could find some wild vlydh to fly us across the river," I snapped. It was, I thought, about as likely as getting help from anyone on the Expanse. Even Taral.

Doran's ears flattened and she took a step back, surprised by my tone. I waved a paw in apology and added, quietly, "What if it's not the Guardflight? What if Kalis sends the Elite Guard again? I doubt they'll net us anywhere, except into the river, or the middle of a clump of brambletrap."

"We're wasting time." Shaya's voice squashed our squabble, and had an edge that ensured no-one else interrupted her. "Let's all get something to eat, and rest till moon-zenith. That will give us half the night to travel."

"With the Spiral watching over us," I added, feeling I ought to salvage something from the conversation.

"The Spiral." Limar's voice, behind me, all but spat the words. "It's done a grand job of watching over us so far, hasn't it?"

Before I could find a response, she had turned on her heel and stomped off toward Rewsa's fire. The tip of her damaged wing trailed in the slush.

We slogged on for another five days, trying to push ahead on as direct a course as possible, while the river and the terrain made straight lines impossible. The hills we had climbed and descended gave way to flatter terrain that would have made for easier going if not for the stubborn drifts of snow and rivulets of muddy water that trickled from the Deadlands as they gradually emerged from their icy coating. The younglings who had lost dams in the storm whimpered in the night, and clung by day to the nest-nurses – though none, I noticed, went near Limar. There were squabbles and howls, bites and clawing, and each day, each night, we moved with slow reluctance, every breath an effort, every step a strain.

"We'll die in the Forest anyway," I heard more than once. "Why are we putting ourselves through this?"

I think it was only Shaya's chivvying and my retelling of the Vision of Dru's destiny that drove some of them on.

And still, with just three days left before moon-end, we were not within sight of the Eye. Not from the ground, anyway.

"I just don't see how we can get everyone across the river in time." Doran flew alongside me as we headed upriver to scout ahead. The sky was lightening from black to dull grey, but a gap in the clouds revealed a thin slice of moon to the west. Below us, the ground south of the river formed a series of hummocks, rising toward the hills and mountains in the west. The snow that had made progress so difficult a nineday ago had all but vanished as a steady drizzle had pecked at it; the river was running higher and faster, fed by melting snows. A few spans further south, the Deadlands were no longer cloaked in white, their familiar grey and black patches of brambletrap and mud already giving off a stench of death. We would need to make sure no-one strayed anywhere near the marsh.

"You sound like Rewsa," I said, in a weak attempt to make light of her words.

Doran flicked an ear, dismissing my poor joke. "Just because she's negative all the time doesn't mean she's always wrong." She raised a paw to point ahead. "There's the Eye, but I don't see how it's going to help, even when the groundlings get there. Look how high the river's running now."

My heart sank like a drax in a downdraught. The river was wider than when I had last seen the Eye, parts of its banks vanishing beneath surging grey water, which heaved and twisted as it was channelled around the islet. The waves beat at the roots of a leaning vine on the northern shoulder of the Eye, churning round them to chop away the clumps of soil they clung to.

"It's going…"

If Doran said more, I didn't hear it, as her words were drowned beneath the creak and crash of the falling vinetree. We were not quite high enough to avoid being spattered with cold water and bits of twig, and I instinctively adjusted wings and tail to move up and away from the splash zone. Beside me, droplets flew from Doran's fur as she shook her head, and her yip of exhilaration carried notes of both excitement and awe. I'd not heard her bark like that since we were younglings, but the sight of the enormous vine crashing across the river, its fall so slow yet so unstoppable, was a remarkable sight.

For a few heartbeats, there was nothing but the wind, the rush of water, and the smack of the vinetree's upper branches smashing to rest at the base of a low, vine-free slope on the edge of the Forest. Branches swayed and snapped, some of them breaking off to scatter along the ground, leaving a litter of leaves and splinters across the damp moss.

"Look!" Doran was already angling away and gliding downward for a better look. "It's made a fly-under."

Sure enough, with the tree's roots still anchored to the Eye, and its upper branches on the riverbank, it had come to rest just far enough above the surging water to produce a challenging gap to fly through. Doran had already picked her course, wings steady as she glided beneath the trunk with a whoop of delight and triumph.

"Doran, that's a youngling's game," I called, even as I turned to follow. As I levelled out, the surface of the water seemed to rise to meet me, the churning waves twisting and churning, hurling spray into the air wherever it collided with the bank or with hidden underwater obstacles. If I flapped my wings, the tips would slap the water and destabilise my flight. If that happened, I would have to pull up, and swerve hard to avoid crashing into the riverbank, the vinetrees, or the fallen vine's sturdy trunk...

Younglings on the vinetrunk. Wingless younglings, walking across...

The Vision came and went in a moment, but I had lost my flight line. Gnarled black bark loomed ahead of me, and I pushed my wings down fast and hard, flapping them just enough to push up and over the vinetree. Above me, Doran's howl of alarm turned to laughter. "I win!" As I flew closer, something about the set of my ears, or perhaps my raised fur, signalled what had happened, and her ears twitched with curiosity. "You Saw something?"

My spirits had lifted like wings on a warm wind. I circled, checking the lie of the vinetrunk to make sure that what I Saw was indeed possible. "The Spiral provides, Doran," I called, pointing at the fallen tree. "A pathway. You see? It makes a pathway over the water." Circling a paw over my chest, I offered up a brief prayer of thanks. "All we need is to cut down a vine on the southern edge of the island to make a path from the Deadlands side to the Eye, and the wingless can walk across the river."

"Yes." Doran's twisting ears indicated ambivalence, and for a moment I thought she was unsure about allowing Cavel and the other younglings to set foot on something as unstable as a fallen vinelog. Just as I was about to assure her that we would make sure the walkovers were properly secured, she put my momentary elation into context by pointing to the crimson canopy beyond the hill on the northern bank. "All we have to do then," she called, "is worry about the Forest."

Sixteen

"Come on! Hurry!"

Milat's call from somewhere downriver was almost drowned by the rush of water and the rasp of seatach-tooth saws on vinewood. Even so, I detected the note of impatience in her voice. It had taken some time to identify and topple a suitable vinetree from the Eye's southern bank. Now its upper branches were resting on the river bank and I was busy helping to trim the branches that twisted beneath its trunk. Despite the keen wind that ruffled fur and rattled leaves, I was ember hot beneath my winter tunic. My arms ached with unaccustomed effort and my fingers were sore where they had gripped the saw's handle. But today was moon-end: we had to get everyone to the Forest bank by the end of the night, or…

Well, we didn't know exactly, except that whatever Kalis had in mind would likely be painful at best, and crippling at worst. That was why Milat and Doran were circling over the wingless and those accompanying them, picking out the quickest route, and warning of dips, hollows, and clumps of brambletrap.

From the depths of the foliage on the Eye, the rustling of leaves and the 'thock' of a cutting blade on vinetrunks indicated the progress of the nine females who were hacking a path through the vines from the south side of the islet to the north. Other flyers were already on the Ambit's far shore, gathering kindling and damp sticks from the riverbank and forest edge. No doubt there were plenty of dry firelogs beneath the canopy, but no-one had yet ventured beyond the first line of vines, and I'd noticed that a good deal of the kindling was being set out in a curve that matched the Forest's edge. Once on the mossy hillside on the far bank, we would have a line of flames between ourselves and whatever lurked beneath the vines. After that...

I shook my head. We had to get there first – and the sun was already sliding toward the mountains in the west.

Beside me, two females in copper tunics were working on one of the bigger branches, pushing a saw back and forth between them. Hearing Milat's call, Winan spared a brief glance upward, then looked along the riverbank in the direction the groundlings would be coming from. "We'll never get everyone across in time," she said, voicing my own thoughts. "Those poor pups, what will happen to them if they're still on this side of the river?"

As she spoke, I saw Dru and Cavel crest the rise to the east – the last hillock the wingless had to negotiate before they reached us. "They're almost here. Let's get this finished." I squashed the thought that Dru and Cavel would be spans ahead of the other younglings, and that they in turn would have bounded ahead of the remaining ground-bound adults. Instead, I concentrated on the thought that we could soon start getting our groundlings across to the northern bank, where they would be safe from Kalis' threats. I'd rested long enough. I gripped my saw with a huff of determination and returned to the judder and scrape of cutting through the branch.

We got the first of the younglings over the makeshift crossing just before the sun vanished behind the mountain peaks. As the sky purpled towards full dark, the Spiral glowed beyond wisps of torn cloud. The moon was a mere suggestion of light on the eastern horizon: moon-end. Tomorrow night, the darkness that clawed at it would be a sliver thinner as the next moon began.

Tomorrow, Kalis would send troops to ensure that we had all left Drax territory.

Fires had been lit on the Forest side of the river, their warm glow and the smell of hot stew beckoning to those who were still on the southern side. Shaya had suggested that the absence of warmth and food on the southern bank would encourage everyone to cross faster, but it seemed to me that all it encouraged was more than the usual grumbling.

Beyond the whoops and squeals of excited younglings, jostling to be next over this new invention, there were mutters in the darkness: "... don't see why we can't have a bit of warmth..." – "... here all night..."– "... feet are freezing..."– "... alright for them, flying about..."

A clatter of wings to my right marked the arrival of a hunter, Trati, who had regained the use of her wings just a few days before. She looked tired, and I recognised the early symptoms of fur-clump in her matted black fur and the way she scratched at her neck. Once we were all safely on the north bank, I would make sure Trati, Flori, and the others who were sickening got the medicine and poultices they needed. Trati scratched at her neck again and set her ears respectfully as she addressed me. "Doran and Winan are getting the younglings over there settled," she said. Then, raising her voice to call to the others: "There's tea and stew on the other side. Keep moving, everyone!"

The line of younglings shuffled toward the log, waving and calling to their dams, pushing and nipping each other in their impatience to use the walkway. They reeked of excitement and anticipation, with barely a hint of trepidation. The fear that emanated from their dams would hit them later, when the adventure of crossing the river was behind them. Once on the far bank, the sounds and smells of the Forest would remind them that our journey wasn't over, and that a myriad of unknown dangers lay ahead.

Shaya had been standing beside the sawn branches of the vinelog that rested on the southern shore, overseeing the initial crossing. "One at a time!" she barked, as two younglings scrambled onto the branches. "Nixel, wait there till Oztin has crossed. The vinetrunk isn't wide enough for both of you."

Oztin turned to wave a paw, barking, "Watch me, Trati-muz!"

"I'm watching – go along now, and be careful," his dam called back and he skittered across, claws scratching at the bark.

As Nixel squirmed with impatience under Shaya's restraining paw, I read discontent in the hunter's twitching whiskers. "If the vines on the Eye had grown thick as well as tall," she called, "we might have risked sending more than one at a time. As it is…"

I scanned the numbers on each bank. Anyone who could fly had been encouraged to go straight to the northern bank, but many dams preferred to wait till their own youngling was ready to cross the log. They'd then take off and hover a little way downstream, paws outstretched, as though their concern alone might keep their offspring safe. Then there were those adults whose wings still weren't healed properly – almost a ninety, Galyn reckoned. They'd have no choice but to follow the younglings over the logs – as would Varna and Limar.

Sniffing the breeze, I detected the two scents I was searching for at opposite sides of the waiting group: Varna's wounded pride; Limar's hurt and anger. "I think we should send Limar over first, after the younglings," I said, "and Varna last. Keep them as far apart as we can."

Shaya's ears swivelled upright as she grunted agreement. "No argument from me about that. Let's just hope that Varna's on the other side of the river by the time the sun comes up."

"Zarda, wake up! They're coming!"

"What…?"

At moon-zenith, I'd flown to the northern encampment for a beaker of tea and a bowl of stew. I'd not intended to sleep, but the preparation and sawing and waiting had exhausted me. My brief rest had become a doze, and then a good night's sleep. As I blinked my eyes open to check the position of the moon, I discovered that it had already vanished with the dawn. Clouds scudded overhead, bruise purple in the early light.

"Who's coming?" I shook myself, rubbed my snout and whiskers in an effort to come awake and focus my thoughts. "Guardflight?"

Liquid sloshed down my blue tunic as Doran passed me a beaker of tea. "Too far away to tell," she said, dabbing at the spill with a cloth, "but they look to me to be coming direct from the *Spirax*, not from Guardflight Rock."

I pushed her paw and the cloth away, took a gulp of tea – bitter, brewed from stale leaves – and stood up. Around me, younglings and adults alike had their snouts turned skyward, watching as Milat led six females south-east, beating their wings against the breeze. Moving toward them, high enough to brush the low cloudbase with their wingtips, was a V formation of fast-flying drax. Scarlet? Crimson? I couldn't be sure of the tunic colour, not at that distance, not in the false colours of early light.

I glanced at the walkover logs and the southern bank. The logs were swaying under the weight of the adults still walking across them, but almost everyone had crossed safely. Only a nine or so drax remained on the far shore. Surely we had done enough to satisfy Kalis' demands. Hadn't we?

"Milat's gone to try to delay them," said Doran. Her ears were almost flat with anxiety. "Shaya's over there on the south bank flapping her wings – she's beside herself that she still can't fly."

I made a conscious effort to set my own ears to a less alarmed angle. Behind me, Dru and Cavel were arguing about the colour of the tunics in the sky:

"Scarlet."

"Crimson."

"Scarlet. They're Guardflight."

"They're *not*. They're Elite Guard."

There were eight drax left on the southern bank. I spiralled a paw over my tunic and muttered a prayer: "Let them be Guardflight. Please."

Milat and the group with her were climbing now, wings blurring as they worked to gain height so they could meet the oncoming group on equal terms. "What are they hoping to do?" I asked, even as I prayed that they would be able to reason with the guards.

Scarlet? Crimson?

There were seven drax on the southern bank.

Six.

Crimson. Not scarlet.

"They're Elite." Doran's voice was flat as she said it, but I caught the scent of her dismay and saw her take a step back, hackles raised. Murmurs and whimpers, the scent of trepidation and hate swirled and mingled on the breeze as the sky brightened and the oncoming flyers came closer.

There were five drax on the southern bank. Curse that snowstorm! If we'd not been delayed, if the melt hadn't caused the river to rise... But then, the vinetree might not have fallen, and we might still be making our way upstream to find a place where the river was narrow enough to risk carrying the wingless across.

An adult female in faded trader blue climbed onto the log. There were four drax on the southern bank.

Milat was flying ahead of the others. As they closed with the Elite, I saw her spread her paws in a motion that might have been a welcome, or perhaps was intended as a gesture of goodwill.

Whatever it was she meant, the Elite Guard didn't want to know. A bow bent and a copper-headed arrow flashed in a shaft of sunlight. Milat fell from the sky, wings folding toward the clouds as she dropped. Even as the howls began, I saw more arrows fly, and one by one the group who had flown with Milat fell like stones toward the black marsh beneath them.

Seventeen

Doran's fur was all on end, and I didn't doubt mine was the same. "They killed them." Her voice was a whimper, almost inaudible through the howls and screams of everyone around us.

"We'll die." Rewsa's whine cut through the noise, and I pulled my gaze from the sky to find her wringing the tip of her tail in her paws. "We'll all die." As I watched, she let go of her tail, sat down, and pulled Ellet into a protective embrace.

"No we won't." My first thought was to snatch up a spear or a bow and fly to meet the Elite head on, but that would be futile. Only the hunters had learned to shoot well enough to hit a moving target, and three of those had just been shot out of the sky, along with one of our healers and two artisans. "Into the forest." I'd barked it out before the thought had fully formed, but when I cast about for alternatives there were none that were viable, because the option to take off and fight would not work unless every flyer we had was able and willing to use a spear or a bow. To judge by the howls and scents, the will would be there – but I knew that the ability was not. I glimpsed Nixel being comforted by one of the nest-nurses, and my jaw ached with the desire to close my teeth around the throat of the Elite Guard who had shot his dam, but attempting it would be futile. No. The only sensible choice was to run and hide, like mud-burrowers scared by a passing cloud. "Take a torch if you can, leave anything you've unpacked. Just get under the vines."

"And keep together," Doran called. Her ears and whiskers were vibrating with alarm, but she smelled of pure hate – as, I suspect, did I. For a beat or two, no-one moved, and I realised that the last of Milat's group was still falling. Odd. It seemed as though several lifetimes had passed since the first arrow flew, yet the aftermath was still playing out.

"Trati-muz, Trati-muz, use your wings. Fly!" The youngling's choked yelping carried across a campsite that was utterly still. Only the rush of the river and the slap of the wind against loose cloth broke the silence. Winan set her hefty frame in front of Oztin and held him close so he wouldn't see his dam's final moments. The scent of anger and hate curdled the air, along with... I sniffed. There was something else there, something I'd not scented for some time. As it spread, overlaying the aggression and the hatred, I realised what it was: determination. Resolve.

"Zarda's right, they can't shoot at us if we're under the vines." Galyn picked up her carry-pouch and handed her youngling, Dugaz, a torch she'd lit from the embers of one of last night's fires. With her free paw, she gripped her spear and shook it. "If they try coming after us, they'll regret it. Come on!"

With a collective roar, everyone moved at once. Pouches were gathered, younglings were collected, torches were lit. Those who had spears or bows snatched them up; others picked up stones or looked about for heavy branches they might use as clubs. "Don't go too far in," I called. "Stay where you can see the riverbank. And make sure some of you check what's around you, we've no idea what's under there."

As they began to move toward the cover of the vinetrees, I turned again to the river. Everyone should have crossed by now – at least as far as the Eye – but the females on the southern bank had been as mesmerised as the rest of us by events in the sky.

The Elite Guard were drawing closer with every wingbeat, and there were still four drax on the river's southern bank.

I snatched at Doran's arm as she moved past me to head for the vines, Cavel and Dru at her wingtips. "Make sure no-one strays too far in," I said, as I unfolded my wings.

"Where are you going?"

"To hurry the others along." I didn't wait to hear her reply. Spreading my wings, I ran through the campsite, kicking over an empty beaker and bruising a toe on a discarded pot before I managed to lift off.

Shaya was halfway across the log that led to the Eye, howling with rage and grief, her body swaying with the effort of moving fast, wings half-extended to help her balance. When she reached the islet, she adjusted her hold on the spear she carried, seizing one end double-pawed. Whipping it right and left as she moved along the cleared path, she smashed the spear to pieces in a frenzy of growls and snapping teeth, throwing the remains into the water when she climbed onto the second log.

There were three drax on the southern bank.

"Hurry!" I swooped low over their heads as I called. I thought I heard whoops and yips carry on the breeze from the Elite, hoped I was imagining it. I flapped my wings to gain height, and saw that the Guards were close enough to pick out individuals. It was no surprise to see Murgo leading the way, but it was a shock to see Difel on his right wing. Difel, who had still been a hardworking zaxel farmer when we left the Expanse. I remembered how desperate he and his nest-brother Hamor had become after the Koth took their crop on the day Dru hatched – desperate enough to slaughter and eat kervhels, beasts which were traditionally killed solely for sacred rituals. I remembered too that Difel had blamed the wingless for their ongoing problems, but I had not guessed that his hatred ran so deep. Murgo – or rather his sire, Fazak – had no doubt promised food and safety in exchange for Difel's change of trade.

Their poison had spread far indeed.

Beyond them, beyond the mottled grey landscape of the Deadlands and the faint blue line of the distant bay, was a black cone, smudged to grey in the early mist. The *Spirax*. We had travelled for a whole moon, but we were still within sight of it;

still close enough that the Guards had reached us with a single night's flight.

The northern river bank was a riot of activity, a tide of colour scurrying up the tongue of trampled moss toward the line of vinetrees. If everyone had moved that fast during our journey, we would have been over the river a nineday ago. Smouldering fires, heaped blankets, and discarded beakers and pots littered the ground behind them. A ladle glinted; a solitary blue tunic lay draped over a rock.

Only Azmit and Varna were still on the southern bank.

Shaya was already half-way along the second log, barrelling toward the northern bank where Trati's spear lay.

"Shaya," I called, "don't do anything foolish." But she didn't even glance up, and I shook my head and looked again at the drax on the southern shore. "Come on, come on." I murmured the words like a personal prayer as Azmit vaulted onto the first log with a sinuous, easy leap and started to cross. I realised, belatedly, that Varna – the last drax left – was burdened with a carry-pouch and a bow, and flew down to land beside her.

"I'll take your things," I said. "You'll be able to move faster without them."

"How close are they?" She threw down the bow and pulled at the carry-pouch straps, tightening them instead of undoing them. "Can't gauge the distance from down here."

I tugged at the knots she'd tightened, switching my attention from the straps to the walkover, making a conscious effort not to look over my shoulder toward the oncoming Elite. "You've got time," I said. "Don't panic."

"Isn't that what everyone else is doing?"

The strap loosened under my fingers and I tugged it free, taking the weight of the pouch as she pushed it at me. "That's a precaution," I said, hoping my ears didn't betray me, "not a panic."

Azmit was almost at the Eye. The Elites' wingbeats were slaps on the breeze, getting louder with every flap.

"I'm not waiting any longer." With that, Varna turned to climb up the sawn branches onto the vinelog. It creaked a little, and Azmit's ears signalled alarm as she wobbled slightly, her wings automatically adjusting to compensate – something Varna would not be able to do if she lost her balance.

Still, Limar had made it safely across earlier. No reason why Varna should not. As Azmit gained the sawn end of the trunk on the Eye and began to climb down onto firm ground, Varna started her crossing. The Elite were close enough that I could hear their howls and whoops. It was time to take off.

I glided low over the river, Varna's bow and carry-pouch gripped firmly in my paws. As I landed to put them down, Shaya stepped onto the northern bank and moved up the hill to snatch up Trati's spear. I drew in a breath to call to her, to tell her again that there was nothing we could do – especially from the ground – but I didn't need to. Shaya's wings shuddered, her ears drooped, and I saw her look south toward the oncoming Elite. She hesitated, her paw outstretched to take the spear. Then she snatched it up, ears rigid with frustration and anger, and marched up the hill to join the others beneath the canopy.

On the Eye, Azmit was climbing onto the fallen log, ready to cross it. Through the vines, I glimpsed Varna, clawing her slow and steady way across to the islet.

Which meant that we had all left Drax territory, as Kalis had commanded. As Shaya scurried beneath the vinetrees, I looked up at the oncoming Elite. Would they understand that we had carried out Kalis' orders? Would they care?

With a clap of wingbeats, the guards turned in formation to swoop low over the log nearest to me, dangerously near to Azmit, who swayed and spread her wings as wide as she could till she had regained her balance.

"Come on!" I yelped, holding out a paw as though that would be a help. At least there hadn't been any more shooting. Yet. I realised I was alone amid the scattered belongings, and felt my hackles prickle in anticipation of an attack, but I couldn't leave Azmit and Varna alone out there. Running for the vines was no longer an option.

The Elite were following Murgo up and around, turning sharply once they reached vinetop level and then swooping low again. This time they were heading for the log that Varna was halfway along. If she fell in...

I found myself running, flapping, feeling the lift under my wings as I gained the air and started to climb. I needed to see what was happening and I couldn't do that from the ground. Azmit was almost at the end of the log; she would be safe in a beat or two. But Varna...

Three of the Elite were hovering over her, yipping insults, while Murgo and Difel had landed on the felled vinelog, one in front and one behind Varna's crouching figure. They began to jump up and down, using their wings to help lift off, barking with laughter. Varna's ears were upright, signalling that she was angry rather than afraid, but I felt my own breath catch as the log bounced and swayed, bending beneath Varna as she clung on.

I glimpsed movement under the vines, and saw Doran and Galyn edge out between two sturdy trunks. Both were signalling frantically for me to land and join them under the canopy, and I suppose I might as well have for all the good I was doing flitting about over the Eye, but it felt wrong to make for safety myself when Varna was in danger, even though there was nothing I could do to help her. I didn't even dare call to her for fear of drawing attention to myself.

The log creaked alarmingly, and Varna let out a howl of sheer terror. There was a smell of triumph in the air, carried from the Elite as Murgo flapped upward for a couple of wingbeats before dropping his full weight onto the log. A branch snapped, the log twisted, the sawn end gave way with a ripping sound – and the whole thing rolled into the river.

Murgo and Difel beat their wings to fly upward and the entire Elite rose into the air, whooping, as the vinelog – and Varna – were engulfed in a mass of fountaining water.

Numb with shock, I did no more than keep my wings outstretched for the wind to blow me where it would. I was half-aware of the Forest vines beneath me as I watched the swollen waters roil past and half-heard Difel shout: "What about the rest?"

"They're in the Forest. Let it take them," Murgo barked in reply, his ears still twitching with glee. "We'll go and deal with that group on the Ambit peninsula. Come on!" With a last yip of triumph, he turned on the breeze and led his guards east.

"Carma," I murmured. I spiralled a paw over my tunic in prayer as I watched them go, though my supplications had not saved Milat or those with her, and I doubted they would save Carma's group either. "At least make it quick," I whispered. "Take them to your arms, Great Spiral and may their lights look down on us always."

Downstream, a splash of black vinetrunk and white water snagged my attention. The log had surfaced – and alongside it, clinging to a branch, ears flat with shock and fright, was Varna.

"Doran, Galyn, fetch a net," I barked, and set off in a frantic chase.

The current was swift, but I didn't have to follow the river's twists and turns and it didn't take many beats to position myself above the log. "Hold on, Varna," I called, "there's a net coming." Though how we would manage to catch her with it I hadn't figured out.

The log had rolled while it was underwater, the shorter roots and branches that we had cut to stabilise it now sticking out above the surface, the whole thing half-submerged as it glided lengthwise through the water. I realised that from Varna's point of view, the riverbank would be rushing past in a blurred, wet haze.

My Vision. I'd Seen this moment when I took Varna's arm ninedays ago, but I hadn't Seen the outcome. Would the log be pulled under again and Varna with it? Would she be carried all the way back to the ocean?

The river was broadening. If the log stayed in the middle of the stream, I could see no way to rescue her. The way she was holding the branch and the size of the log alongside her reminded me of a trader guiding a vlydh. Might the log be steered in a similar way?

"Varna," I called, "use your tail. And your feet. See if you can push the log toward the bank."

She spared me no more than the merest ear-twitch to acknowledge that she'd heard me, but the blurred outline of her lower body was visible beneath the surface, and I watched as she began to wave her feet about. Her tail angled away from the northern bank and to my joy and amazement the log veered slightly in the other direction – toward shallower water and the safety of the shore.

"It's working," I shouted. "Keep going."

"What's working?"

I'd been so intent on following Varna's progress that I'd not heard Doran and Galyn flying up behind me. I spared a glance over my shoulder. Doran clutched a net in her paws, Galyn a blanket. Beyond them, already distant, columns of smoke indicated that drax were rekindling the fires they had abandoned when the Elite Guard sent everyone scurrying for the vines.

I pointed a paw, gasping an explanation, while Varna and the log she clung to drew nearer to the river bank till, with a suddenness that almost jolted Varna's grip loose, the vinelog jerked to a halt.

"Its branches are caught on the bottom," said Doran. "Now's our chance."

She angled her wings and dived, Galyn and myself right behind her. Varna, with the presence of mind that had once made her an exceptional guardflight member, used the branches to pull herself along the log and nearer to the bank. By the time we had landed with the net, she was wading through the shallows to make her way to dry land.

"Look," said Galyn, jerking her snout in the direction of the next hill as we folded our wings. "The Abandoned Cluster's just over there."

It was close, so ridiculously close to the Eye, when approached on the wing. Yet it had taken over a nineday for the wingless to make that short journey.

"Good thing we brought the net," said Galyn, voicing my thoughts.

Varna was wet through and shivering, but as she climbed from the water her ears were upright, and through the reek of wet fur I smelled relief and – strangely – exhilaration. She shook herself, covering Doran, Galyn, and myself in ice cold droplets. "Did you see that log?" she said, getting to her feet. "It floated! Just like a twig, though it was so much bigger and heavier."

Bedraggled as she was, Varna's stance and scent left no doubt that she had left behind the howling wreck Kalis had reduced her to. In her place stood the clever, decisive female he had once chosen as a worthy mate.

Varna rubbed her snout to warm it and stamped her feet, while Galyn wrapped the blanket round her and rubbed Varna's back, wringing out the long fur beneath the wing-stubs.

"I don't see that it matters," said Doran, "except that it was the log kept you afloat."

"Yes," said Varna, "I clung to it and it kept me afloat. That's my point." She turned to me, her ears set with excitement. "You understand, Zarda, don't you?"

I was not entirely sure that I did, but Varna plunged on. "We already knew that vinelogs floated, but now we know that they'll bear the weight of a full-grown drax while they are in the water. Don't you think that's interesting?"

I began to understand. The wingless could not move far or fast, the air being closed to them, but if they could move on a river, with the help of floating vinelogs, progress would be swifter. Though the knowledge was not much use to us without a body of water.

"There's a river in the Forest," said Varna, as though reading my doubts. Then, seeing my surprise, added, "Oh come on, I was young once too – we all flew to places we were not supposed to go, did things we shouldn't have..." She shook herself again, though I wasn't sure whether it was to warm herself, or was an involuntary reaction to a bad memory. She extended an arm toward the mountains in the west. "The river runs from the mountains and winds through the Forest, northward. I don't know how far it travels, but it must lead to whatever is beyond the vines."

Beyond the vines was nothing but ocean, but this did not seem the right moment to mention my Dream. In any case, she was surely right – if a river did indeed flow north as she said, then it would make sense for us to find a way of travelling on it using felled vines.

"We have to find this river," I said, "before we can float on it."

"We can worry about all that later," said Doran, ever the practical one. "Right now, we need to get you back to the campsite, Varna – everyone was frantic when you fell in. Besides which you'll need a warm tunic if you're not to catch a chill.

Galyn, fly back and let them know that we are all safe, would you? Zarda and I will bring Varna."

The sun was halfway to zenith as we landed, and Galyn handed me a beaker of hot broth, which I seized gratefully. Dru bolted across to hand his dam a dry tunic, and I left them to lick each other while I took a look at the makeshift camp. The fires had been rekindled, the younglings who had seen their dams killed had been gathered up by other females or the nest-nurses; the aroma of hot food mingled with the smoke and the Forest's smell of peat, bark and slime. The broth in my beaker tasted of salted seatach and herbs, and I gave it an approving sniff as I detected the fiery aftertaste of hoxberries.

"I didn't have many – I was saving them to make berrywine when we found a new home, but I thought they'd be better used now to warm us," said Galyn, as I took another sip of the hot liquid.

I nodded and waved my free paw at the camp. "Who do we have to thank for getting this straight?"

Her whiskers twitched as she pointed to Dru, who was bent over the pot on the nearest fire, ladling stew into a beaker. "When I got back, he was already bounding about getting everyone organised. I expect it helped keep his mind from Varna, thinking of what needed doing."

Dru's ears twitched as she spoke. Handing the beaker to Varna, who ran a paw over his white mane, he turned and came over to us. "I knew Varna-muz would be alright. I Saw it, when I got on the log to walk over the river." As I opened my mouth to ask why he'd said nothing to me about it, he went on: "You were airborne, Zarda, or I'd have told you." Turning to Galyn, he said, "Shaya and the hunters were angry, roaring at everything. Everyone else was panicking about the Elite and Varna-muz. I thought that getting them to set up the camp again would help."

"You did well." I stared about at the spans of trampled moss between us and the vinetrees, and sniffed the air again to try to sense what lay beyond the twisted trunks, but my nose detected so many strange smells that I couldn't choose one from another. All I could tell was that none of them smelled pleasant.

Galyn must have sensed some change in my demeanour for, as I turned my attention back to our camp, she said, "Do you smell something, Zarda? Are we in danger?"

"We've been in danger since we left the *Spirax*," I reminded her, "and I smell many things in the Forest – but I can't tell whether any of them are an immediate threat. The Sight eludes me, and my nose tells me nothing." I drained the last of the broth and licked the beaker clean. "All the same, I think perhaps we should make sure everyone remains near the fires – and tonight we'll set a watch along the Forest edge. Just to be sure." I turned to look over the river, in the direction Milat and the others had flown before they were killed. "I'll put my black tunic on," I said. "There's a death-rite to howl."

Eighteen

The watchers saw nothing that night, but despite our exhaustion, I doubt there were many who slept well. The pups whose dams had been killed had whimpered through the early part of the night, while my memory saw the flyers fall again and again. After a while, the wind had changed to the north-east, and the sound of grieving younglings was no longer so acute; in its stead, came the rank stench of mould and decay, along with a host of unfamiliar sounds – screams, chittering, odd groaning noises, the rustling of a million leaves, and the unmistakable cries of a creature in pain. Flattening my ears didn't help – I could still hear the louder noises, and I was anxious that I might miss some softer sound that would warn me of imminent danger.

I dozed eventually – I was too tired not to – but I woke frequently, and each time I did so it was to find some other member of our company adding a vinelog to a fire, or sitting up beneath their blankets to stare over at the Forest edge. We didn't even have the comfort of the Spiral to gaze at, for the wind had brought cloud with it, and the sky was obscured behind a depressing grey veil.

And with the morning came the moment that we had to face the Forest.

"You know, it's odd," said Doran, as she pushed the last spoon into her carry-pouch and fastened the straps. "I never quite believed we would actually have to go into the Forest. I don't know what I thought would happen to prevent it, but somehow it never seemed quite real." She stood, adjusted the straps around her shoulders and added, "Till now."

I fastened my own carry-pouch, and pushed an unlit torch into my belt as I dipped an ear in acknowledgement. I knew exactly what she meant, and I suspect that we were not the only ones who had daily expected some sort of miraculous intervention that would prevent us reaching this moment – a death at the *Spirax*, a change of heart on Kalis' part, some sign from the Great Spiral that it was displeased with our treatment.

I glanced upward at this last thought, but the sky was still covered with a damp curtain of dark grey which matched the mood of the camp.

"No use looking up there." Doran's voice was tart, her whiskers quivering with disappointment. "It's not listening."

"The Spiral always listens," I retorted, "and it answers. But the reply—"

"—may not be the one we want to hear. Yes – I heard Vizan speak too, remember."

I did. I'd been alongside Doran when we took her dam, her sire, and her nest-brother to their last nests after the Sickness took them. Each time, Vizan had used some variation on the words I'd just spoken; each time, they had been enough. But that was before Cavel hatched, wingless; before Miyak discarded Doran in favour of another nest-mate; before this wretched exile, with its daily footslog, its terrors, its horrifying, random deaths.

Looking around, I saw Doran's despair reflected in the drooping ears and lowered heads of all too many; the smell of sorrow mingled with agitation and alarm. The younglings were subdued. Some wandered aimlessly about the camp, whimpering; others stayed close to their dams, helping to pick up beakers and roll blankets. A few had made their way to the riverbank and were throwing bits of burned twig into the current.

"What's that terrible smell?" Rewsa's shrill, panic-edged voice carried from the campfire nearest the Forest, and everyone stopped what they were doing and sniffed the air.

There was nothing there that I'd not been scenting all night – damp vineleaves, rot, slime – but cries of agreement and murmurings of anxiety spread through the camp faster than a wind-driven flame. I could have cheerfully bitten Rewsa right on the nose, but reminded myself that it would serve no useful purpose other than venting my frustration.

Limar took up the lament: "There'll be nothing safe to eat," she wailed. "Nothing to add to the meat or the stews. We'll starve."

Flori, who already looked starved, though I'd tended to her fur-clump the previous evening, chimed in: "Or we'll be the ones who get eaten."

"We'll die." Rewsa again. "We'll all die!"

I ran a paw over the front of my crumpled black tunic and wondered, just for a heartbeat, whether I would be better off taking my chances back at the *Spirax*. Then I caught sight of Dru, rocking from side to side as he stood next to his dam, his ears upright. It was obvious he wanted to speak, to bolster morale, to allay what fears he could: but he was too young. He would have no clear idea what to say.

I wasn't sure I knew either, but I was the one wearing the black tunic. With little wind, and limited room on the cramped tongue of land for me to take off, I had to make do with climbing to the top of the rise, spreading my wings, and beating them up and down for attention.

"Listen to me." The voices nearest to me subsided and I called again. This time, everyone heard and I stilled my wings but left them outspread. Now I had their attention, I sent up a brief prayer to the Spiral that I would say the right thing, and began to speak: "I know we've already had an arduous journey, and too many of us have not survived it. But the Spiral sent the seatach, and it will send us more food when we need it. For now, we still have enough dried meat and herbs to last for another moon – longer if we're careful. As for the Forest, Vizan taught me what can and

168

what cannot be eaten – and what can, and cannot, eat us. There will be strange vegetation, yes, but some of it will be familiar – orenvines and camylvines, maybe some kestox too. But don't touch them unless you're *sure* there's nothing lurking under the leaves or around the trunk. Keep your feet clear of the ferns – most of them are harmless, but if you step on a Sucker Fern it will kill you." No need to explain how. Everyone had enough nightmares, real and imagined, to deal with. Bending low, I plucked a small blue leaf from a low-growing bush near my feet. "These are Sweetleaf plants. They're medicinal, they grow in clearings, and they'll help to soothe bites and stings. But don't eat them, they're poisonous."

I waited while my words were relayed to the drax nearest the river, who were straining to hear, then continued: "We will need to be alert, we will need to be careful what we touch and what we lick – but we will not starve." Murmurs and the faint smell of consolation told me that I had allayed that fear at least, but there was still the Forest to face with all its dangers. I raised my head and my voice again and added: "We can't know what awaits us in the Crimson Forest, but we *do* know what is behind us. We can't stay here and we can't go back, but remember the Vision that Vizan and I Saw for Dru. He has a future – a great future – and if Dru has a future, then so do we all."

It was not the stirring speech Vizan would doubtless have conjured, but it seemed to serve. The smell of anxiety still lingered, but now it was overlaid with hints of determination and – faint, but unmistakeable – hope.

Limar stood a little apart from the rest, her ears shifting in sulky agitation. "You'd best go first then, Zarda, since you know so much about it."

She had spoken loudly enough for everyone near her to hear, and as much as I baulked at being the first to step into the unknown, I could hardly refuse her challenge. Besides, it made sense, much as I hated the idea. "By all means," I said, pushing my ears upright to convey more confidence than I felt. I lifted the torch I had stuck in my belt. "Let's get the torches lit."

While the adults ignited the torches and gathered the younglings they were each responsible for, I turned to Shaya.

169

"We'll need someone with keen senses at the rear. Would the hunters take turns?"

Her grip tightened around the shaft of the spear she held, the spear that had been Trati's, and her ears twitched between grief and resolve. "There are only three of us left," she said, "Azmit, Marga and myself." She took a breath, and her scent shifted as she set her ears to a determined angle. "We'll do what we can – and keep training some of the others, along with the younglings." She glanced upriver in the direction we would be travelling. "What about scouting ahead? Finding a place to camp tonight?"

"It won't have to be very far," I said. "The vines will be horribly tangled once we get away from the forest edge – we'll make very slow progress."

She dipped an ear. "I'll send a couple of flyers to check for clearings. They can report back on the possibilities before they start building any fires."

As she turned away to put our plans into action, her tail was still rigid with anger and grief. I suspected it would be that way for some time. Smoke from nines of torches rose into the still air; I heard caws and squeaks from the Forest ahead, the wash of the river behind me. No-one spoke, no-one moved. Everyone was looking at me.

"Tread where I tread," I called. "Stay in line, don't venture off anywhere. Those of us at the front will need to stop and cut through vines, so when the line halts, don't panic. Keep your torches high, watch where you're stepping, and above all *don't touch anything.*" What had I forgotten? Oh! "May the Spiral watch over us and keep us. As it has always been."

"May it so remain." The response was little more than an automatic mutter, but at least it had been said.

I'd run out of reasons to stand still, and the sun was well on towards zenith already. With a last glance up at the sky and a sniff of the water-reeds, I turned and stepped under the canopy.

It was easy to see where everyone had hidden earlier: trampled fungi and bruised moss stretched right and left beneath the vines.

The smell of terror lingered in the still air – though that might just have been my own scent rising to haunt me.

In both directions the vines ran to meet the curving riverbank and clung to it. Regardless of which way we went, we had to go further under the canopy, but Varna had spoken of another river, far to the west, and it gave us a goal to aim for, if nothing else.

I took a single step, my torch illuminating the grey bark of tanglevines, spotted with scarlet lichens and black moss. Above shoulder height, the trunks twisted round each other, blocking the way in several places, but creating strange twisting tunnels in others. Where their trunks weren't twined together, their branches met over our heads and wrapped around till it was impossible to see where one vine ended and the other began. The sky was already lost behind the layers of crimson leaves that stretched upward groping for the light; all that was left was an eerie red glow – and even that faded as I took another step. My claws sank into soft black mulch, which squelched underfoot. The stench of rot and slime assaulted my nostrils, and I peered into the gloom in expectation of finding a spiny slug or a suckerpod lurking there. I twisted my ears about, listening. Screeches in the distance; the faint susseration of the vineleaves rustling as something bounced through the branches; a fur-raising scream that rose and fell in pitch for several beats before ending with a series of cackles.

When a paw grasped my shoulder, I almost bit it. "Don't do that!"

"Sorry." Doran sounded even more frightened than I felt, and I flicked an ear to apologise for snapping. "What was that?" she whispered.

The screaming began again, this time from a different direction.

"Gumalix," I said. "Mating calls, I think."

"Sounded like they were being eaten alive."

"It's a normal sound in the Forest at this point in the cycle." The words were Vizan's. He'd said them when he'd brought me here to teach me what he knew of the Forest and its ways. I'd been curled into a ball at the base of a gigantic whipvine at the time, whimpering.

"You sound like Vizan."

"Then you know that I'm right." I took a steadying breath. It was normal. This was the standard by which we would have to gauge future threats; this was the situation we would have to live with and camp in, day after day, night after night, for the Spiral knew how long. "Pass the word along that it's safe, that we'll have to get used to the noises."

"I doubt I'll ever get used to that," Doran muttered, as a third and then a fourth gumalix began to scream. But I heard the crunch of the mulch under her feet as she turned to call over Cavel's head to Varna, who was the next in our straggling line. "It's fine. Just a few mite-eaters playing."

I took a moment to tamp down my own fright, bundling it up in my head and pushing it aside. This was the commonplace now. Keep the fear, but don't let it overwhelm.

Another breath. Another step. A gap between twisting trunks opened up on my left. West. With the torch held ahead in my outstretched paw, and my other paw resting on the knife in my belt, I moved toward it.

Progress was almost non-existent. When we weren't skirting twisted roots and trunks, we were avoiding hollows choked with brambles, or evil-smelling dips where dank mud sucked and bubbled of its own accord. I learned the quickest way to slash through head-high branches and knee-high ferns, found the optimum height to hold my torch so that my shoulders and arms didn't constantly ache, and used Vizan's teachings to ensure that we kept heading west. Beneath the canopy, there was little chance of seeing sun or stars, but the sight of fungus on the southern side of the vinetrunks – and the calls of our flyers overhead – assured me that our direction was correct.

For a nineday, we did little more than stumble from riverbend to riverbend, making camp each night on mossy tongues of raised ground. With access to the river, plus the reeds and the cut branches we had collected as I cut through them, at least we didn't want for water or hot food. But our progress, already pitiable, grew slower as the smaller and weaker members of the party fell further and further behind.

"Have you noticed that that the grumbling and complaining has stopped?" asked Doran, as we flew ahead on the tenth afterzenith to scout for an overnight camping spot. It was my first flight since we had stepped into the Forest, and it felt good to stretch my wings and feel the breeze beneath me, though a steady drizzle misted my fur, the low clouds making me wary of flying too high for fear of floaters. It was warm enough now, I thought, for them to start following the clouds.

"Yes," I called, in answer to Doran's question. "They are all saving their breath for the journey." As I spoke, I saw a small hillock of reedgrass below us, fringed by vines, a span or two inland from the river. "Down there." I pointed, turned into the wind, and glided lower to take a closer look. Landing, I glimpsed the river through the scrawny vines at the base of the rise, its waters churned and swollen from the rain. The ground beneath my feet was soggy, but that would be the same for any point along our route – unless we were prepared to spend the night beneath the Forest canopy. "Do you think there'll be room here for everyone?" I asked, as Doran landed beside me.

She eyed the vines, giving a start as something chittered in the shadowed tangle of branches behind us. "It'll serve," she said. "It will have to – it's the first clear ground we've seen since we took off, and I'm not sure the groundlings will make it even this far before dark."

At least the rain had eased, though a fine mist still hung in the air and clung to our fur. I turned a slow circle, mud sticky beneath my feet while I sniffed the air and listened: screams, mulch, chitters, fungus, whistles, lichens, ferns and vineleaves. Nothing beyond the usual Forest scares. "Perhaps we should try a bit further north," I said. "See if there's anything closer to the walking group. I'll—"

I never finished my sentence. The alien sounds of the Forest were suddenly cut through by a sound that both Doran and I knew far too well: the sound of a youngling, howling in terror.

Nineteen

We flew with the wind, our wingbeats cutting the air with an urgency born of nightmare imaginings. Ahead of us, the screams had multiplied, the noise of adult cries mingling with the shrill squeals of the younglings, but they were hidden beneath the mist-wreathed vinetrees and I couldn't see what had caused such horror.

As I angled my wings for the glide down, I pulled my knife from my belt and twisted it so that the sharper edge was toward the ground.

"How are we going to land?" Doran's concern for Cavel gave her voice an edge of hysteria. She hovered over the vinetrees, looking and sniffing for a gap in the leaves, while beneath us the howls were loud enough to make my ears vibrate – and to draw every predator within earshot. "We can't even see through this."

For spans around us, vinecreepers bounced across the topmost branches of the vines, screaming with alarm as they headed back to their nests. I remembered what had happened the last time

Doran and I had encountered what we thought was a vinecreeper nest, and thought about how I had hurtled groundward to retrieve the dropped knife when Doran had been bitten. "We'll go through." Just as I had done as a youngling, I angled my wings back and stooped downward, keeping my arms and paws outstretched to punch through the top layer of leaves. Twigs and small branches clattered against my wings and bruised my shoulders as I hurtled groundward much faster than was usually considered sane. A hurried switch to night-vision showed me that larger branches were stretched across my flight-path, and I pulled my right wing up, twisting my tail to jink between them. Another course correction as a clump of tangled vinetrunks appeared ahead of me, and then I was on the ground, skidding on a tuft of moss. I'd have landed face-first in the mulch if I hadn't skinned a paw on a vine in an effort to steady myself, but that didn't matter. I was close enough to the howls that I had to fold my ears against the noise, and I glimpsed movement among the vines – tunics and torches dodging and swaying, just a few spans away – and I hurried toward them.

When I caught the stench of spiny slug, I faltered. I might even have stopped altogether if Doran hadn't landed behind me and started her own run toward the danger. Fighting nausea and the strange cold fear that made my fur stand on end, I pressed on, hacking through strands of tanglevine, keeping my eyes, nose, ears alert.

The creature made a horrible sucking noise as it slithered about, and as I pushed through vines and into a gap in the howling crowd, I saw that it had already made one kill: a youngling in a blood-splashed blue-striped tunic hung from the slug's horn, dissolving in the slime it excreted from its skin. As I watched, a slew of arrows flew toward it – and every one of them bounced from its hide and dropped harmlessly to the ground.

"Take off!" I heard someone shout. "Get above it!"

"We can't!" Shaya's voice answered. "There's not enough breeze here, and the vinetrunks are crowded too close to spread our wings."

She was right. The slug has chosen its attack point well – the vines were dense here, the Forest canopy forming a crimson tunnel overhead, the twisting branches blocking all but one narrow route through the tangle. The creature had made its strike near the back of the straggling line, and as I watched, it slicked over the trampled ferns and advanced toward the group backing away through the vines – all save one female in pale blue, who moved toward the slug. It was Jonel, the first trader to make Dru welcome at her cluster so many moons ago. Her screams of anger and anguish confirmed that the dead youngling was Manda, while her actions were heedless of danger.

"Back! Get back!"

Jonel didn't appear to hear my warning. Armed only with a cooking-knife, she edged forward toward the squirming creature.

"It's too late, Jonel." It should have been a shout, but my words came out as a murmur of distress, and a moment later it was too late for Jonel, too: the slug jerked its tail up over its head, in a movement too quick for the eyes to follow, and speared her through the heart. As the creature used its tail to lift her body onto its back and impale her on one of its spines, everyone turned and fled – including me. Twigs snapped, branches were crashed aside and sprang back to slap at heads, bodies, legs; squeals and howls gave way to panting and sudden cries of pain or surprise; pots and pans rattled, belongings came loose from their packs and dropped unnoticed into the ferns that brushed our ankles as we bolted.

It wasn't exhaustion that stopped us; it wasn't even the return of reason. It was a wall of knotvines. Thin and supple, the vines were as densely entwined as a reed screen – but this screen stretched for spans on either side of our trampling dash, while its topmost fronds were lost in the canopy above. Shaya and three or four others pulled out knives and hacked at the barrier, while others jostled and pushed in an effort to keep away from the thicker trunks of the tanglevines which enclosed us, and urged them to hurry. The entire company was wailing and keening, dams and nest-nurses attempting to comfort younglings even while they howled themselves. Everyone was sniffing the air for the slightest whiff of spiny slug.

"We'll die!" cried a familiar voice, which carried over the hubbub. "We'll all die!"

"Oh, do be quiet, Rewsa." I'd said it quietly, almost to myself – too breathless to shout. My stomachs roiled at the memory of those two bodies hanging from the slug's spines, and I dropped to my knees, overwhelmed by loss, failure, and disgust. I'd failed again. I hadn't Seen this coming, and I had no idea what lay in wait for us beyond the knotvines.

Knotvines.

The thought broke through my horror and self-pity: knotvines were bright yellow, and their uppermost tendrils wove themselves through the highest branches of the vines surrounding them, making them easily identifiable from the air.

"Doran." She sat to my left, carry-pouch discarded, paws clutching a trembling Cavel while she licked him, but showing no sign of having heard me. I reached over and placed a paw on her shoulder. "Doran. Did we see any knotvines while we were scouting?"

She stopped in mid-lick, tongue lolling and ears twitching while she gave it some thought. Her ears were set back as they stopped flicking, signalling her renewed distress. "No." She sat up straight, blinked, and looked hard at the knotvines, as though to assure herself that they truly were that colour, then glanced back at me, whiskers quivering. "No, we didn't."

I looked again at the nearest tanglevine, and checked for the grey fungus that coated the southern side. There was no doubt about it: our panicked, headlong, instinctive run from danger had taken us north – deeper into the Forest.

We had run the wrong way.

Doran must have realised it too, but she waggled her ears to signal caution. "Say nothing," she said, indicating the chaos and panic that still swirled around us. "Everyone's petrified enough as it is."

I nodded, got to my feet and took a long, deep breath before letting it out with a roar: "Quiet!"

Howls died away, the crash of bodies against branches ceased, and the smell of alarm subsided, though the scent of distress and fear lingered, as did the bleats and whimpers of younglings.

I'd got their attention. Now I had to work out what to do with it.

"It won't follow us this far." I spoke with more confidence than I felt, especially as we had left a spans-wide pathway for it to follow if it wanted to: but it would be gorged, surely, and wouldn't need to hunt again for some time. I pointed to the knotvines. "We have a natural barrier here – nothing can come through those. I suggest we keep them at our backs and build a semi-circle of fires around us. Use the spaces between the tanglevines where we can, and make camp here till morning." I dipped my ears and head as I added, "There's nothing we can do for Jonel and Manda but mourn them. Let's get the fires lit and have some tea to calm us. Then we'll howl the ceremony."

Shaya approached with a blazing torch in one paw and a spear in the other. "We have another problem," she confided, her voice so low I had to twist both my ears her way to make out her next words. "We're not all here."

"What?" I looked around again, trying to count individuals, nines, larger groups. I felt ill as I realised Shaya was right: we were at least half a ninety short. "Where are they?"

"You tell me." Shaya peered into the gloom beneath the vines, sniffed, set her ears to listen. "They could have run anywhere, in any direction. Or all directions." She turned her attention back to me. "Can you See where they might be?"

I rubbed my snout as I shook my head and dipped an ear in regret and sorrow. "It doesn't work like that."

A sigh, the merest twitch of an ear told me Shaya wasn't happy about it but accepted what I said. "Then we'll have to hope they find us." She indicated the whimpering, shaking drax surrounding us as she added, "because we can't go searching for them." Her own paw was trembling as she pointed her torch back in the direction we had come. "I won't ask anyone to go back there." She shook herself in an attempt to flatten her fur, and her voice was firm as she went on: "I'll take Azmit and Marga, and check the boundaries once the fires are set."

Cavel wriggled free of Doran's arms and stood up, his tone and posture hostile as he pointed to Shaya's spear. "Why didn't you throw that? You could have saved them."

Doran reached out a paw. "Cavel…"

Shaya shook her head. "Did you see how the arrows bounced off? It would have been the same with the spears."

"They wouldn't have made any difference," I assured him. "Not against that hide."

"You could have tried." He pulled away from Doran and stomped away, threading his way through dropped carry-pouches, murmuring adults, and leaf-gathering younglings till he reached Varna and Dru, who were building a fire on the northern edge of the group.

"I know." Shaya held up her spear and examined it as though it might turn to flame at any moment. "I know it wouldn't have made any difference, but I should have thrown it anyway. The truth is, I'd never seen anything like that thing. It was..." Shredded leaves and tiny twigs flew from her fur as she shook herself again. "It was horrifying. I couldn't think—"

Doran stood up to place a paw over Shaya's, where she gripped the spear's shaft. "Don't blame yourself, there was nothing any of us could have done."

Shaya's acknowledging ear-flick was the merest twitch, the scent of her receding fear overlayed now with the distinctive smell of shame. Then, just as she had done back by the river, before we entered the Forest, she gathered herself and began to plan: "Tomorrow, we'll reorganise the way we move," she said. "No more stragglers, no more walking in one thin line. In future, we should stay in groups – nines, if we can – with more torches, and at least two armed adults in each group. Perhaps that way we can keep everyone safe."

I nodded agreement, but as she turned and walked away to find her two surviving hunters, my concern was not how we grouped ourselves.

It was where we would go. With the canopy above us, none of us could take flight to scout for clearings, to find the river, to find those who had run in a different direction, or even to make sure we were heading the right way.

We were grounded. All of us.

Twenty

Keeping the knotvines to our right, we pushed on the next morning, huddled in small groups as Shaya had suggested. Noses twitched, ears twisted to catch every sound, and eyes strained to check every shadow that wavered beyond the reach of the blazing torches.

At first, I endeavoured to head south-westward in what I guessed was the direction of the Ambit and the chance of finding a clearing near the river, but almost at once we found the way blocked by an oozing swathe of swampy ground that was pocked with clumps of suckerpods. Even there, the tanglevines had found enough of a foothold to take root, and the canopy over our heads remained unbroken.

"There's higher ground to the north-west," said Shaya. "We'll have to go that way."

I remembered seeing the undulating hills in the distance as I had flown along the river. Apart from their height, they had looked no different from the rest of the Forest – covered in

180

swaying, shimmering crimson where the vines reached for the clouds. I'd hoped that by staying close to the Ambit we'd be able to take advantage of bankside clearings and the bounty of fresh fish. We'd also have avoided the steep hills that marched toward the spine of mountains that had lined the western horizon – when we'd been able to see it.

Fate – or, as I reminded myself, the Spiral – had other ideas. As the knotvines thinned and disappeared, and the ground under our feet began to rise, I prayed that there was some meaning to our new course, and that there would be a clearing or a source of food ahead of us.

But, as we made camp for a second night – and a third, and a fourth – under the relentless canopy of vines, my prayers went unanswered.

The slopes we toiled up and down were steep, slippery with rotting leaves and knotted with roots, but we had left behind the suckerpods and the air seemed warmer – though that might have been due to the lack of breeze beneath the vines. Sunlight provided an occasional glimpse of brightness, and warmed the canopy to a brighter red, giving hints that there might be enough space ahead to take off – then reneged on the promise as the branches closed overhead and the trunks ahead of us twisted into knotted barriers once again.

The smell of burning torches masked the scents of whatever kept chittering in the branches though occasionally, when we halted to cut our way through another jumble of tanglevines, we would catch a glimpse of something youngling-sized moving fast through the canopy. The screams and high-pitched cries that had so frightened us when we first moved under the vines had become nothing more than background noise by day.

The nights were a different matter.

Every night, we had to clear a space for each group between the vinetrunks, set a watch and light a fire for each, as well as lighting fires every half-span, in a circle. At least there was no shortage of fuel. Nor did we need the seatach-hide shelters, as the weather remained dry – though we were soon to regret our lack of overhead cover.

By the fifth night since our grounding, my wings were growing cramped from being folded for so long and, while those around me slept – or attempted to – I stood up and gently stretched them. My feet were sore and the ache in my legs was worse than it had been since we first set out. Climbing hills, I decided, was much better done on an updraught.

Beyond the campfire flames, the chittering went on, a well-worn chorus I had grown used to. The usual screams and roars would break in at irregular intervals, occasionally accompanied by a rustle of leaves or a creaking branch. Once or twice I thought I saw paw-sized green eyes staring at us from the darkness, but when I blinked they were gone.

Settling myself back on the ground next to Doran and Cavel, I closed my eyes and tried to banish thoughts of spiny slugs, mouldworms, and imaginary sucking creatures from my mind, but when my nose detected a peculiar oily smell mingling with the smoke, I opened my eyes. Nothing there. Nothing! I closed them again.

And jerked awake as a high-pitched howl drowned out every other sound in the Forest: "Get it off me! Get it off! Help!"

In a heartbeat the entire encampment were on their feet. Younglings were herded into the centre of groups and adults snatched up torches, everyone hurrying closer to the light and safety of the nearest fire.

No. Not everyone.

The flaring torches pushed the shadows back to the edges of the encampment, and illuminated the dreadful sight of Galyn the healer being pulled upward into the canopy. Eyes glazed, head lolling, silent, it was clear her light had already fled. There was a brief, violent movement in the leaves overhead. Then silence, save for the cries of Dugaz, Galyn's youngling, who was standing a short distance from me beyond the next vine. Both Limar and Winan had their paws on his shoulders, and the light from the fires behind them showed their fur was standing on end.

So was everyone else's.

More torches were lit and thrust upward. Some probed and circled beneath the branch where we had last seen Galyn; most remained still, a fearful barricade against another aerial assault. Then, like a sudden gale, the questions began:

"What was that thing?"

"Did you see it?"

"It looked like a vinebranch!"

"Aren't we even safe from the plants?"

The questions were flung in my direction, some of them with an accusing tone that suggested I ought to have known what would happen. Perhaps I should – after all, I had told the story of the vine-serpent often enough, but I had not realised that such things might descend almost to the ground, or that they might use a tail to snag an unsuspecting victim.

Holding my torch aloft, I checked the canopy above me as I turned on the spot in the vain hope of seeing Galyn somewhere overhead. "It wasn't a branch," I called, stifling the rising note of panic that had been starting to swell amid the questions. "It was a serpent."

I realised even as I spoke that my words did not offer much in the way of comfort. While I had quelled fears about the very vines attacking us, the idea of unseen, silent coils descending on us from above was just as terrifying a prospect – as the howls and whimpers that followed my announcement proved. The reek of horror and fear filled my nostrils.

"All the younglings should sit down," I said. "Or better yet, lie down. We'll cover them with the seatach-hides, and the adults can take turns with these torches, standing watch."

My arm was already beginning to ache from holding the torch over my head, and when I swapped paws, I saw that Doran was doing the same. "I'll take our first watch," I said to her, and she nodded. In the glow of the flames I could see that her fur was still sticking up in alarm, her ears set back in shock and fear.

I looked up again, sending my thoughts beyond the dark leaves that held such dangers, praying that the Spiral would take Galyn's light to itself, and keep us safe from further harm.

Whimpers and snuffling at my feet bore testament to the terror of the younglings, while even those adults who were not on watch sat bolt upright, noses sniffing for any possible hint of danger, eyes darting from the shadows beyond the fires to the undulating cloak of leaves over our heads.

I moved the torch back to my right paw and flexed my left shoulder, which was already throbbing.

It was going to be a long, long night.

Twenty-One

"Why do we even bother to keep going? Why don't we just stay here?" Rewsa's wail may have been louder than most, but as I looked around at the half-packed belongings and smelled the dejection and sorrow, I guessed that she was simply voicing what many felt.

"And wait for the Forest to kill us all?" Shaya's tone was sharp, her ears set firm and upright. She shook out her blanket as she spoke and rolled it carefully. "You stay here if you want to, Rewsa, but I'm going to press on thank you very much."

"There's a river somewhere beyond these hills," I said, pointing up the slope we had to climb that morning. "The sooner we can reach it, the sooner our flyers can find clear space to get airborne."

"And what about us?" Pain and resentment dripped from every syllable as Limar spoke, the set of her ears reinforcing her feelings. "Those of us who can't fly. What are we supposed to do while you flap off along this river? Assuming we ever find it?"

"We're heading west, Limar." I thought it best not to hedge round the point with approximations. "The river flows north between these hills and the western mountains. If we keep going in this direction, we can't fail to find it."

"And when we do find it, we can cut logs and make them float. We can sit on them and let the river take us north." Dru had stepped up onto a protruding vineroot as he spoke, bringing his head almost level with mine and allowing his voice to carry further.

Limar snorted, contempt bristling in every whisker. "I'd heard that rumour, but I thought it was just some silly idea that had been twisted from an old legend." She turned her attention from Dru as though dismissing him, and glared at me instead. "I can't believe you'd think it was a viable option."

"We don't have any others," I said, fighting the urge to give Limar a nip on the nose. "The alternatives are to stay here – as Rewsa suggested – or keep walking through these vines. If you'd prefer to do either of those, go right ahead." I made sure I was speaking loudly enough for the message to be heard beyond Limar's ears. I was tired of arguing, of justifying the few clear plans we had. If Rewsa wanted to stay put, I'd not stop her; if Limar wanted to crash off into the Forest, I wouldn't stand in her way. I put a paw on Dru's shoulder and added: "The Lordling and I are going to the river, and we're going to make floats for any wingless who come with us. If you don't want to do that, any of you, then you're welcome to find your own flightpaths, and I'll pray that the Spiral will watch over you."

Perhaps the mention of prayer reminded them of my place as Fate-seer; maybe it was the indication of Dru's importance. Either way, there was no more outspoken dissent. Though there were murmurs and mutterings as everyone turned to their packing, no-one made any move to head in a different direction, or indicated that they would stay put.

Limar's ears twitched a reluctant acknowledgment, and she turned her attention to her carry-pouch. Dru stepped down from the root and I saw his ears droop. "You shouldn't call me 'Lordling'," he said, sadly. "I'm not a leader. The other day..." He choked off, his mane standing on end again as he remembered what had happened. He went on, though I could barely hear him: "When the slug…I ran. I ran with everyone else."

"Of course you did! You're a youngling, no-one expects you to take on a spiny slug! For that matter, no-one expects anyone to take on a slug – but I should have anticipated that we might encounter one. If there is any fault for what happened to Jonel and Manda and Galyn – and all those who got lost when we ran – it's mine."

"No-one was at fault," said Doran, firmly, looking up from lacing her stewing pot onto her carry-pouch. "We couldn't have known that the things would strike like that – so fast, no warning. Not unless you Saw it?"

I shook my head. Dru had Seen blood-covered tunics in the Forest, but that was all. He'd not Seen a spiny slug, nor anything else specific – and I'd Seen nothing at all. "I wish I had. All the same, we knew the Forest was dangerous. We should have been better prepared."

"Well, I don't see how." Doran pulled the straps tight, gave the pouch a pat and hoisted it up to put it on her shoulders. "From what Winan told me, Manda had fallen behind because she'd seen something that looked like a toy egg. Shaya thought she heard something behind her and had turned to look, and the thing plunged out from the ferns. As for Galyn – well, I'm the one with the scar from the serpent-bite. If anyone should have thought of the danger they might pose it should have been me. But I didn't know they could do that! None of us did."

"Perhaps if…" I shook my head. No point going through the 'ifs' or the 'what might haves'. My ears were drooping, and I made an effort to set them to a straighter, more confident angle. We could do nothing to change what had happened: we could only learn from our mistakes and try to make sure they didn't happen again. Spiral willing, we would reach the river without losing anyone else.

I spiralled a paw over my tunic and looked up.

The backlit leaves of the canopy swayed and rustled in a breeze I couldn't detect; beyond them, slivers of blue suggested a fine sunny day for those in the open – or in the air. I extended my wings again, stretching them wide while I imagined clear ground and space enough to take off. I glanced uphill, at the route we must take, my legs protesting at the thought of spending another day climbing hillsides through unrelenting tangles of fern and vine. Then, hauling my carry-pouch clear of the damp, mouldering leaves underfoot, I picked up my torch and checked my knife was near to paw and ready to use.

Slowly, steadily, I started to climb.

Two ninedays passed in a torment of climbs and descents, grumbles and whimpers, cutting and slashing. There were no proper clearings, and no water except the little that dripped from the trees during sudden downpours. We were reduced to licking the drops from the fat, shining tanglevine leaves, or chewing juicy ferns to pulp to quench our thirst; our cooking pots stood idle every night while we chewed cold patties and dried curls of seatach meat beneath our hide shelters, as there was nothing to make tea with or cook a stew. Flori's fur-clump worsened by the day and spread to others. Three younglings and two females were lost to the Sucker Ferns, and another four females to rotberry poisoning. Two entire nines disappeared one afterzenith without so much as a whimper. They simply didn't appear when we made camp that night.

At least we no longer had to contend with the snow and ice. The further we walked, the warmer it became – or perhaps it was just that we were not built for clambering up hillsides in our winter fur.

Even Shaya looked tired and ungroomed, though her ears and scent betrayed her burning anger for every death, every disappearance we suffered. I'm sure it was the anger that kept her going – that kept many of us going. If we stopped, if we waited in the Forest to die, then Kalis – and Fazak – had won. But every morning it took a little longer to summon the willpower to stagger on.

"How much further is this river of yours, Varna?" Shaya paused as she led the way up another great hill, pricked her ears and sniffed the wind. I took the opportunity to snatch a brief rest and did the same.

No sound or smell of running water. No odour of freshwater plants. We were barely a quarter-way up the rise, but my legs were already issuing their usual protest.

"I don't know!" Varna bared her teeth as she plodded past us, head down, body swaying with the effort of the climb. Her words came in gasps. "We flew there. We flew back. It was almost a day's flight from that wild orenvine grove on the southern bank of the Ambit. On foot? Who knows?"

"Well, it hadn't better be much further," Shaya murmured to me, glancing round to make sure no-one could overhear. "I doubt we can go much longer without a proper source of water."

Aching, thirsty, and gasping for breath, we pushed on, cursing as the incline became steeper and rockier. The vines thinned along with the topsoil as we moved higher, till at last we stood on a ridge in the open, looking west into the valley beyond.

The fresh smell of shower-soaked leaves was overpowering, though it was no longer raining. Across the valley, a dark fist of cloud was heading for the hills in the west, trailing a mist of rain beneath it. I filled my lungs again and again with the aroma of damp foliage, of wet, gritty rock. My tunic flapped in a steady north-easterly and I stretched my wings, enjoying the feel of the breeze caressing the membranes. With howls of joy, the hunters Azmit and Marga threw down their carry-pouches and took off.

I stayed on the ground, remembering the last time I'd flown off and left people in the Forest. I couldn't take to the air till I knew everyone was safely in the open.

We were high up – higher, possibly, than the balcony on the *Spirax*. As I thought it, I turned to look over my shoulder in the direction where the *Spirax* lay, and realised with a shock that I couldn't see it. I called up to Azmit as she glided overhead, "Can you see the *Spirax*?"

She angled a wing, turned to take a look. "No. No, I can't." Her voice carried a hint of astonishment and a hair of trepidation. To not see the *Spirax* – to not see 'home' even from the air! It was a new experience, one which reminded us of how far we'd been forced to travel, and what we'd left behind. "I'll fly a bit higher."

"Be careful, then. Watch for floaters, it's warm enough for them."

She flapped her wings and for a few beats I watched her rise higher, then I turned my attention back to checking how many others had reached the safety of the ridge. No longer were the younglings ahead of the adults – they kept together in their groups without prompting now, scared and sobered by the events that had befallen us. Slowly, group by group, nine by nine, they climbed out of the vines, gasping and exclaiming with the joy of being under an open sky. As more and more flyers took to the air, I turned my attention to the view ahead. Vinetops stretched skyward from the slope below as though reaching to pull us to them. Further down the hill, and on the far side of the valley, their close-clustered tops looked like soft crimson cushions, embroidered here and there with the yellow threads of knotvine. Beyond them, the hills reared steeper and higher than anything we had yet climbed. The forest's relentless march ceased part way up the furthest of them and their summits, dull with drizzle, were patched grey and purple with rock, lichens, and moss. In the distance, the mountains stood, massive peaks of grey and black, their snow-laden upper slopes disappearing into the high clouds that habitually clung to them.

"I'm glad we don't have to climb those," I said to Doran, who had arrived, panting, beside me, with Winan at her tail.

As I spoke, a shaft of sunlight appeared between fleeing rainclouds, and something sparkled through the crimson in the valley bottom. "Is that—?"

"The river!" To my right, Varna was leaping up and down as she pointed, howling with delight. "What did I tell you?"

Dru and Cavel joined in, yipping with glee and bouncing about. Within moments every youngling on the hillcrest was doing the same, and I folded my ears against the din. "Is everyone here?" I shouted, checking to see whether Shaya, who had insisted on bringing up the last group, had emerged from the vines. Seeing her faded ochre tunic ascend the last few spans towards us, I leaned close to Doran's folded ears and barked, "I'm going to take a closer look at the river."

Water tumbled from a high ledge into a vast pool that swirled and eddied in a rock-strewn basin before steadying into a wide, pebble-lined river that flowed away toward a tunnel of overhanging vines. Between the pool and the vines, where the riverbank curved, a wide, mossy meadow promised rest and respite.

Glumps hopped about near the water's edge, croaking an alarm as I landed and plopping into the river as more flyers swooped in.

"If we're all they're worried about, it must be safe," said Shaya. She kept her wings outstretched for several beats after landing, no doubt savouring the feel of flight, air over wings, after over a moon on the ground. With a satisfied sigh, she folded them and made for the water's edge. I followed, the smell of sweet, fresh water overwhelming everything else. As we sank our snouts into the water and drank, I thought that I had never before tasted anything so good.

Many of the other flyers filled flasks and flew back to the hilltop to share the bounty with the groundlings and wingless, while Shaya and I began to set up camp. "Do you think the non-flyers will make it this far before dark?" I glanced up as I spoke. More clouds were scudding westward, gathering together as they moved and shifted. The scent of the breeze promised more rain to come, but there were pockets of blue amid the clouds, and for a few glorious moments the sun warmed my snout. It was already past zenith. I thought of the pitiful progress we had made through the vines each day, and thought it likely that the groundlings would have to make camp in the Forest again. Surely they would not make it this far before nightfall.

"They'll be here." Shaya's ears were alert, listening for any sound – friendly or otherwise – from the Forest while she made her way along its edge gathering twigs and branches. Every few paces, she dropped what she had gathered and piled them into rough heaps to mark the spots where we would light fires and erect the shelters.

"You can hear them? Over the noise of that waterfall?"

"I can barely hear you! But they'll be here. We have water, open space, and somewhere we can set shelters and be sure nothing will creep over them. No-one will be sleeping under the vines tonight."

As we settled into a rhythm of stick-gathering and fire-building, the glumps ventured from the water in ones and twos. After sending out a few tentative croaks to test our reactions, they decided we were no threat and settled into a rhythmic chirp that counterpointed the deep roar of the falls and the gurgle of the river.

The ground was wet from the spray and the earlier rain, and had that pleasing, clean odour of fresh moss. While we had fought our way through stubborn vines, tripped over roots, and avoided puddles of dank mud, the Melt had arrived.

Dropping an armful of twigs near the pool bank, I sniffed again at the water, testing the air for something other than melted ice, wet rock, and glump-waste. "Do you think it's safe to go in?" I asked as Shaya stepped onto the rocks.

Her gaze swept over the pool, the river, and the tiny splashes where the glumps had jumped back in. "Quite safe," she said. "Those glumps wouldn't be nesting here if there were any predators nearby." Guessing my next question, she glanced round at me and added, "It'll be perfect for washing in – us *and* our tunics." Scratching delicately at the fur round her neck, she held up several strands of long winter hairs. "Moulting," she confirmed, as the strands blew away on the breeze. "We'll be glad of the water over the next few ninedays."

It did feel good to wade into the pool and have a good scratch and scrub, even if the ice-cold water did take my breath and make my limbs cramp. As other flyers returned for more water and to bring carry-pouches from the ridge, they wasted no time in flapping into the water as well. Before long, the pool was heaving with chattering females, splashing themselves and each other. The air was filled with yips of shock as they entered the water, howls of delight as itching, dirty fur fell away, and even barks of laughter. It was not a sound I had thought to hear again, and as I climbed from the pool and shook myself dry, I thanked the Spiral for finding us such a refuge.

As dusk fell, we lit the campfires, scooped water into cooking pots, and opened carry-pouches to find the last of the avalox. At the sound of footsteps approaching through the Forest, the glumps began to croak again, and a few beats later Dru and Cavel led the first of the groundlings onto the bank, yipping with glee as they bounded to the pool and leaped in.

Shaya eyed the vines, counting as nine after nine of younglings and their accompanying dams and nest-nurses emerged from beneath the canopy, blinking in the evening light. "If they'd walked that far every day, we'd have been here ninedays ago," she grumbled, "and been at the Eye with time to spare."

"All they needed was to be thirsty enough," I said, indicating the tumbling water and the pool in which nines of drax still bathed and filled beakers. Dru bounded over, his damp fur and mane on end from the brisk rub-down Varna had given him.

"This is a much better place to spend the night," he said, taking a torch from Shaya to help light the fires we had set across the vinetree line. He looked up. "No serpents to worry about. The Spiral overhead – and just a single line of defence needed." He pointed at the flames that already burned bright against the background of dark vinetrunks.

He was learning well; I nodded agreement and approval of his assessment. Shaya, though, with her hunter's skills, was more cautious, turning to point at the surging water that glided north from the pool. "We can't afford to be complacent," she said. "We don't know what might lurk in the river. I'm sure it's safe here – those glumps would not be chirping so calmly if there was any danger – but still, we'll post sentries tonight to make sure."

I nodded agreement and saw Dru mirror the action. It was a precaution we had taken every night, but even so we had lost people, including younglings, to the Forest. I was determined that the river would not lay claim to any more.

Twenty-Two

"Why don't we just stay here?" It was Rewsa who asked the question, but there was a group of several nines gathered around her who appeared to feel the same way. "It's quiet here, safe. Kalis wanted us in the Forest, that's where we are. I don't see why we have to go any further."

Shaya shouldered past me. "Look around," she barked. "Tell me what you see that we can eat."

Rewsa hesitated, but Limar spoke up from the middle of the group. "There's some wild kerzh grass over there near the falls."

"We've seen fish in the water," added Hariz, hopefully.

"And there must be vinecreepers in the canopy," Norba the cluster-cryer piped up.

"What about those glumps?" Rewsa ventured. "There must be nineties of them. Nineties of nineties."

"And all of them inedible," said Shaya, raising her voice to ensure she could be heard above the noise of the falls. She fixed Rewsa with a glare that would have felled a Koth. "Trust me, I've tried one. Once. Never again. As for the rest…" She turned where she stood, arms extended in a sweeping gesture that took in our surroundings: the waterfall, the river, the vines, and the trampled moss on which we stood. "With what's left of our supplies and what we can find here, we have enough for about two moons. No more. After that we'll have to move from here or starve. So I suggest—" the set of her ears indicated it was not a suggestion "—that we stay here for one moon, and gather enough extra food for another." Only then did she glance at me. "What say you, Fate-seer?"

She hadn't left me much to do but flick an ear and nod to indicate my agreement, but I felt I ought to add something. If we were to collect food for an additional moon, we would need to be better organised, so… "Gatherers—" I raised my voice to carry beyond the immediate group. "Gatherers, pick eight females and nine younglings each, and collect any kerzh seeds or other edible vegetation you can find. Divide it into three piles – one to eat here, one to take with us, and one to preserve for planting when we find a place to stay. Shaya, the hunters—"

She was already stalking away. "I know. Vinecreepers and fish. I'll get a nine of younglings to help."

"Catch anything you can find that's edible," I called, though she didn't acknowledge that she'd heard me. I looked around. That still left nineties of females and younglings with too little to do. I pointed at the vines at the edge of our campsite. "Anyone who's not going with the gatherers or hunters – let's start cutting down vines."

We began to call the place Falls Camp, and the moon we spent there probably saved many lives. Everyone was weary and upset after the trials of the Forest – we needed to rest, to come to terms with our losses, to treat the sick and the lame, to patch and lengthen tunics, to gather our wits along with more supplies – and we needed time to cut logs for our floats.

To avoid bringing the vines crashing down on our camp, we began with those at the river's edge, furthest from our fires, and worked our way carefully downstream, cutting a swathe along the bank that was four or five vinetrees deep. Once the adults had felled the vines, the younglings trimmed the branches, ensuring we had a good supply of kindling and fuel stacked along the forest edge, even as we hacked that edge back from the river.

"What do we do now?" asked Doran, smearing salve on a paw that was raw from pushing a saw to and fro. "Sit on a log each and point them downstream?"

Shaya scratched her snout, ears flicking, her head tilted first to one side then to the other as she gave it some thought. "I don't see how that will work," she said. "I don't know about you, but I'd like something a bit more stable than a single log under me if I'm going to trust myself to the river. And I'm definitely not putting Ravar on one by himself!"

"Bind them together." Winan, with her artisan's eye, saw the solution. "We can use the reeds from the river bank to make ropes. And we still have the nets, as well as the bindings we made from the seatach."

Through trial and error, and a good deal of bickering and quarrelling about the best size of log, and how many should be lashed together, we finally completed the first float five ninedays after our arrival at the Falls. It immediately began to drift downstream, and as we watched it vanish round the bend of the river we realised we needed some means of tying the floats to the riverbank when we wished to make camp.

"This is new to all of us," I said to Dru, as he brought more reeds for the adults to weave together into a thick cord. "No-one has made anything that floats on water before."

"There has been no need," said Varna, her voice bearing the dull edge it had had when we first left the *Spirax*. "We have always flown over the water, why would we want to travel on it?" She sighed, her ears drooping, and I feared she was going to revert to the miserable state she had been in when her wings had been removed. But then I saw her shake herself and rub at her whiskers. When she spoke again her tone was lighter. "Zarda is right, of course. We have to learn as we go along."

"Let's hope that we don't lose anyone in the learning," said Limar, cutting as ever, "as we did in the Forest."

It was a jibe, but not an entirely unjustified one. Choosing not to take the remark as personally as I'm sure it was meant, I nodded. "We have to try the floats while they are still tethered to the bank," I said, "so that we can establish how stable they are and how many drax and packs each one can carry."

"Then it would be sensible to put those who can fly on the first ones," said Doran. "That way, if there is a problem, they will not have to worry about falling into the water."

It was a good plan, and one we carried out thoroughly as soon as we had constructed a second float – one with a tether like a vlydh's leading-rein to secure it to the vines on the bank. Shaya handed Dugaz and Oztin – two younglings who had lost their dams – a broad tanglevine leaf each, and put them in charge of noting the loads. "Those leaves won't keep for long," she said, "but we only need the scratchings for a few days." With Doran and myself checking that they were recording things accurately, and several days of trials and testing, we eventually calculated that a nine-log float would carry a maximum of six full-grown drax, plus the same number of younglings and their carry-pouches.

"Now," said Shaya, hopping on to the bank from the float, having satisfied herself that it would not sink even if a grown drax flew onto it from a height, "how do we push it away from the river bank and keep it pointing the right way?"

"Keep your paws and feet out of the water!" I cautioned, as we broke camp at dawn one cloudy morning. "We still don't know what might be living in there."

As it turned out, there was nothing particularly vicious beneath the surface, but as we used the steering poles we had designed to push off from the riverbank, and moved into the middle of the river to allow the current to carry us along, what none of us anticipated was that the water itself would prove to be the greatest danger we would face.

Twenty-Three

Our first day on the water was peaceful, restful almost. The flyers among us took turns in the air, but with the river wide and calm, and the sky over our heads, it was more to stretch our wings than to look for potential dangers. From above it was easy to see that the river meandered in wide slow loops through unrelenting forest, which converged on both sides of the water in rustling veils of crimson. Here and there long branches from each bank met over the water and every float kept a bow and spear ready, watching for vine-serpents as the river took them beneath the tangles. The contented croaking of the glumps had been left behind, and the sounds of the Forest surrounded us once again – the screech of vinecreepers, the rustle of leaves, the clicking of insects and, at least once a day, the roars of predators claiming their screaming prey.

After zenith, Shaya and the other two hunters flew on ahead to try to find a landing place for the night. They were gone for so long that I began to worry that something had happened to them, but eventually, as our shadows lengthened across the water, Shaya swooped from a cloud-free sky to hover over each float in turn. "There's a bend up ahead where the river has carved a new course and left the old one behind," she called. "The old route has filled in with mud and moss. We should be safe enough there once the fires get going. Marga and Azmit are already making a start, and they'll look out for the floats and guide you to the bank."

By the time we had set our fires that night, I knew that even a flight from the head of the Ambit would take more than a day to reach us. No-one would be coming after us now. All we needed was somewhere safe to stay, to settle, to make a new home.

"It's a pity the vines grow so close to the banks," I said to Varna and Dru, who shared a float with me. "If we could find space where there's room to spread out and get some cuttings and seeds in the ground, we could ignore Kalis's orders and build a new settlement on the river's edge. No-one on the Expanse would know – and even if they guessed it, they couldn't reach us. Not by flying."

Varna looked pleased with herself, as well she might since the whole idea of floating on the water had been hers. "If we find a suitable clearing," she said, stroking Dru's unruly white mane, "we will land. And we will build."

On the second night, we rested on a vine-free island in the middle of the river. Alas, it was too small to consider staying there for more than a night, and it was clear from the grooves on some of the rocks that most of it would be underwater if the river flooded.

"But it is good to know that such havens exist," said Doran, as we boarded our floats the next morning, "If we could find a bigger one…"

"And higher," said Azmit, who was preparing to take off on the warm breeze that blew upriver.

I nodded. "The river runs to the sea," I said, "and it will broaden as it nears the ocean. That may be where we find what we are looking for."

Doran glanced over at me. "Have you Seen such a place, Zarda?"

"No." I waved a paw at the vinetrees that still marched along each bank. "All I have Seen is Forest. But I didn't See a river either – yet here we are."

Three more days and nights passed peacefully, while the Forest rustled and roared on each bank. On the fifth afterzenith, we found the mite-mounds – nines of them, built on the bankside from the silt of the slowly-winding river and stretching upward to the height of a full-grown drax. Shaya took the hunters, Varna, and the few younglings who could hit a target with an arrow, and killed nine gumalix which had gathered to feed on the mites. Added to the evening's stew, they made a greasy meal, but a filling one.

Then, on the morning of the sixth day...

"Pole to the shore! Pole to the shore on the next bend!" The cry came from Winan, who had been in the group flying ahead. She was flapping wildly, gesturing with her paws, ears upright with excitement. "On the bank," she called again. "You'll see!"

The river slowed in another broad curve as Shaya and I leaned on our float's pole, steering toward the bank where Azmit's lean grey figure and Hariz's black-and-green tunic stood out against the scrubby bushes and patches of red moss that covered the rising ground behind them. Both females were waving and calling, mirroring Winan's agitation. They appeared to have found a possible camp site, but we had barely left the previous one.

"Surely they're not expecting us to stop for the night just yet?" I said, sniffing the breeze in the hope of determining what had caused the excitement. Avalox! Was that a hint of avalox amid the odour of moss, mud, and vine, or was I imagining it?

"Well, there's obviously no danger." Shaya accompanied her dry remark with an ear-flick that indicated she'd already realised that from Winan's initial call and was not being serious.

"Do you think they've found a place we can stay?" The wash from Doran's float almost drowned her words. Her ears and tail were twitching with anticipation. Not even a soaking from a rogue wave that drenched us as we turned could dampen the scent of hope that poured from everyone on our float and those alongside us.

"What is it?" called Shaya. Impatient to be on the river bank, she spread her wings to glide to shore before we were close enough to throw our tether. "What have you found?"

I split my attention between Azmit, who was gesturing at something on the steep incline behind her, and Hariz, who had hurried to catch our rope, and I almost fell over when the float bumped against the bank. Leaving Hariz to tie up, I leaped onto solid ground, Dru at my wingtips, and hurried to catch up with Shaya. At the top of the rise, the reason for all the excitement became clear.

"Dwellings!" Shaya halted where she stood. The crest of the hill was dotted with boulders, rotting logs, and circles of fallen stone. "Look at the way they're laid out." She spiralled a paw across her tunic – a gesture I had not noticed her make for some time.

I didn't have Shaya's training or keen eye for detail, but once she'd told us what to look for, I could see beyond the jumble of stone, ignore the hacklebrush and twisting vines that grew through the ruins, and see the pattern. "They're set out in a spiral," I said, moving a paw over my own tunic.

"And there are more clusters in the Forest," said Winan, landing beside us with a thump. "They're not easy to see with the vines growing round them, but there are some gaps in the canopy where you can glimpse white stones."

Doran arrived beside me, panting from the climb up the hill. "Who would live in the middle of the Forest?" She gazed up at the rustling leaves, and the branches that swayed just a span or so beyond the remains of the hilltop dwelling.

"Perhaps it was not always Forest." I remembered what Vizan had told me of his flight over the Frozen Wastes, his tale of the dwellings beneath the ice. If that was indeed true, then drax had not always lived solely on the Expanse as we had been taught. Perhaps it had not 'always been'.

"How could that be?" There was scorn in Hariz's voice, and her black ears were set to a sceptical angle. I shook my head and shrugged a shoulder. I didn't know. I was still trying to come to terms with the idea myself, I had no words to explain it to others.

"All we know for sure," I said, bending to pick up one of the fallen stones, "is that these dwellings are…"

Sun on water. A wide river valley filled with the scent of the avalox plants that swayed in the breeze. Clusters, nine clusters just like the one we had found, all of them busy with...

"Koth!" I staggered and dropped the stone I held, while everyone around me ducked their heads and looked skyward, some of them reaching for bows and spears. "Not here," I called, then – realising that was not entirely true – I added, "Not now."

"You mean the cluster was abandoned because the Koth destroyed it?" Shaya stood at my wingtip, spear in hand, ears alert for danger.

"No." I spread my arms to encompass the dwelling and the Forest beyond it. "This was a Koth dwelling, a Koth cluster. Long ago – before the vines grew here." I spiralled a paw across my tunic and my next words were spoken quietly as I realised the full significance of what I had Seen. "The Koth built in spirals too." That being so, they honoured the Great Spiral as we did, and if they worshiped the lights, we had something in common. It was not a comfortable thought and I pushed it aside, reaching for something more trivial. Raising my snout, I sniffed the still air. "They grew avalox. There – can you smell it?" I pointed to where the vines pushed through the next dwelling. "Gone to the wild, long since."

Shaya's whiskers quivered as she sniffed, delicately, her ears still alert for the merest hint of danger. Around us, the usual forest cacophony went on, but we had grown used to it and listened now for the silences rather than the screeching, searched for stillness not movement. Our noses told us what was unusual, what was out of place – and right now, they were telling us that wild avalox lay beneath the vines.

Doran sighed, her own snout busy sniffing the air. "Do you think it's safe to pick some?" she asked, when Shaya made no move. "I'd take on a Koth for a proper brew."

Shaya considered for a moment longer, then dipped an ear. "Take torches," she said, "and stay in threes – one to hold the torch and two to pick the leaves." She switched her attention to the broken stones and leaf-littered ground that lay between the hilltop and the floats, and I knew she was gauging the area's size and safety. "It will be cozy," she said, "and we haven't travelled far from the last camping site. But there's avalox here, and some decent tea would cheer us all. We'll overnight here."

Hariz seemed unsure about that idea, and I watched her scurry off to Limar and Rewsa who were walking up the bank from their own float. Others gathered about them as Hariz, fur on end, pointed and gesticulated, snout tilted skyward, as though to search for angry Koth come back to claim their own.

"I'm not staying here," Limar announced as she stomped up the hill to where Shaya and I stood. Her ear-flick of greeting was just the right side of civil and I returned it in kind before turning my attention to the damless younglings who trailed in her wake.

"There's avalox under the vines," I called to them. "Who wants some tea?"

They all did, and I pointed them in Winan's direction while Limar went on: "It's much too dangerous."

Shaya sighed. "Limar, we are in danger every beat of every day. Making camp near the ruins of ancient dwellings is no less dangerous than picking avalox under the vines." She extended a paw in the direction of Winan, who was already dividing the younglings into pairs and handing torches to the adults who would accompany them.

"Let her leave if she wants to," Varna called from the middle of the dwelling behind us. Spear in one hand, blazing torch in the other, she had Galyn's youngling, Dugaz, and Dru at her wingtips as she picked her way over fallen stones toward the vines beyond. "If she takes a few of her friends with her, there'll be more room here." She stalked away, Dru giving his half-sibling a cheeky tail-waggle as he followed.

Limar's own tail went rigid with anger, and without another word she spun on her toes and marched off toward the river.

"Are you going further downriver?" Shaya called. "Wait a moment, there might be others who—"

"I'm going to get my carry-pouch," Limar snapped. "Rewsa – save me a spot."

"It's a shame these dwellings aren't intact." Doran glanced up from combing Cavel's fur as she spoke. The camp hummed with activity, everyone making ready to move on – licking bowls, fastening carry-pouches, washing pans in the river – and wrapping our new supply of avalox in leafy twists. "It would be lovely to have stones over our heads again and a real hearth."

The murmurs of agreement were squashed by Limar, who stood beside the next campfire tugging angrily at her own still-moulting coat. "Yes, lovely. Surrounded by screaming animals, vinetrees that hide the Spiral-knows-what, and a boggy dip that smells like a waste-pit."

This last had been my discovery the previous evening, when I had almost fallen into it while reaching for a particularly fine stem of wild avalox. Shaya had poked at it with a stick to ensure there were no surprises lurking beneath the surface, but the resulting stench had spoiled appetites and made the younglings gag.

"That wasn't what I meant." Doran gripped Cavel's shoulders to prevent him wriggling, and started to brush his mane, ignoring his protests that he could do it himself. "I mean, if the dwellings were intact, the vinetrees wouldn't be growing through them, would they?"

"If the dwellings were intact, the Koth might still be in them." Rewsa, at Limar's broken wingtip, echoed her friend's determination to be contrary.

Doran sighed. "I just meant…"

"We knew what you meant," I said, indicating those nearby who were glaring at Limar and Rewsa. "And you were right. A night indoors with a comfortable nest and a warm fire – it would have been wonderful to have the makings of that ready for us."

"Perhaps you should make an offering to your precious Spiral." At Limar's words, even Rewsa took a step back, shock written in the set of her ears and tail.

"The Spiral watches all of us, Limar." The words sounded feeble even to my own ears, and I gestured at the nearest dwelling and the vinetrees beyond. "We've learned more about the Koth – that may be useful in the future. We have found a supply of avalox, and we have had another night of safety. I can't answer for those who have been taken from us – or why we are out here at all – but we are surviving and we are learning. The

Spiral needs us to be exactly where we are, it is not for us to question the wisdom of the lights."

"Limar..." Over to my right, Varna took a step toward her older offspring, one paw outstretched, ears set to a contrite, apologetic angle.

"Stay away from me, Varna-muz, you've done enough damage."

They were the first words I'd heard the two of them speak to each other since Varna had slashed Limar's wing. Better they had maintained their mutual silence, I thought – poor Dru looked crushed by Limar's hostility, while Varna simply ignored him and turned back to rolling her blanket. He had been spending time each day with each of them in turn; would he now be expected to choose between his dam and his sibling? As Limar snatched up her carry-pouch and stomped off toward her float, I called Dru over to me. "Come and help me with this blanket, would you? It's got in a tangle again."

Behind me, I heard Shaya call to Rewsa, asking her to take off and scout ahead. "Azmit's already up there. Don't worry, Ellet can come with Ravar and me for a while."

Rewsa looked annoyed, doubtless irritated that her opportunity to gossip with Limar about overnight events would have to wait, but she dipped an ear in acknowledgement, handed her pouch to Ellet, and took a few short bounds along the mossy ground in front of the ruins. She was aloft in moments, circling upward, and levelling off at a height just above the bankside vinetrees. Once, it had been easy to fly ahead of the grounded, as the wingless ones made their way step by painful step over sand and snow, and through the treacherous tangles of the Forest, but the river current was proving to be a swift carrier. I knew that Rewsa and Azmit would struggle to keep up with the floats, but I was not unduly worried. The width of the river meant the vinetrees were spans away and there had been nothing seen in the water that might harm us. Even the weather had turned our way, with the icy blasts of two moons ago now a distant memory.

I should have known better than to lower my guard.

Twenty-Four

"Look!"

Dru was travelling on my float, which I hoped would satisfy both Limar and Varna. He had spent the morning pointing out the different types of vine on the bank, looking for fish in the water, and taking a turn holding the steering pole. He was sitting at the front of the float when he shouted and sat up, pointing with paw and snout, and making the float wobble.

I couldn't blame him for his excitement. Red cliffs reared up ahead of us on both banks of the river, climbing vertically far beyond the tops of the vines – though the trunks near to them had sent branches upward to cling to the lower rockface. The crimson leaves moving in the breeze against the sandstone made the whole face seem alive. Shrill calls from the air drew my attention, and I looked up to see a colony of melidhs on the wing, swooping and squawking in a cloud of irridescent blue.

"What are they?" said Dru, his voice quiet with awe.

"Melidhs," I said. "It's rare to catch sight of one in Drax territory – though you could usually hear them squawking at sunrise. But see how many there are here!"

"They must nest in the cliffs," said Winan, who shared our float along with her own youngling and three others she had taken under her wing. "See, there are dark spaces near the top – are they burrows, do you think?"

I nodded and turned my attention to the other floats for a moment. Everyone was looking upward, save Shaya and Azmit, whose turn it was to fly above us. "The cliffs!" Shaya called. "Look at the cliffs!"

The cliffs grew further apart as they rose higher, pushing back the Forest and leaving wide shingle beaches for the river to meander through. Sloping stripes of reds, yellows, and greys patterned the vertical rock faces, but as we travelled past them I realised it was not the height of the cliffs or their patterns of colour that had drawn Shaya's attention.

It was the carvings that had made her call and point – carvings of spirals, huge and magnificent, lined the escarpments on either side. Some, confined to a single band of rock, were relatively small; others ran from the top of the bluffs to the base in one gigantic whorl. All of them were worn and chipped, almost weathered away in places. I traced a paw across my tunic and saw others doing the same. Who had done this? Some long-forgotten drax? The Koth who had built the ruined cluster? Or the same gods whom the Spiral had sent to create the *Spirax*?

"Stop!" I called, loudly enough that others would hear me as well as Winan at our own steering pole. "We need to stop."

A faint smell of alarm made me look round. Winan's ears were twitching and I realised she was struggling to steer the float.

"The river's running faster," she shouted. "Lend a paw here."

Even as she spoke, the shingle beaches vanished, the gorge narrowed, and the shadows swallowed us as the sun was lost behind towering crags.

The water was running swift and strong – had in fact been gaining speed insidiously over the past ninety spans or more – and I no longer felt safe, clinging to the edges of the float as it began to bob and heave on churning waves.

"What's that noise?" called Dru.

It was an odd, echoing hiss, with a deep, threatening note behind it. I had never heard the like before, and looked for Shaya overhead – but our floats had outpaced her frantic flapping, and we were being borne away from her, pitching and tossing about at a speed that was beginning to make my stomachs churn.

The deep rumble grew louder, more ominous, and everyone was beginning to look about in alarm, hoping for some quiet inlet or sloping, shingle-covered bank to manifest itself, but there were only cliffs and more cliffs, the colours of which were becoming blurred as we hurtled past. Floats reared up on tossing waves and smacked down in bone-jarring jets of spray, soaking us, and I wondered if I dared let go of my hold on the float to reach back for the straps of my carry-pouch.

Then we hurtled round a bend and I saw what was making the noise.

Ahead of us, water foamed and swirled as the river carved downward through boulders and rocks to a lower level. "Hold on!" I howled, wondering whether my voice could be heard even by Dru and Winan, let alone anyone on the other floats. "Don't let go! Whatever you do, keep hold of the float!"

I toyed with the idea of taking off, but realised in a heartbeat that it wasn't possible. The wind here, funneled by the canyon, swirled almost as dangerously as the waters beneath us. If I attempted to take off, I might be plunged into the water or slammed into a cliff. And what of those, like Dru, who couldn't fly? The best I could do was to wrap my claws tighter around the float's bindings, pray to the Spiral that they held, and extend my wings a little, in the hope that it might help stabilise our craft. The younglings were all holding on to the float's bindings with paws and claws, while Winan used one paw to hold on and wrapped the other round Chiva's waist. Her eyes were closed; the youngling was howling.

I don't know how long we tumbled through the rapids. I suppose it did not take many beats, but it seemed that our ordeal would never end. I was aware of nothing save howls, a continuous thunder of noise, the tug of wind on my wings, the sting of water against my snout, sodden fur, and the taste of river water as I gasped and panted. From the corner of my eye I glimpsed another float upending, caught sight of bodies and packs being hurled into the water. I tried to look for them, but it was all too fast; in any case it was not as though there was anything we could do.

When finally the river swept out of the gorge and slowed as it broadened into a lush, vinetree-lined valley, it took some time for me to release my grip on the float and pull myself together sufficiently to look around. There were no other floats ahead of ours, though both Varna's float and Flori's had entered the gorge ahead of us. Upriver, downriver, where had they gone? As I checked again, frantic to find them, two broken logs bobbed to the surface, and I spiralled a paw over my tunic before twisting carefully around to look behind. Battered floats were still popping out from the bottom of the rapids, some with only one or two drax clinging to them. A quick glance told me that we had lost entire floats, and there were howls and squeals of shock as several bodies floated past, borne along in a tangle of bobbing carry-pouches and smashed logs.

The shadows of the canyon had receded and the sun was warm as the river swept us along, but I felt colder than I had at any point on our journey. The coldest night of ice and snow had not chilled me in the way that that disaster had. For disaster it was; as the noise of the rapids receded, and those cruel cliffs were lost to sight around a river bend, I sat clutching at the float, numb with the knowledge that we had lost nines of females and younglings.

More supplies too, I thought, then felt guilty that I was worrying about such things when drax had lost their lives. Somehow, my own carry-pouch was still on the float, its trailing straps caught between the logs, though it was soaked through and I doubted any of my herbs would be usable. Nor the avalox we had so carefully gathered...

What was I thinking? Drax had died, what did herbs and tea matter? I shook myself, inadvertently spraying water over the younglings and Winan, who responded by doing the same; some of them snuffled with laughter, though there was an edge of hysteria to it.

I took a breath. "It's good to be alive," I said. "We must give thanks to the Spiral that so many of us made it through in one piece."

The younglings had stopped snuffling, and Dru pulled his paws free of the bindings he had clung to and edged closer to me. "Where's Varna-muz?" he said. "Where's Cavel?"

Varna. I remembered my Vision on the beach, moons ago. *Tumbling water, a riverbank reached for and lost.* I had thought that Varna's ride down the Ambit on a rolling log had seen the Vision fulfilled. I had been mistaken. As for Doran...

I had not realised that Doran's float was one of those missing, and I looked more closely at the survivors. Dru had to be mistaken – Cavel and Doran must surely be among them. Surely? I couldn't see them, and shook my head, flicking my ears with annoyance that I had missed them somehow. I checked again, looking back along the line of bedraggled floats for a yellow-striped tunic with a green-and-black check alongside it. The realisation that they were not on any of the floats hit me almost as hard as the rapids had. "I don't know, Dru. Perhaps..."

I could think of no 'perhaps' and silence enveloped the float as we allowed the river to carry us further from those terrible rapids. I was tired suddenly, and told myself that we needed to get to the bank and take stock, dry out, perhaps organise a search. The cliffs had given way to steep hills, with clumps of tanglevine clinging to their flanks, and patches of hacklebrush and scrubby purple-leaved bushes filling the gaps between. Here and there, tumbles of small red stones scattered down the slopes, doubtless disturbed by the gumalix whose burrows showed up as raised mounds of soil amid the vegetation.

"There's a clear patch of ground up ahead." I looked up to see Shaya pointing to a tongue of land further downstream, where the river curved left. "You should land, dry out."

She didn't add the rest, nor did she need to.

I waved an acknowledgement, and Winan leaned on the steering pole, while Dru and the younglings waved to the other floats and pointed.

As we pulled up the last of the surviving floats on the mudbank, pieces of vinelog bobbed past in the middle of the stream: the remains of another float.

Of the missing drax there was no sign.

Twenty-Five

Azmit arrived, bearing in her slender arms a youngling she had somehow managed to pluck from the water.

"It's Cavel," said Dru, bounding up as the hunter lowered the bundle of fur to the ground.

"Hurry with those campfires!" I called, skimming over to squat next to Cavel's limp form. My first impression was that Azmit's rescue effort had been fruitless – Cavel's eyes were closed, his head rolled to one side, tongue lolling. But when I put an ear against his chest there was a faint heartbeat, and as I sat up and rubbed at his paws, he coughed and took a breath, gasped, then took another.

"Well done, Azmit," I said. "That could not have been easy in those gusting winds."

We didn't have a dry blanket between us, but I felt another surge of gratitude as she pulled off her own dry tunic and placed it gently over Cavel.

"It was thanks to Doran that I was able to grab him," she said. "When I saw the float go over, I swooped down as low as I dared. Doran was clinging to the logs, trying to keep both of them afloat, but when she saw me she pushed Cavel up as far as she could. I took the youngling, and the current took Doran..." Her grey ears drooped with regret and sorrow. "I'm sorry, Zarda. I know the two of you were friends."

I could barely speak. "Since we hatched."

I was still trying to come to terms with the scale of our losses, as well as the shock of losing my oldest friend. Yet, as I stood back from Cavel and spiralled a paw over my tunic, I realised that, once again, everyone was looking to me to say something – do anything – to ease the hollow, sick feeling their scent and postures told me we all shared.

I looked back up the river, as though expecting Doran to round the bend waving, unscathed. "I'll fly back," I said, "and see if I can find any survivors. It may be that they're lying at the foot of those cliffs with nothing worse than a headache."

I knew it was futile, but I had to try. I couldn't simply sit by a fire – let alone paddle away – without knowing that all those drax were truly gone. There was no protest, not even from Limar, who had her arms around Dru as they both gazed out over the water, looking for their dam. There were so many others missing too – Norba the Cluster-cryer; Flori, the gaunt trader I had met by the campfire on my first morning with the exiles; everyone on Doran's float except Cavel ...

Others were beginning to wander about, calling for friends and younglings; the odour of denial mingled with those of shock and mourning on drying fur. I needed to fly, needed to be somewhere I could howl myself hoarse without anyone seeing that the Fate-seer was a broken mess. The losses in the Forest had been bad, but this was worse – so much worse. Even without the loss of Doran...

I pushed that thought away and endeavoured to present a steady, determined front as I turned to Shaya. "When I've checked the cliffs and riverbanks upstream," I said, my ears rigid and tail locked straight, "I'll fly further downstream, in case..."

In case their bodies had somehow washed to the bank further along.

I left the thought unspoken, but Shaya's whiskers twitched in understanding and I saw her nod.

"I'll keep everyone busy," she said, her voice high and brisk, a paw on her youngling's right shoulder. "We need to find out what we have left in our packs – what can be salvaged, what can't. And everything needs to be dried."

"Including us," said Ravar, looking down at his wet, ochre-striped tunic and wringing the patched hem, before shaking himself again to rid his fur of the more stubborn droplets that made his coat glisten in the sun's warming light.

Leaving them to start unpacking the bundles, I stretched my wings to check the breeze, and took off at a run.

There was nothing. I searched the canyon from end to end, skimming the waves and flying as close to the cliffs as I dared in the swirling wind, but there was no sign of Doran, Varna, Flori, or the rest. The river, and the Forest surrounding it, had swallowed them as surely as serpents swallowed creepers. I checked twice, and then flew up to make one last pass over the area from a greater height.

Clear skies. No floaters. A perfect day for flying high.

I spiralled upward, howling, wings beating furiously in my grief and anger, till I could see the river's course winding through the forest. It looked so peaceful – a sparkling, deep blue trail through the crimson – and I wondered how something so beautiful could turn so ugly, so treacherous. Turning on the breeze, I looked south, and realised that the edge of the Forest was no longer in sight. There seemed no end to it in any direction, save to the west, where it came up against the mountains. Truly, the river had been a swift carrier, even before…

Grief overwhelmed me again, but I was beyond howling, beyond feeling anything as I turned to fly downriver. I flew over the encampment, noticing that fires had been lit and tunics were being laid out to dry – splashes of faded colour against the scattered red pebbles and purple weeds of the valley floor.

As though exhausted after its run through the gorge, the river slowed and broadened. I caught glimpses here and there of tiny patches of blue flowers growing near the water's edge, saw melidhs swooping about below me, and guessed they were feeding on the tiny insects that hovered over the river-reeds that lined the banks. But still the Forest marched on, the vines growing in places right to the river's edge, and I wondered how much longer we must journey: a few days? A moon? A whole cycle?

My wings were tiring and I knew that I must turn back if I was to reach our refuge again before dark. I had just started to feel for the right wind current to make my turn when I saw it, several twists of the river ahead: a vast lake, big enough to cover half the Expanse, and on it a scattering of islands. I hovered, noting the vine-free, moss-covered isles which would provide plenty of space for all of us, safe from the Forest and its dangers.

But none of those factors were what drew my attention.

What made me stop, hover, and continue on toward the lake, my fatigue forgotten, was the sight of a column of smoke.

The islands were inhabited.

Twenty-Six

The smoke issued from the largest island, a triangle of land a little bigger than the *Spirax* peninsula. Roughly tooth-shaped, it had a steep-sided hill at its narrowest end and a notch at the other which formed a small inlet. As I descended toward it, I saw there were nine stacks of vinelogs set round the base of the hill, with a tenth, larger stack at the top. Smoke was rising from several of them, and I realised they were not bundled logs at all, but dwellings – or shelters of some kind at any rate. How odd they looked, with their boxy shapes and reed-covered sloping roofs!

Where the island widened, to the south of the dwellings, the ground had been tilled, and two drax were walking over the broken soil, dropping seeds from carry-pouches. On a mossy bank near the inlet, a clutch of younglings were testing their wings and each other in mock-fights, and there were floats too – individual hollowed-out logs, tethered to a horizontal line of cut vinelogs that extended into the lake from the inlet.

Angling my wings to slow my descent, I yipped the age-old cry of greeting, and swooped lower, keeping my paws extended to show that I was unarmed. I had no wish to be shot down by a fellow drax after surviving so many difficulties over the past few moons.

The reaction from below was immediate. Drax emerged from the dwellings; the younglings took off and headed toward the hill, while the two drax scattering the seeds dropped their carry-pouches and took to the air. Those still on the ground gathered the younglings and climbed the hill to form a spiral that led to the shelter – the dwelling? – at the crest of the rise.

The two drax flying to intercept me – one a huge, brown-furred male, the other a slighter, mottled-grey female – both wore roughly-woven purple tunics. Purple. The colour I'd Seen nineties of drax wearing. As I dipped a wing and spiralled downward, I could see that those on the ground were wearing the same colour. Were there guardflight here? Hunters? The two airborne drax both wielded knives, but might they have carried other weapons if they'd not been surprised while they sowed crops? Or were these two farmers?

They gave me no clue to their identities as they tucked in beside me, one on each wing, calling only to tell me to land at the bottom of the hill.

"This way," the big male grunted as we folded our wings, and he led the way up the slope, past the strange dwellings. Towards the top of the hill, I entered a corridor of silent drax in purple tunics, whose raised fur, scent of doubt, and half-spread wings told me that they were deeply suspicious of my sudden arrival. Keeping my own wings folded and my snout down in a gesture of supplication, I could hear the escorting female behind me as I continued to follow the male through the spiral of drax, circling inward till I reached the mossy space to the front of the hilltop dwelling.

Now that I was able to take a closer look, it was clear that it had been constructed from vinelogs, set one on another and coated with mud and moss to seal the gaps. Spirals had been carved into the doorposts, and as I stepped onto the cleared ground in front of it, the two drax who had accompanied me drew aside to join the others, and one of the half-growns blew a *spirorn.* I recognised the notes, though they were not quite pitched correctly – it was a Summoning, an announcement that the leader of this group was about to appear.

A heartbeat later, the door to the dwelling opened and a large, imposing drax in a patched tunic that might once have been cream stepped into the sunlight to face me. His grey mane was magnificent, his bearing regal, and his features were so familiar that for a beat I mistook him for Kalis. Then, as he unfolded one large wing to spread in the greeting-challenge, I realised my mistake. This was not Kalis, the younger shell-brother who had become Prime when his older sibling was killed in battle.

This was the supposedly-dead older sibling I had Seen in a Dream-cave Vision.

This was Kalon.

It took a beat or two to recover from the shock, but once I had regained my senses, I dropped immediately to one knee and bowed my head so low that my snout almost touched the ground at Kalon's feet.

"My lord Kalon! We thought you dead! Your shell-brother..."

"My shell-brother and his groundslug of a flight leader tried to take my wings while I slept."

I was so astonished that I raised my head without permission to look up at him, then, catching myself, dropped my gaze again as he went on: "We were on our Proving Flight – the two of us, hunting Koth in the Copper Hills with nine friends and two guardflight each. On our first night, Kalis said he would take the first watch with those who flew closest to his wingtips." His voice was a growl, his scent bitter. "Kalis, Varna, that groundslug Fazak who he always listened to – they put zenox in the tea to drug everyone else, then slashed their wings as they slept!" His voice rose to a howl of anguish, and I heard growls of remembered pain and humiliation from some of those around me.

I waited, setting my ears to a level which symbolised the sympathy I felt, and after a moment, Kalon continued. "As for me, Kalis wanted to cripple me himself, but he was always slow on his feet and I had found the tea too sweet. I heard him approach and woke to find him poised to strike." He growled, the low sound of anger, though I understood it was for his brother and not for me. "If I had not been wrapped in my blanket I would have bettered him, but he had chosen his moment well, the coward! We struggled, I beat him off, and took to the air, but his friends helped him chase me with a net, curse them all. I must have had enough of their drugged tea to slow me, otherwise they'd never have caught me. But catch me they did, may they all rot in darkness. Kalis severed my wing, and he and his wingflyers took off and left us to die."

That had been, what, two cycles ago? Three? As Kalon's feet halted, I recalled the tale that Kalis and his friends had told when they returned from their flight, the report that Kalon and the others had died in a Koth attack. And when Gavar had gone to his last nest, Kalis had become Prime, with Varna at his side. Varna who had told me that she had seen an aerial chase before the one that netted Limar. Clearly, she had done more than witness it – she had taken part in it. This then had been the secret that had kept her safe for so many moons: she and Kalis, along with Fazak, had maimed the rightful heir, and two nines of others, and left them to die.

"I knew that drax would not follow a leader who couldn't fly," Kalon went on, "so we made for the north-bound river I had discovered with Kalis and Varna on an earlier flight. We learned. Some of us survived. We had thought ourselves far enough from Drax territory that we would not be visited by Kalis or any of his lackeys. Yet here you are, Fate-seer, torn tunic, unbrushed fur, muddy paws and all. Tell me why I should not cripple you and send you to walk back whence you came."

I took a deep breath. "Because, Lord, that is how I came to be here – on foot, with a group of wingless younglings and their dams, banished by Kalis for an accident of hatching that condemns them to a life on the ground. His heir is among them."

"Wait – banished by *Kalis*?" Kalon's ears flicked back and forth. "Kalis is Prime?"

He stammered the words, and too late I realised the import of mine. I kept my head bowed, set my ears to apology and mourning, and spiralled a paw across my tunic.

"I regret, Lord, that your sire was taken to his last nest a cycle ago, by a terrible Sickness that killed nineties of drax. The surviving females laid eggs in the harvest season which hatched wingless younglings."

"Including Kalis' own pup?" I glanced up, for it was not Kalon who asked the question, but a well-groomed female with near-black fur who moved to Kalon's side and placed a paw on his arm. Her snuffle of laughter had a cruel edge to it as she added, "I'm surprised Kalis didn't drop him in the ocean."

I dared to raise my head. "He would have," I said, "but for a Vision that the youngling will one day defeat the Koth in battle."

The female – Kalon's nest-mate, I assumed, though she had not given her name – snorted. "And you still believe your Vision? Here, thousands of wingbeats from drax territory, in the middle of a Forest that holds death and horror for any who venture too far into it, and in the company of exiles and the lame...you still believe?"

"Yes, ah...?"

"Elver. Nest-mate to Kalon."

"Yes, Elver," I said. "My visions have always proved true, and Vizan – lights rest him – Saw this too. I do not know how it will come to pass, but..." I spiralled a paw on my tunic again, "I know that it will."

To my relief, Kalon folded his wing at last, and turned his right paw palm upwards, gesturing that I should get to my feet. "Perhaps my own heir will give him the task." As he spoke, Kalon gestured to a half-grown with a shaggy white mane who left the spiral formation and moved to stand at his right wing. "This is Urxov," he said, "my youngling, and my heir."

I made the appropriate bow and set my ears to signal respect and loyalty, even while my mind spun to take in this new revelation. If Kalon was the Prime and Urxov was his heir then how was it I had Seen Dru in the white tunic of a Prime? Best not mention that to Kalon. "An honour, Lord," I said instead. "It will be my pleasure to serve as Fate-seer should that be your wish." *Probably not a good idea to mention my limited skills either.*

"I have had no Fate-seer," said Kalon, his ears at last set in welcome, "till now." Looking around at his people, he went on: "We have managed, somehow, the twelve of us who survived the journey here. A fortunate few, like Jotto and his nest-mate Manel who flew to meet you, have healed well enough to fly, and our pups all have strong wings, Spiral be praised, but your skills and those of the others who travel with you will be most welcome."

"Thank you, Lord." It occurred to me that perhaps it was just as well that the Spiral had already taken Varna's light. I doubted she would have lasted long under Kalon's teeth. But the others...I fought back a howl of grief and returned my attention to Kalon, who spread his arms to indicate the islands that encircled his own.

"There is not much room on the hillside here for more dwellings, but all these islands together will hold nineties," he said. "And no predators to worry about, save those on the shore where we go to cut vinelogs. Your exiles may make their homes where they wish, though you, of course, must have a dwelling built close to my own. Now – where are these drax of which you speak?"

"Upriver from here. Downstream from the rapids." I lowered my head and looked away, suppressing a whimper of grief as I said, "We lost people there. I was looking..."

To my surprise, I felt Kalon's paw on my arm, and looked up to see his whiskers twitch in sympathy. "I understand. We too lost drax at the rapids before we found our sanctuary." Releasing my arm, he called to a winged half-grown in a patched tunic that looked to have been cut down from a larger one. "Yaver! Fly upstream and find these wingless drax. It will be near dark when you reach them, and no doubt they'll be too tired to travel further today, so remain with them overnight. Guide them here in the morning."

The half-grown nodded and raised his snout to sniff the breeze, then turned in the most favourable direction for take off and spread his wings, while Kalon returned his attention to me. "Fate-seer, be welcome. Your flight from Kalis is ended."

Far from home. Far from the Koth. Far from fulfilling the Vision we had had for Dru. Our flight had indeed ended – but surely our journey was not yet complete.

Twenty-Seven

A fire was kindled on the mossy bank near the inlet, fish were pulled from the lake, and I offered damp herbs from my tunic pocket to flavour them. I spent my first evening on the lake telling Kalon and those with him all that had happened in the past cycle – the Sickness, the hatching of the wingless, the Vision for Dru, Fazak, the Night of the Two Moons. The exile. The journey.

When I tried to tell what had happened at the rapids, I broke down and howled, and Kalon suggested I should get some sleep. There was no Welcome Place and no spare nests, but I was more than content to huddle in a makeshift nest of blankets by the fire. I had reached a place of safety when so many had not – what did it matter if I spent another night under the sky?

In the morning, the stunned, exhausted survivors of our journey arrived at the lake by float and wing, whimpering with relief, uncaring of anything save resting in safety. Kalon's Island, as it swiftly became known, was largely given over to crops – the kerzh grass I'd seen Jotto and Manel sowing and, praise the Spiral, avalox – but there were plenty of islets surrounding it where drax could settle. Nine by nine, group by group, our survivors – nearly two nineties of females, and just under ninety younglings – made their way to stand on the hill outside Kalon's dwelling for a formal welcome and a ritual gift of fish and water. They were then directed by Varel – Kalon's tawny-furred adviser – to different islands. At Varel's wingtip and in front of me stood his nest-mate Hynka, Kalon's appointed Record Keeper, who held broad purple leaves in her paws on which she scratched notes.

"What are those leaves?" I asked, leaning over her crippled right wing to sniff at them. "I've seen similar ones on our journey, along..." My voice caught as I remembered anew what our journey had cost us. "Along the river," I managed. "Before the rapids."

Varel grunted. His ears were set sympathetically, but his scent told me he was wary of me. He had been appointed as Chief Adviser in the absence of a Fate-seer; now here I was, speaking of visions and talking of destiny. No doubt Varel was anxious about his position in the new order of things, but he spoke politely enough. "Death River we named it. Lost four of our own travelling along it. Would have been more if Kalon hadn't seen a log floating past, and had the idea of travelling on the water. Even then we lost drax at the rapids, as you did."

My own ears still drooped with sorrow, but I flicked one in understanding and acknowledgement. "'Death River'," I repeated. "It seems an appropriate name to me."

Hynka scratched at another leaf as Hariz and Azmit paused to give their names, chewing the fish they'd been given by Kalon, and ushering their younglings ahead of them. "These are moontrap leaves," she confided, as the two females were assigned to an island near the lake's western shore. "At least, that's what we named it. The plant flowers at each full moon."

She broke off to listen and scratch as a shocked and whimpering Rewsa gave her name, and Varel spoke up again: "The petals form an orb which seems to glow, and attracts insects and moths. Once they get inside the flower..." He opened his paw, then closed it in a quick snatching motion. "If you get close enough on a quiet evening, you can hear the trapped insects buzzing – for a while."

"And do the leaves keep well?" I asked, recalling my own mishap in the Records Cave, moons ago, when I had forgotten to spit on the scroll before removing it from its casing. "They don't disintegrate?"

"They seem to be fine at the moment," said Hynka, "so long as I give them a good licking before putting them on the shelf. She paused in her scratching and returned her attention to Rewsa. "We're putting artisans on that island over there," she said, pointing a claw north and west toward a rounded hump of red moss that looked large enough for at least half-a-ninety of dwellings.

"The one that looks like a groxen's rear end?" Rewsa's drooping ears twitched half-heartedly, and she grumbled in a low mutter: "Seems about right. Come all this way, avoid death by a whisker, get assigned to Rump Island."

"Perfect," murmured Hynka, scribbling. "We hadn't given it a name till now."

As Rewsa huffed and set off down the hill with Ellet at her wingtip, I turned to Varel. "Why are all the artisans being sent to the same island? Who decided such a thing – and why was I not consulted?" After all I'd been through, had I simply exchanged one Prime who didn't listen to me for another?

My teeth snapped together a little harder than I'd intended, and Varel took a step away from me, setting his ears to full apology. "Forgive me, Fate-seer, but you were so tired after your journey – you were asleep and, well, Kalon felt...that is, I advised...I mean..."

I waved a paw, made an effort to set my own ears to a conciliatory angle, then raised my voice so that Kalon, standing outside his dwelling on my left, could hear. "You're unused to having a Fate-seer to consult," I said, "but if you'd spoken with me about this, I would have told you to assign the females to the islands at random. Not only have we been learning skills from each other for moons now, but I had a Vision of all these drax in purple tunics. One colour, together under one Prime. Splitting them by trade and skill..." I groped for the right words. "That will not help any of us learn."

Kalon, with Elver and Urxov beside him, had twisted an ear my way. Elver was holding a basket of fish and Urxov a flask of water, ready to pass to Kalon when the next female plodded up the hill. I could see Elver's tail was rigid with disapproval at the idea of mixing trades and skills, but Kalon's ears twitched while he considered it. "It seems reasonable to me," he said. "After all, when we arrived here, those of us who survived the journey, we all had to learn new skills. The dyers improved our floats, the hunters cut the logs for our dwellings—"

"That was a matter of necessity." Elver still didn't look happy. "We have wood-shapers now, builders, weavers." She waved a paw in the general direction of the queue that spiralled down the hill. "Why dilute those skills?"

"When we set out," I said, "we had just one female who knew how to use a bow and arrows. Now, we have nines of females and younglings who can hunt with them. The hunters and gatherers, the weavers, the healers, they've taught their skills to so many others during our journey. The Spiral sent me a Vision of a crowd of drax wearing purple. Surely that suggests that we should not be separated by skill or trade?"

Marga the hunter, silver fur fluffed and her torn tunic flapping in the breeze, appeared around the final bend in the hillside pathway. Hynka tucked a scratched leaf into her tunic pocket and licked a fresh one. The splash of floats and the distant cries of females and younglings carried over the water on a fresh southwesterly.

"A Vision you say?" Kalon ignored Elver's proffered basket, and turned his head to look over at me.

"Yes Lord. All but the Prime, his heir, and the Fate-seer in purple."

A grunt, an ear-twitch of affirmation. "Very well." He turned his attention to the hunter dipping a weary bow, passed her a pawful of fish, and splashed water into her beaker. "Assign them randomly, Varel." He rumbled a laugh. "And make a note of Rump Island, Hynka. We should make that official."

For several days, those who had survived our journey did little except eat fish from the lake, wash and patch grubby tunics, groom their young, and sleep. The seatach hides were unrolled for the last time and cut into smaller pieces, which were divided among the islands. The islands acquired names: West Island, where Azmit and Hariz had been sent; its opposite, East Island, an undulating mound just big enough for two nines of dwellings; Itch Island – infested with mites and swiftly abandoned; and Doorway Island, which had an arched outcrop of rock at its southern end, and which was large enough for nine nines to settle.

I took Dru and Cavel under my own wings for a few days, while Limar wandered about Rump Island, bleating that she should have been kinder to her dam. "You must talk about them," I said to the younglings, "and howl if you wish." But if they spoke of Varna and Doran it was not within my hearing, and they clung to my wingtips like small pups, keeping me grounded for much of the time.

Murmurs and whimpers, silence, and bowed heads populated the islands in those first few days, while Kalon used one of those hollowed-out log floats to visit each new settlement and speak with as many drax as he could.

On the fifth day – the first of a new moon – we carried out the Ceremony for the Dead. It was the most difficult ritual I had ever had to carry out. It was bad enough that I had no notes on the ritual and had seen it done just once, when Vizan had performed it for the missing Kalon and his presumed-dead friends, but infinitely worse was that one of the names on the list was that of my best friend.

While Winan looked after Dru and Cavel, Kalon allowed me the use of his dwelling to make my preparations. For a while I put off my task by examining the strange construction with its four straight sides. Inside, the bark had been stripped from the logs that formed the walls, and the place smelled of vinechips and dry resin. White pebbles spiralled across the western wall, but there was no see-shell to let light in. I left the door open and set a torch over the trimmed log that served as a table, but it did little to lighten the gloom at the back of the dwelling. Blinking to night-vision, I saw that there were nests there – one large enough for Kalon and Elver, the other sized for Urxov – but there were no screens. Clearly the weavers, and those who had learned from them on our journey, would have much work to do. As would the wood-shapers, I thought, as I settled onto a makeshift stool. How many of them did we have? I knew two at least had died in the rapids. Along with...

I fought back a howl. It would not do for the others to see the Fate-seer yowling in misery; I had to store my grief for the ceremony. Spiralling a paw, I began to scratch names on the waxy moontrap leaves.

I also scratched what I could remember of the ritual, and consulted some of the older females who had been at the ceremony for Kalon. "But I'm still not sure I remember every gesture, every howl," I confided to Kalon as we stood outside his dwelling watching the other drax gather on the mossy ground to the south of his island. "I was very young when I saw it done, and I was still expecting to be a Trader, not a Fate-seer."

Kalon flicked an ear, dismissively. "If it is all done with sincerity, I'm sure the Spiral in its Greatness will accept it," he said.

I almost remarked that if Kalis had taken that attitude we would not have been sent into exile, but decided it would be best not to mention his shell-brother if I did not have to. As he stood in the waning sunlight looking over the number of drax he now led, Kalon looked somehow even bigger than he had when I first encountered him. Then, he had been a leader with a pawful of drax, driven by anger, surviving on fish, a few scant crops, and hatred. Now, he was a well-groomed, upright Prime, ears alert, nose busy sniffing the various odours the evening breeze carried. His own scent was of pride, of belief in himself, and I saw it carry through to Elver, Hynka, Varel, and to the half-grown Urxov who stood at his sire's left wing, his own ears and tail quivering with the excitement of it all.

The night was clear, the Spiral bright overhead as I read the litany of names – everyone who had died on our journey, from Colex to Varna. I kept my voice steady, my words clear till I had completed the chants; then I lifted my head to begin the Death Howls. All my grief, all my anger, all my loathing of Fazak and his schemes, I poured into my howls, breathing deep and howling long, ears and wings set to full mourning. As the crowd responded with howls of their own, filling the night with sound, the moon rose – a sign that our ceremony had been accepted – but I howled on till my throat roughened with effort. Young

Urxov, I noticed, had to be nipped by his dam to continue adding his howls to the noise, but everyone else followed my lead. Only when I folded my wings and lowered my head, too drained to continue, did the noise cease. I doubt anyone heard my final words clearly, but it didn't matter. The ceremony had been completed, our dead mourned.

"Tomorrow," I said, "we start our new lives."

I should have known that it would not take long for those lives to descend into jealousy, annoyance, and squabbling.

Bidra and Yedri, the two female dyers who had worked out how to make individual hollowed-out floats for Kalon, insisted that our wood-shapers could learn from them, while our wood-shapers were equally adamant that it would take little effort to improve on the rough work of untrained pot-stirrers. The pot-stirrers' younglings, Yaver and Danza, half-growns who had known no other life but that of the island, attempted to show our gatherers how to cut reeds; while Jotto – who had once been Guardflight – and Shaya argued about everything, from the easiest way to trap vinecreepers to which speartips were the sharpest. Myxot and Gimel, nest-mates of Bidra and Yedri for the past few cycles, strutted and preened for the nineties of females they could now choose from, upsetting those they threatened to discard as well as those they rejected.

And Urxov took an instant dislike to Dru, demanding that the wingless youngling should take off the cream tunic he had no right to – and which was now too small for him anyway – and insisting he should be sent to Rump Island to live with Limar.

"I would rather he was not," I said, keeping my ears set respectfully though my voice was firm. When I had accompanied Dru into Kalon's dwelling on our ninth morning, I had been dismayed to find Elver, Urxov, and Varel waiting for me as well as Kalon. As Kalon's adviser, Varel said little to me beyond what politeness required, and I still detected a sour odour whenever I went near him that indicated he did not enjoy stepping aside for a new counsellor, even if that counsellor had the Sight.

"I see no harm in allowing Dru to remain on this island under my supervision." I waved a paw as I spoke, indicating the youngling beside me, who stood with ears set to the correct angle of respect, his head lowered in a half-bow. "I joined Kalis' exiles of my own choice because both Vizan and I had Seen that Dru will defeat the Koth. I've had little opportunity to give him guidance while we were busy trying to stay alive. He's just lost his dam—"

Elver stood on Kalon's right, where his wingtip should have been. "A conniving, underhand, knife-happy—"

"Elver." Kalon's growl was enough to silence her. "Varna has gone to her last nest. Be content."

I'd lost the thread of what I'd been saying, but dipped a grateful ear in Kalon's direction before placing a paw on Dru's shoulder. "Please, Lord, allow me to keep him close, now that we have found safe haven under your protection."

Varel stepped from the shadows near the table, ears flattened and tail moving in a way that indicated mistrust. He favoured his left leg, a legacy of his own journey through the rapids, and he limped across to give Dru a doubtful sniff. "He's Kalis' youngling—"

"Who is here because his own sire banished him, along with all the other wingless younglings. He didn't choose his dam any more than he can choose his destiny, but if he is to defeat the Koth he must learn!"

I understood the reluctance to make an exception. Staying with me, learning from me, would elevate Dru above the other younglings, and remind everyone that he was a possible rival to Urxov for the Prime position – but that was precisely why I wanted him alongside me. It was not Urxov I had Seen defeating the Koth.

Kalon flicked an ear, considering, and I saw his ears shift to a more amenable angle. Sensing I was beginning to make my point, I was about to press home my argument when Elver spoke up again. "He is just one more wingless youngling here. I don't see the need to give him special treatment because he was once regarded as a Prime heir." She stepped into the pool of light formed by the torch on the wall, and I knew I had lost my argument. Here was a drax who would rip open a Koth for her offspring if she had to. Straight-backed, straight-eared, and implacable, she would never countenance any suggestion of a rival for Urxov.

"As I indicated, Elver, it is not what he *was* that is important, it's what has been foreseen for him that matters."

She reeked of scepticism. "And have you had this Vision since you left the Expanse?"

"I saw it in the Dream-cave after Dru's banishment. It had not changed."

"And since then?"

I shook my head. "I can't summon Visions at will—"

"Then you've not Seen this..." she said, waving a paw as though brushing away a persistent flisk, "this *destiny* for some time. Perhaps that means it is no longer true."

"If I believed that, Elver, I would have flown home to the plateau when the Guardflight came looking for me," I said, "and taken my chances with Kalis."

"All the same," she said, returning to Kalon's side and placing a paw on his arm, "I don't see that he deserves preferential treatment."

Kalon sighed. "We have just gained a Fate-seer, Elver. I see no need to vex her by refusing her first request."

Elver smoothed his fur, tugged a stray strand of his grey mane back into place, and set her ears to a placatory angle – though there was nothing she could do to disguise the scent of her dislike of Dru. "He can stay with his friends on another island," she said, her voice as smooth as Fazak's, "and visit Zarda when he needs to." She turned to me, her false pleasantries reinforced by a flick of her ears and a twitch of her whiskers. "That would suffice, surely?"

Dru looked up at me, and it was obvious he was trying to keep his tail from signalling his disappointment. "I can stay with Limar," he said, "and Cavel can come too."

Deep breath. Concede the minor points, there would doubtless be bigger arguments to win in the moons to come. "Very well," I said, "but we'll have to make more floats, so that the wingless can move between the islands as they need to."

Kalon's whiskers twitched with what might have been amusement. "I agree, but if you're going to make floats, you must make better ones than those you came here on. I'll ask Bidra and Yedri to show your wood-shapers how to hollow out the logs so that you can sit in them rather than on them. I think you will find it much safer and more practical than those cumbersome craft you floated on. A single drax with a good paddle can tow three or four vinelogs from the lake's western shore. You'll need them if you're to build floats and dwellings for everyone."

I decided not to tell him that the dyers and wood-shapers had already argued the point, and instead dipped a bow and an ear. "I'm sure we can all learn from each other, Lord," I said.

We never stopped mourning our losses, but there was much to do that kept our ears up and our howls at bay.

Younglings were tasked with collecting the reeds that grew along every island shore, and the weavers showed the islands' half-growns how to crush the fat stems and separate the fibres inside. New tunics were soon replacing the patched, torn garments we all wore. The wood-shapers improved on Bidra and Yedri's float design by narrowing the front and rear ends of the logs, making them appear almost leaf-like from above, while Bidra and Yedri turned gratefully back to their original trade and dyed the new tunics purple with juice from the moontrap leaves. The rich colour gave everyone the uniform look I had Seen – though Kalon insisted on a new black tunic for me, a white tunic for himself and a cream one for Urxov. There were no vlydh to produce the waste needed create a pure white, so our Prime ended up with a pale cream tunic instead, but fortunately he was content with the result.

Those who were not involved in shaping floats or producing tunics were occupied with learning how to build dwellings from vinetrees. Hunters, artisans, and traders alike all flew to the western lake shore to fell the vines, which formed a thin strip of crimson between the lake and a jagged formation of cliffs. As the vines toppled, and we pushed the vineline back from the water's edge, the logs were towed to the islands by younglings in their new floats.

Kalon insisted that the Fate-seer's dwelling should be built first, constructed on the hillside not far below his own. In my determination to help, I was probably more of a hindrance, cutting my arm quite badly when I endeavoured to assist Myxot with the log-trimming, and bruising a finger when it got trapped as two logs were set one on another. Winan and Hariz, who did much of the heavy lifting, huffed and sighed at my efforts, though they didn't voice any direct criticism. "We're all learning," said Winan, nipping Chiva, who had sniggered at my bruised paw. "These dwellings are such an odd shape! And who ever heard of building with vinelogs?"

"You're welcome to try looking for stones to build a proper dwelling." Myxot's voice was tart, his ears and mane bristled. "Maybe you flyers can find enough for several nineties. But we paddled right round the lake, and went upriver and down, and we couldn't find enough large stones to build even Kalon a decent dwelling."

"No-one's criticizing your workmanship." Limar appeared on the slope below my half-constructed dwelling, a basket of fresh-picked moontrap leaves in her paw. Her fur was groomed and sleek, the patches on her old pink tunic artfully arranged to form a pattern. What was she up to? I knew our wood-shapers had already suggested several ways of improving the original design. "We're just not used to seeing dwellings constructed in this way."

Myxot ran a paw through his mane and rubbed the claws of his right paw on his tunic. "Took some thought, I can tell you, working out how to do it."

Limar leaned closer to him, tail quivering, ears turned to take in his every word. Hariz and Winan exchanged a weary glance and lifted another log into place.

"Well, I think they're clever," said Chiva, setting a paw at one end of a trimmed log. "Much better than sleeping in the open or under that smelly seatach-hide anyway."

"That smelly seatach-hide kept us dry on many a night," her dam retorted, bending to lift the log's other end, "and don't think you've seen the last of it. Some of us are going to use the pieces as a roof."

"But we have to get this one finished first," said Hariz, as Chiva signalled her disappointment. "What was it you wanted, Limar?"

"My new tunic's not been woven yet." Limar slid a paw down her front and hefted the basket. "But I've picked some leaves to dye my old one. I was hoping Myxot might show me how it's done?"

Myxot preened again. "Well, Bidra's the expert really, but I'd be happy to give you a few pointers – if the females here will excuse me?"

Hariz waved a dismissive paw. "We can manage." She watched as Myxot and Limar meandered away together down the hill, and snorted derision. "Do you think she could be any more obvious?"

"Obvious?" Chiva looked up at her dam, not understanding. "Obvious about what, Winan-muz?"

"Never mind." Winan flicked an ear at Hariz to signal agreement, and lifted another trimmed log. "Come on – let's get this shelf safely fixed."

So it was that barely a moon after our arrival I was able to place my beaker on my own table and build a fire in my own hearth. A trimmed log served as a stool, and I found a last twist of unspoiled avalox at the bottom of my carry-pouch. I brewed it strong and bitter, as Doran would have, and raised my beaker to her memory before sipping it with more relish than I would have believed possible. Outside, younglings barked and yipped, excitement in their voices, while the constant murmur of their dams' voices was as restful as the gentle lap of water on the shore. The logs surrounding me gave off a fresh resin smell that was reminiscent of fresh-cut zaxel. Putting my beaker aside, I closed my eyes and took a deep breath. It was not home. It would never be home. But it was a warm, dry sanctuary, and I spiralled a paw over my tunic as I thanked the Spiral for sparing me to see it.

I pushed away a howl at the thought of the many who had not been so blessed. They had been mourned. They would be remembered.

And, if I ever saw Fazak again, they would be avenged.

Twenty-Eight

The moons passed, and the islands on the lake grew dense with dwellings that became spiralling clusters. Gimel, perhaps wary of mating with females who had hatched wingless younglings, elected to remain with Yedri, while Myxot continued to dither between Bidra and Limar, ensuring that none of them were happy. The vinetrees on the western shore were cut back as far as craggy bluffs, which the wingless younglings promptly took to climbing. By setting nets over the entrance to melidh-burrows in the sheer faces, they were able to catch the creatures for our cooking pots.

Kalon was surprised and impressed, Elver less so. "Those things can certainly climb," she acknowledged, in a mutter I was not supposed to overhear.

Shaya grudgingly agreed that Jotto's method of creeper-catching was more efficient than her own; Jotto conceded that Shaya's gumalix traps were superior to his. I endeavoured to smooth Varel's ruffled fur by asking his advice on the strange plants that grew on the islands and around the lake, and made a point of conferring with him about where the new dwellings should be built, as well as how best to organise tasks, distribute food and gather together for rituals.

From the few nines of pouches that were salvaged from our plunge through the rapids, we planted the damp roots and seeds by the light of the Spiral on the cleared western shore, and were rewarded moons later with several fields of vari-coloured shoots. Chalkmoss, camyl, and kestox all grew rapidly in the warm sun, watered by occasional downpours, which Hynka told me were the norm for the growing season on the islands.

Four moons had passed since our arrival on the lake, and most of a fifth, when Varel knocked on my door to summon me to Kalon's dwelling. "He wishes to discuss the arrangements for the Feast of New Life," he said, as I hastily gulped down a beaker of tea and brushed crumbs from my tunic.

"I'm glad the weavers and dyers were able to produce a warm-season tunic for me," I said, as I stepped outside into the heat of another cloud-free day. "Is it always this hot so early in the cycle?"

Varel nodded, his ears set at the slightly cocky angle he used when he could tell me something I didn't know. He used it quite a lot. "The entire cycle here is warmer than it is on the Expanse," he said, brushing away a flisk that had buzzed up from the hillside moss. "I think perhaps that is why so many of the wild plants here are different from the ones on the Expanse. We haven't seen snow here since we arrived."

"No snow?" I couldn't imagine such a thing. No cold, no snow, no ice – what sort of place was this? "How is that possible?"

Varel shrugged a shoulder. "I simply tell you what is," he said. "I thought perhaps you would know why, being Fate-seer."

I shook my head, unsure whether he was genuinely mistaken about my abilities or whether he was goading me. Again. "If I could see the 'why' of things, the wingless would not have been banished," I said, falling silent as we hurried up the winding path that led to Kalon's dwelling. I was grateful for the breeze off the lake which ruffled my fur, and I opened my mouth to draw cooling air over my tongue, snapping it shut in a hurry as another flisk circled my snout. If I'd had breath to spare, I'd have asked Varel how Kalon's group had previously celebrated the Feast, for it was clear that the mountains were too far distant even for our flyers to hunt down a kervhel, but when we stepped inside Kalon's dwelling, I'd no sooner blinked to night-vision than the Prime provided the answer.

"Ah, Fate-seer!" He jumped to his feet from his makeshift Throne-stool. "Come and join us." He indicated Jotto, who stood respectfully to his left, and Elver who remained seated on her own Throne-stool to Kalon's right.

I scented excitement and anticipation, noting twitching ears and swishing tails.

"We need to discuss arrangements for our serpent-hunt."

I halted a few paces from the Prime and dipped a bow to cover my confusion. "Serpent-hunt, Lord?"

"Did Varel not tell you?" He waved a paw, dismissing the question, and went on: "We have no kervhels here, and the mountains can't be reached to get one. So we celebrate our feast-days here with a serpent for the spit." Spiralling a paw, he added, "It is what the Spiral provides. I trust you find it acceptable?"

I was floundering. Hunt *serpents*? Deliberately go out and find the things? And eat them? Still, I could hardly deny that Kalon's group did not appear to have suffered unduly for taking such an unorthodox approach to feasting. They had not even had the Sickness! So... "The Spiral has blessed you all with healthy younglings and abundant crops," I said. "Since the Spiral is content with your offering, I can but agree to bless the Feast in the usual way."

What else could I say? And how else would our exiles mark the occasion? All the same, I sent up a brief and silent prayer as I spoke.

For answer, I was sent a roar of delight from Kalon, an ear-twitch of approval from Elver, and a punch on the shoulder from Jotto, which nearly felled me. "Wonderful. Thank you, Fate-seer. I trust you will join us on the hunt?"

There was little I'd have liked less, but right then I could think of no possible answer save: "It would be an honour, Lord."

Armed with arrows and spears, the hunting party set off at sunrise, the flightless paddling floats north across the lake, the winged among us riding the air currents above. There had been some dispute about who should go along, with Elver arguing that only those who had been hunters or guardflight should accompany the Prime and the Fate-seer. "That's the way we've always done it here," she'd said, ignoring the fact that Kalon had had few with him who had *not* been hunters or guardflight.

"With respect, Elver," I'd said, dipping a bow and setting my ears to a courteous angle, "the traditional kervhel hunt from the Expanse included representatives of every trade and skill." Most of them had done little but gossip, chant, and flap about at a safe distance while the hunters netted the kervhel – the largest male they could find, usually one with majestic horns and a temper – but still, everyone had felt included.

"Drax from each island, then?" Varel suggested, "As well as the hunters and guardflight?"

"In that case, should there not be younglings too?" Elver's remark was accurate, but spiteful. On the kervhel hunt, younglings had been able to fly above the action, well away from any danger. With the exception of the younglings and half-growns that Kalon's group had hatched, ours would be on the ground, in the most dangerous place of all, but I could hardly use tradition as an argument with one breath and deny it with the next.

So it was that the half-grown, Yaver, and several island-hatched younglings flew alongside Hariz, Winan, and myself as we rode the air-currents over the lake. Ahead of us were Jotto, Shaya, Azmit, and Marga, while below on the water, Kalon led the maimed and wingless in floats, Urxov circling over their heads. I spiralled a paw over my tunic as I watched Dru paddle hard to keep up: he looked very small from where I flew, though I understood his determination to take part. So did Limar, though she had done her utmost to try to persuade him to stay behind in safety.

"I'll come with you, then," she'd declared, when he pointed out that he had to prove he could do everything Urxov did. "Urxov is a half-grown, and he has wings. You shouldn't expect to match him."

Cavel paddled in their wake, alongside Myxot and Gimel, Elver and Varel, with the other younglings trailing behind. I recognised Nixel, Ravar, Dugaz, and Oztin among them, hoped they would all stay out of harm's way, and heard Shaya call to Ravar to do just that.

Even if they all joined the hunt, it still seemed to me to be a very small flock for confronting a serpent.

At the northern end of the lake, two separate channels cut through the forested bank, both streams meeting and mingling a few wingbeats into the vines. The triangle of land that lay between them and the lakewater was our destination – 'Hunt Isle' Kalon had called it, though it looked to me to be little more than another low mound covered with vinetrees. If not for the water surrounding it, it would have been just another section of unrelenting forest. Certainly it looked little different to me: vines soared skyward, creeper nests – or serpents, perhaps? – swayed in the topmost branches. Grief gripped me like a sudden downdraught as I remembered my flight to the Forest with Doran, so many cycles ago. Why had I agreed to fly with the hunters? Was I a fool, trying to impress an exiled Prime with bravado because my talent for Visions was so poor? Would Kalon have thought less of me if I had declined his invitation?

I shook my mind free of memories and speculation as we reached the isle and angled our wings to circle it while we waited for the floats to catch up. I needed to concentrate on the plan: the hunters would identify a good-sized serpent hiding amid the creeper nests and attack it, distracting the thing while Kalon and those alongside him searched for its eggs. Once we heard the howls of success from the ground, the branch the serpent was wrapped around would be cut and lowered to where the flightless members of our party waited. "Usually, they cling to the branch they're on," Jotto had said, when he explained the plan to me, "and when they do that, they are easy to pick off. But sometimes they slip off and slither down a vinetrunk – and when they do that, they could descend anywhere, on anyone. The skill is in listening, to know where the creature is – to be ready."

"What about those horrible things on the ground?" Dru had asked. "The…mouldworms? The spiny slugs? The suckerpods?"

"There are none," Kalon had assured us. "We found a few suckerpods when we first discovered the place, but we killed them and filled in the swampy ground they like. They can't swim anyway, so the water prevents others taking their place. The danger lies with the serpents – and with the Sucker Ferns. Be sure you never step on one of those!"

Below me, the floats had nudged up against the bank of the island, and I watched Kalon, Dru, and the rest tie them to the trunks of the nearest vines. Kalon extended his wing – the signal to start – and Jotto waggled his own wings in acknowledgement. Then Jotto and Shaya flew low over the vinetops, circling the creeper nests.

Within a few beats, every false nest had sprouted an evil black-and-magenta head, swaying on the end of mottled necks that would have been indistinguishable from the branches they clung to if they had not been moving independently of the wind. As the heads turned and swayed to keep us in sight, I followed Shaya's lead in concentrating our attentions on a particularly large specimen, which had claimed a tangle of branches almost at the top of the tallest vine near the centre of the island.

As we closed in on it, the serpent opened its jaws, displaying a formidable set of curved fangs, and it began to sway from side to side in its quest to drive us away.

"Magnificent!" called Jotto.

The word that had sprung to my head was 'frightening', but I thought it best to keep that to myself. The slithering beast was huge; it kept pulling more and more of its slick scales clear of the vinetop. I guessed it must be at least ten wingspans long and as thick around its widest point as Kalon was. It would certainly have swallowed a youngling whole without any problem, and I thought anxiously of Dru. If he was not careful, and if those looking to his welfare were not vigilant, there was every chance he'd end up as the serpent's next meal.

The beast's forked tail appeared, its two prongs opening and closing as it sought to snare one or other of us in its grip. I remembered Galyn, who had been snatched from our camp in the Forest, and my fur bristled with dread, even while Shaya and Azmit distracted the creature by flying round its head at a ridiculously close range. Jotto, meanwhile, flew in past its thrashing tail, dodging and weaving. I concentrated my attention on the serpent, so was not able to follow Jotto's every move, but I heard his call plainly enough when the wretched thing was confined to one branch. As he flew upward, paying out the rope that was now attached to the tangle of woven leaves and branches, there were cries from below: they had found the eggs. Marga, who had been hovering above us, waiting for the signal, pulled an axe from her tunic belt, folded her wings into a dive and swung the axe at the single branch the serpent had wrapped itself round.

To my relief, one blow was enough to sever it, and I flew with Azmit to help Jotto and Shaya hold the weight of branch and serpent, while the younglings circled about at a safe distance, calling encouragement. Together, we lowered it through the canopy, feeling it bump against branches as it descended. A sudden relief from the weight told me that it had reached the ground, and a beat later, Jotto pulled up the rope and coiled it round his waist.

My part in the adventure was officially at an end, but I couldn't remain in the now-safe comfort of the air. I needed to know what was happening on the ground. Where was Dru, and was he in danger? Leaving Shaya and the others to circle the vinetops to alert those below to any more serpents, I flew down to land beside the floats. I was relieved to see some of the younglings at the edge of the vines, peering into the gloom, ears flat and tails rigid, their early bravado having subsided to apprehension once they'd seen the vines. But Dru and Cavel were not among them. As I folded my wings and switched to night vision to follow the beaten trail through the dark canopy of vines, cries and squeals in the gloom told me the serpent was putting up a fight.

I prayed that it had not taken anyone by surprise.

I edged into the clearing – into chaos.

The grounders had taken the eggs they'd found and scattered them across the clearing, their smooth grey shells easy to spot against the dark loam. The serpent was coiled around a low-hanging branch, its tail darting one way and its head another, as it snapped and struck at those surrounding it.

Myxot was on the ground, nursing his left shoulder where a growing patch of blood that matted his grey fur spoke of a nasty wound. Gimel, Cavel, and Varel stood over him, spears raised to ward the creature away, though they all looked and smelled terrified. Kalon and Dru were circling beneath the serpent's jaws, jabbing at it with their own spears, and Limar...

Limar, who had strutted and preened for Myxot, who had moaned, complained, and gossiped her way from the Expanse to the lake; Limar, Dru's nest-nurse and half-sibling, who had once attempted to betray a Fate-seer...

Limar hung lifeless from the creature's coils, her head at an unnatural angle. Urxov was pulling on his bow, attempting to aim an arrow at the writhing beast which, to judge from the number of shafts that were already jutting from its scales, was proving difficult to finish off.

As Urxov loosed his arrow, he staggered a little from the recoil and stepped back onto one of the eggs, which broke under his foot with a snap like a breaking vine. Instantly the serpent turned its attention to him, coiling itself toward the half-grown with a speed that defied its vast size. Elver sprang forward with an axe at the same moment Kalon lunged at the thing with his spear, but I was sure they were both too late, that the serpent's jaws would close around Urxov's head even in its death throes.

But Dru had other ideas.

Howling with rage and grief, he jumped, powering upward to a height that no winged drax could dream of attaining without using its wings to assist. In mid-air he twisted about, landing behind the creature's head and, with a cry of triumph, plunged his spear directly into its skull.

As the serpent gave a last shudder, Kalon put his head back and sent forth a triumphal roar. "You are a true warrior," he called to Dru. "You too must roar your victory."

Dru was panting with effort, ears drooping as he glanced at Limar, though his tail and snout were a-quiver with the exhilaration of the hunt. "Like this?" He raised his head and made a good try at reproducing the multi-tone deep-throated roar that Kalon had made.

Kalon waggled his ears with approval, and bent to pull Dru's blood-encrusted spear from the skull. "A little more from the second stomach," he said, "but not bad for a first try." He looked down at the dead serpent for a beat, and extended his paw toward Elver. "Axe."

His nest-mate had been glaring at Dru, but at Kalon's command she handed the axe to him and he hacked at the creature's head till he parted it from its body.

"Your trophy," he said, dragging the head toward Dru. "Have it preserved. Zarda, you know how?"

One of my first duties as an apprentice had been to assist Vizan as he worked on one of Kalis's hunting trophies. I had never carried out the process myself, but I was fairly sure I could remember how to do it. "I know how, Lord," I said, giving the serpent a kick. "I can suggest a recipe or two for the remainder of it, too."

"Why are you giving Dru the credit?" The roar of outrage was accompanied by the snap and crunch of something breaking, and I turned to find Urxov jumping up and down on the serpent's remaining eggs. "I shot it! I killed it! Look, that's my arrow in its jaw, right there!"

"You hit it, certainly," said Kalon, ignoring Elver's indignant stance, "but your arrow didn't kill it. Dru did – and bravely, too." Kalon smelled disappointed about the outcome, but he sounded sincere enough.

Urxov, though, was not appeased. "It would have died anyway," he insisted. "If you're going to give him the head, I want the heart."

"That is not how it's done," I said, remembering the kervhel hunts. "The drax who slays the beast must eat the heart, and Dru—"

"It's alright, Zarda." Dru pushed at the serpent's great head, oblivious to the blood dripping from his tunic. "I'll share the heart with Urxov. If he had not hit the serpent with his arrow, it would not have been distracted enough for me to jump on its back. We should share the prize."

"You are generous, Dru," I said, and Kalon nodded. "Come, we must get back to Kalon's Island. The serpent will take all day to prepare, Myxot needs his wound tending, and we must give Limar the death-rites she deserves."

Dru jumped onto the serpent again, and began to climb over blood-spattered skin and twisted coils, making for Limar's still form.

"Beware the tail, Dru," Varel called, limping across the broken ground to call up to him. "There's poison in the barbs. Best let them drain and let the hunters come back for Limar later."

Dru halted where he stood, reached a paw toward Limar, who was still several spans from him, and sat down on top of the serpent. "She was showing off for Myxot," he said, his voice so quiet I strained to hear over the noise of the others gathering spears and eggs. "She wanted an egg of her own."

I spiralled a paw over my tunic and moved across the clearing. "I'm sorry, Dru. I'll ask Kalon again if you can come to live with me. You'll not be left on your own, I promise you."

He flicked an ear, so I knew he'd heard me, though his gaze rested on Limar. "Would you leave me on my own now? Just for a few beats? Please?"

"Of course." I set my ears to sorrow and respect, though it was more for Dru's sake than because Limar deserved it. "I'll see you back at the floats."

As I bent to help Myxot to his feet, Urxov stalked past. His feet were covered in the sticky yolk of the eggs he had destroyed, but he seemed oblivious to the mess as he stomped off in the direction of the floats with his ears set in triumph: he had got the outcome he wanted, or a share of it, anyway.

But the scent I caught as the breeze rustled the leaves overhead was not one of victory. I had smelled it before, in the Council Chamber at the Spirax – the sour smell of hate. In the Chamber, I had not been sure who the culprit was, though I was convinced now that it had been Fazak; here, I knew the scent was Urxov's: the question was, who did he hate most? Dru? Me? His sire, perhaps, who had praised Dru's hunting skills so effusively?

I sighed. There was little I could do about it, even if I knew. As I pulled Myxot upright and he leaned his weight on my shoulder, all I could do was hope that Urxov's hatred did not have the same devastating consequences as Fazak's.

"Where's Urxov?" We had gained the relative safety of the bank when Myxot spoke, and I looked around at the trampled slope, at the floats that were pulled up beside it and the younglings who stood at the water's edge throwing sticks into the lake. Urxov should have been there ahead of us, but he was nowhere to be seen. I looked out over the lake in case he was already flying home, but there was no sign of him. Where could he have gone?

Ravar looked across at us, arm raised in mid-throw. "Is it dead?"

"Yes, Dru killed it. We'll be celebrating later, once we've prepared Limar for her last nest. You can all lead the way home if you'd like to, but have you seen Urxov at all?"

Nixel made a noise that indicated he was not fond of the half-grown, and Oztin snuffled at his daring. Ravar turned away to rid himself of the stick he held, hurling it away with a vicious growl. Dugaz shrugged as he kicked at a pebble.

"Shaya! Jotto?" I called to the flyers, who swooped low and hovered over the water. "Have you seen Urxov? He was ahead of us."

"Lost again, is he?" Jotto sounded unsurprised. With a tilt of his wings, he floated down to land beside me and twisted his ears toward the vines to listen. "He'll be under the canopy somewhere – we'll have to spread out and work our way back through the vines to find him."

"He's done this before?" Shaya glided in to land next to Jotto, carrying the scent of annoyance with her.

"Now and then." Jotto held up a paw, curtailing any criticism of his young lordling. "He lets his curiosity get the better of his good sense sometimes."

I glanced at Myxot, who sat on the patchy moss, clutching his shoulder. He needed healing herbs and a poultice, and sooner rather than later. From the vines behind me came the roars and barks of the hunting party. Surely, if Urxov had lost his way he would simply make his way towards the noise?

Assuming he wasn't hurt. Or worse.

"Ravar, you go on ahead with the other younglings. We'll wait for Kalon and the rest." It was Shaya who spoke, though I saw Jotto flick an ear in agreement. "Zarda, you should get Myxot home."

I was more than happy to agree – but right then, the howling started.

Twenty-Nine

It was impossible to run – vines, roots and the constant fear of treading on something hideous kept our pace to a hurried trot. It felt that lifetimes passed while we moved toward the sound, though I doubt more than a few moments had gone by till we burst into a clearing and found Urxov, flapping his paws, ears, and wings at the swarm of insects buzzing about his face. His eyes were closed, and his howling doubtless indicated that he had been stung. I looked about in hope of finding a sweetleaf shrub, and offered brief thanks to the Spiral when I saw a clump of them growing in the middle of the glade.

I turned to Shaya and Jotto. "The sweetleaf bushes – pull off the leaves, as many as you can. Quickly, now, quickly!"

Hurriedly, I pulled a firestick from my tunic pocket and, dropping to one knee, gathered a few dead leaves and fern stems into a pile. It seemed an age before they caught light, but once I had a flame we piled on the blue sweetleaves. Smooth and shiny, they were not easy to set afire, due to the oily content that made them smell good, but once alight they burned well and gave off a thick, cloying smoke with a sickly sweet odour.

"Urxov! I called, "Over here, Urxov! Come! This way!" The others stopped pulling at the bush and turned to watch as the half-grown staggered toward the sound of my voice, a flapping, howling, swirling mass of fur and insects. "Bring more leaves! Pile them on!" I urged, and Shaya and Jotto returned to their task.

Distant cries and the sound of breaking undergrowth heralded the arrival of Kalon, Elver, and the rest, all bearing torches and spears. I blinked back to normal vision as the flames illuminated the clearing.

"The serpents will have heard the howls," Varel called. "They'll be coming to see what's been stung."

Kalon indicated the clearing with a sweep of his arm. "Spread out," he ordered. "Keep those torches raised!"

As the other adults rushed to comply, I turned my attention back to Urxov. He was coughing in the smoke, still flapping his arms and wings, but most of the insects had called off their attack and returned to the rotting vinelog where they nested.

"You're fortunate, Urxov," I said. "That might have been a Sucker Fern you trod on. As it is—" I put a paw under his chin and lifted his head to get a better look at the damage, "—a sweetleaf paste will stop the itching, and the swellings will go down of their own accord in a few days."

Kalon seized him by the scruff of his white mane. "What I'd like to know," he growled, "is how you managed to stray so far from the trodden way?"

Urxov's answer was lost amid another fit of coughing, and his sire guided him back toward the lake, leaving the rest of us following hard on their tails. As Urxov and Myxot were helped into nets, Dru emerged from the vines and I put a paw on his shoulder, noting with surprise that it was barely a paw-width below my own.

"I'll return with the hunters for Limar," I said, "but her last nest will have to be in the Forest."

A sigh, a tiny ear-flick. "I know. I don't want to think about it. Not yet."

To our left, the serpent's head was dropped into another net with a wet thud.

"Why did you offer to share your prize with Urxov?" I said, glad that a change of subject was so readily at paw. "He won't thank you for it."

I felt Dru shrug. "He'll never stop claiming he killed it, anyway," he said. "Urxov likes to show off, and he never listens." A pause, then: "He'll die because he won't listen." He glanced up at me. "Haven't you Seen?"

I had not. This was not the first time Dru had told me of a Vision he had had that I had not shared. I was certain now that his gift was more powerful than mine. I was less sure what I should make of that.

"We'll discuss this later," I said, as I helped him into his float, "once I've dealt with our wounded – and Limar."

Taking off into a warm breeze, I circled upward, admiring the view as I stretched my wings and set course back to Kalon's Island.

How quickly I had become used to the straight-sided, log-built dwellings that now spiralled across most of the islands. The newer dwellings still had the near-black colour of vine-bark; those on Kalon's Isle, which had been through several cycles of wind and weathering, had shaded to a mottled grey, the reeds that lined their roofs faded to a pale mauve. The distinctive smells of simmering dye, new-cut logs, and drying reeds mingled with the vinesmoke that drifted on the breeze. Kalon's triumphant howls resounded across the water, and were met with answering yips and cries. Already some of the younglings on Doorway Island were heading for their floats, paddling for the main island while their dams circled above.

I thought about what Dru had told me of Urxov's fate, and wondered why I had not Seen the same thing. I found it a little alarming to be out-Seen by a youngling who, by rights, should not even have had his gift awakened yet. But then, I had been barely half-trained when Vizan went to his last nest. There was much I didn't know and much I couldn't See – though, so far, Kalon had not questioned my abilities.

Nor had he questioned my loyalty, and it was true that, as rightful Prime, he had my utter allegiance. But I still couldn't understand how Kalon and Urxov fitted into the Vision that Vizan and I had had of Dru's destiny.

I heard Kalon calling my name from below, and I remembered my duty to Myxot, and to Urxov and his insect-stings. With a snuffle of laughter at the memory of the half-grown's wild flapping, I angled my wings and circled to begin my descent.

I landed on the flat, mossy ground next to the float-platform that extended into the lake. To my left, fish were being strung on twine, their water-fresh smell drifting to my twitching snout. They would be smoked and salted ready for the freeze – if we could call it that here – and put into jars in the food stores, which were being built on The Crag, an islet near the eastern lake shore that was too small and rocky for dwellings.

Gathering a handful of damp, red moss, I glided across the island and walked up the spiralling path that wound round the hillside, till I gained my shelter. Kalon was waiting outside.

"What kept you, Zarda? Hariz is tending to Myxot, but Urxov is breaking out in sores and can't stop itching, yet you wander with the wind."

"I was making the ritual prayer to the Spiral for Urxov's well-being," I lied, opening the door to my dwelling and ducking inside. While its straight walls seemed less strange than they once had, I still missed the spiralling stones and the see-shell of my old home. "It will take a few moments to make the paste," I said, throwing the moss into a bowl and pulling sweetleaves from my pocket, before hunting through jars and containers for the other herbs I needed. As I upended one of the jars, a single leaf fluttered onto the table. "The last of the canox," I said, scooping it into the bowl. "I've not seen the bushes growing since we left the Expanse."

Kalon grunted. "Not an orenvine to be found, either. Perhaps they don't like the snowless freeze."

It still seemed odd, the idea of a cold season without seeing snow, but the Growing Season was certainly much warmer than I was used to, and I panted a little as I crushed the canox together with the sweetleaf and moss, adding a little resin to make the paste. Giving the bowl a last sniff, I pronounced it ready and Kalon led the way outside.

"Urxov is in his nest," he said, as he strode ahead of me toward his own, bigger, dwelling. "Elver is with him."

I glanced down the hill. Dru had moored his float and was hurrying inland, moving much more rapidly over the ground than any winged drax could manage.

Kalon must have been following the direction of my gaze. "The wingless have strengths of their own, do they not?" he remarked. "Their legs are longer, and carry them further."

"Yes." I pointed west to where a knot of younglings were clambering down the rock face on the lake shore. "And you've seen how well they climb." I remembered how Dru and Cavel had climbed the Tusk, in the days before our exile, and thought of my Vision of Dru raising a drax banner over the Koth eyrie. With a jolt, I understood how he might reach it.

And then the view I was looking at faded, and I Saw clearly and for the first time that there was more than one enemy to defeat. "*Before the Koth mountain is climbed*," I said, "*the* Spirax *itself must be taken*."

When the Vision faded, Kalon was standing in front of me, his hands on the bowl of paste that I was in danger of dropping. "Take the *Spirax*? Zarda, you are quite mad!" As he spoke, he glared at me as though I had tried to snap off his one remaining wing, but although I dipped my head, and set my ears and wings respectfully, I did not move away from him.

"No." I raised my head, and lifted the bowl from his paws. "It must be done." Though I had no idea how. Not only was the *Spirax* set atop a vertical-sided plateau on a guarded peninsula that was the most important place in Drax territory, but it was at least a nineday's flight from the island where we stood. Nevertheless... "I have Seen it."

"A Vision?" I smelled Kalon's doubt and heard it in his voice, but unlike his shell-brother he knew better than to ignore a Fate-seer – even a half-trained apprentice in a grubby tunic.

I nodded. "As clear as any I had in the Dream-cave."

He grunted, never altogether happy to be reminded that the Dream-smoke showed Dru, not himself or Urxov, defeating the Koth, but after a moment he set his ears upright and waved a paw to indicate I should precede him into his dwelling. "We'll discuss this further," he growled, "once you've seen to Urxov's stings. And tomorrow, we'll put it to the council."

Thirty

In his torch-lit dwelling, Kalon paced about from angle to angle, back and forth along the straight, shelf-lined walls. The Feast of New Life had been celebrated long into the night, and the serpent – a surprisingly tender meat when roasted and basted with herbs – consumed. Limar had been prepared for her last nest, and Dru had agreed that she should be netted to rest in a clump of Sucker Ferns on the eastern shore. After the feast he had slept beside her in my dwelling, his sleep broken by terrible dreams. I'd not slept well myself, thanks to his howls and my own tumbling thoughts, but Kalon's summons had come with the dawn, so I'd brushed my fur and put on a clean tunic before making my way up the hill to join the rest of the recently-formed council.

As I'd stepped over the entrance-stone, Elver glared at me from her Throne-stool, while Urxov sat, scratching, on a log beside her. Jotto, Hynka, Shaya, Winan, and Varel were seated round the table, snouts moving in unison as they followed

Kalon's pacing. I'd judged it best to remain standing, just inside the door, and shifted uncomfortably from foot to foot as Kalon growled and grumbled.

"There are too few of us to even think of attacking Kalis. I can't fly. Some of my troops can't fly. Your wingless can't fly. How are we even to reach Drax territory, let alone cross it? We would be seen and massacred before we got near the Expanse."

There were ear-flicks of agreement, and I could offer no argument. Hynka scratched on a record-leaf while the torches hissed and sputtered as wind gusted through the open door; Urxov rubbed at his left thigh.

"I don't know how it can be done, Lord," I offered. "I merely state that it must."

"Floats." Jotto leaned forward, paws clasped over the table, ears suddenly upright. "We could use floats."

Shaya's ears quivered as she caught the suggestion's scent and followed it: "They could be paddled up Death River," she put in. "Then perhaps we could make more when we reach the Ambit?"

Jotto agreed. "Once we're on the Ambit, it's a straightforward paddle to the ocean." He waved his paws to illustrate his words as he went on: "Pick a still night, and it wouldn't be too difficult to paddle through the shallows, right to the foot of the *Spirax* plateau. We'd have the advantage of complete surprise."

Varel joined in. "Others perhaps could fly across the Deadlands to the Expanse?"

"And remain unseen? How?" Elver, putting a spear through the idea's flight.

Varel spread his paws, shrugged a shoulder. "A problem for another day."

Kalon raised a paw. "However it's done, we can't contemplate it yet. The wingless won't be half-growns till the Harvest season. Many of them still haven't mastered the bow or the spear. They will need to practice a good deal more if we are to take on Kalis and his Elite troops."

"There'll be the guardflight to consider, too," said Winan, claws drumming on the table, "though their numbers aren't what they were."

I took a breath, about to suggest that the guardflight might be sympathetic toward us...but no. Just because Taral had once protected me from discovery did not mean he would side with me against his Prime. Even if he did, there were plenty more guardflight who might feel differently.

"We can make sure our younglings are trained properly," said Jotto, "and remind ourselves of how to fight – it's a skill that has grown mossy with disuse."

Kalon finally stilled his pacing, coming to a halt beside the spiral of white pebbles that decorated his dwelling's western wall. He reached out a paw to trace the pattern as he spoke: "It would be useful to find out what has happened on the Expanse since you left. Have guardflight numbers increased? How many times have the Koth raided? What's the situation with this new Elite Guard?"

I nodded agreement. "Many drax were unhappy when news of your death was announced, Lord. Some of them were uncomfortable with the banishment of the wingless – there were few clusters who were not affected. Then there are the tithes, which Fazak persuaded Kalis to increase even though the last cycle's harvest was slim."

Kalon turned slowly, ears a-twitch. He smelled of hope. "You believe that the drax on the Expanse may be unhappy with Kalis's rule? That some of them might be persuaded to help us?"

I glanced at Shaya's flattened ears and smelled Winan's scepticism. "It's not impossible," I replied, "but we'll need to know. Perhaps their harvest will be better this cycle, perhaps Kalis has stopped listening to Fazak and been less demanding with his tithes. This cycle may have brought fewer Koth raids, less illness, more healthy nestlings."

"In which case they will forget the lean times," said Kalon. He moved past me to the door and glanced out. "Perhaps we are better off here than we know."

I nodded. "We will need to find out." As he moved away from the door, I caught the scent of waterweed and vinesmoke on the breeze. It was quiet outside – no sounds but the gentle wash of the lake, a melidh somewhere overhead, the yips of younglings playing, and the barks of drax going about their work. No-one spoke for several beats – it was clear that there was only one way to discover what was happening on the Expanse.

Varel broke the silence: "Someone will have to go back."

Kalon didn't hesitate. "Fate-seer," he said, "you must go. Disguise yourself, the way you told me you did when you joined the exiles."

Me? He wanted *me* to take wing on such an errand?

The odour of shock overwhelmed the cramped space, and a quick glance around told me I was not alone in being astonished by his pronouncement.

"But..." Winan dipped her head and ears to indicate she was not issuing a challenge. "Zarda is our Fate-seer. She—"

"She knows the Expanse better than any other drax." Kalon snapped his teeth dangerously close to Winan's snout. "She flew with Vizan, she travelled about the Expanse with Dru." He looked across the table at me. "You know who to speak to, Zarda, who might be trusted, who cannot. You'll know what to look for, where to listen, and how to sniff in the right places. In any case -"

Shaya risked attracting a snap. "She can't go alone. I'll go with her." Of course she would. No matter how far we had travelled together, what we had been through, to Shaya I would always be a half-trained apprentice, unable to fend for myself or to See the way clearly.

"And I." Jotto's stool scraped as he got to his feet. "Though we'll have to learn to be something other than hunters or guardflight." He took a step to stand beside Kalon, and half-turned to dip an ear in Elver's direction. "With your permission, I suggest young Urxov comes with us too. If we wait till the harvest season, he'll be old enough to take his Proving Flight."

Kalon grunted what might have been agreement, and silenced further debate with an upraised paw. "If you wait till the harvest season, then we have plenty of time to plan this properly."

Shaya and Jotto both had enthusiasm pouring from every hair, but I felt unwell. Go back! I'd given no thought to who Kalon might send to discover what was happening on the Expanse. It hadn't even occurred to me that I was the best candidate he had.

Raising my head, I looked out through the open doorway. Out there, serpent-skin was being pegged to the hillside to dry, dyers were stirring pots, and winged younglings were flapping about on the mossy bank near the inlet; lakewater sparkled as the sun caught the surface. But all I could see, in my mind and memory, was the *Spirax*.

How wonderful it would be to visit the Expanse again, to drink hoxberry juice, eat loxcakes, to glimpse Taral perhaps, and sleep in a Welcome Place with stones over my head.

How wonderful – and how dangerous.

END OF VOLUME TWO

Acknowledgements

Ongoing thanks to everyone at Mirror World for their enthusiasm and engagement with both 'Exile' and 'Unreachable Skies'. Robert Dowsett has again done an amazing job with the line edits, while Justine Alley Dowsett has nailed the cover design once more. Thanks both.

I'm so grateful to everyone who bought 'Unreachable Skies', and if you took the time to post a review on Amazon or Goodreads I really appreciate it. Here's hoping you enjoy Volume II as much as you liked Volume I! I have to give a special shout-out to all the ladies of Bognor Regis WI, who bought 'Unreachable Skies' even if they "never read sci-fi", and who told family and friends to buy it too; and to Annie Smith and my dad, Alec McCreedy, who both beta-read the manuscript for 'Exile'.

Thanks once again to James Swallow for the writerly chats and encouragement; and much love to my family for all the help and support.

About the Author

Brought up in Staffordshire, England, Karen now lives in West Sussex where she is enjoying her retirement. When not writing, she enjoys reading, watching films, local WI and U3A activities, volunteering with the South Downs National Park Volunteer Rangers, and spending time with friends and family. She has also flown in a Spitfire!

Karen has written articles on films and British history for a number of British magazines including 'Yours', 'Classic Television', and 'Best of British'. In 2009, her essay on *'British Propaganda Films of the Second World War'* was published in *'Under Fire: A Century of War Movies'* (Ian Allen Publishing).

She also wrote a number of online articles and reviews for The Geek Girl Project (www.geekgirlproject.com), as their British correspondent.

Karen's short stories have appeared in anthologies by Fiction Brigade (2012, e-book), Zharmae Publishing *('RealLies'*, 2013), Audio Arcadia (*'On Another Plane'*, 2015), Luna Station Publishing (*'Luna Station Quarterly'* December 2015), Horrified Press *('Killer Tracks'* and *'Waiting'*, both 2015; and *'Crossroads'*, 2016), and Reflex Fiction (*'Voicemail'*, published online 2017). She also won second prize in Writers' News magazine's 'Comeuppance' competition in 2014 with her short story *'Hero'*.

'Exile' is the sequel to *'Unreachable Skies'*, and Karen is currently working on the third book in the trilogy.

You can follow Karen on Twitter @McKaren_Writer, or check out her website at www.karenmccreedy.com

To learn more about our authors and their current projects visit: www.mirrorworldpublishing.com or follow @MirrorWorldPub or like us at www.facebook.com/mirrorworldpublishing

Why 'Mirror World'?

We publish escapism fiction for all ages. Our novels are imaginative and character-driven and our goal is to give our readers a glimpse into other worlds, times, and versions of reality that parallel our own, giving them an experience they can't get anywhere else!

We offer free delivery within Windsor-Essex,Ontario, an all-you-can-read membership program, blind-dates with books, and you can find our novels in our online store, or from your favorite major book retailer.

To learn more about our authors and our current projects visit: www.mirrorworldpublishing.com, follow @MirrorWorldPub or like us at www.facebook.com/mirrorworldpublishing

If you liked Unreachable Skies, keep an eye out for:

THE DEMONS OF WALL STREET

A Novella By

Laurence Brothers

Coming Spring 2020!

ONE

I was working the action of my compact Ruger, pretending to shoot people I knew, when my phone rang. The ringtone was the opening to *Night on Bald Mountain* so I could tell who it was without looking at the screen. Also, the phone answered itself and switched to speaker. It wasn't programmed to do that.

"Mom," I said. "What is it?" I imagined her face floating in front of me, aimed, and pulled the trigger.

"Nora, dear, would it hurt to be polite?"

"To you? Yes." I keep hoping if I'm offensive enough maybe she'll just leave me alone. But it never works.

"I just wanted to let you know, dear. You have some work coming your way."

"I thought we had an understanding. I don't need your money, especially not for some stupid makework job."

"Nora, please. This is not my idea. And it's not makework at all. This is the Commission's assignment. I just thought it would be nice to let you know about it in advance. I expect you'll have a case before the day is over. Your first in quite some time, if I'm not mistaken."

"Yeah, well. Thanks, I guess."

"Don't mention it, dear. And good luck. I think you'll need it."

She hung up. Talk about politeness. But she was a big one for last words. I felt a point of heat in my chest; it was Spark, responding to my irritation. So I walked over to the little clay pot by the window where it hangs out while I'm at the office and sprinkled some more crushed incense to show I wasn't angry at it. Not that I think Spark really understands that kind of thing, but I like to pretend it does anyway. And it settled down, too; the spike of fiery heat became a pleasant emanation of warmth before fading away completely.

It wasn't half an hour before someone knocked on my office door. I couldn't be sure it was a Commission agent. I do get drop-in clients from time to time. And sometimes people who aren't clients at all. I slotted a magazine into the Ruger and put the gun back in its clamp under my desk. You never know. Then I hit the button to unlock the door. It made a thwocking noise loud enough for the person on the other side to hear.

The man who entered paused uncertainly. He was looking around at a tiny, bare space just big enough to wedge in an assistant or a secretary and their desk. If I had an assistant or a secretary, anyway.

"In here," I said, and he stepped through the doorway into my inner office. It wasn't much bigger than the outer one, a mere cubbyhole, but at least it had a window looking down on 35th street. For what that was worth.

"Ms. Simeon?"

I figured he was a Commission agent; he looked like one, anyway, in his conservative gray suit with its thin red pinstripe. They like to think they project an aura of authority, inherited from their bosses, but really, it's more like smug self-satisfaction at being in on the big dark secret behind all the finance of midtown and Wall Street.

"Yup."

The man pulled a device from a pocket that looked like one of the pistol-grip bar-code readers they use on checkout lines. He pointed it at me, which made me antsy to begin with, then pulled the trigger, almost blinding me with a laser glare. I came *this* close to blowing him away because I had the Ruger in my hand under the desk. And then a moment later, when I realized what he was doing, I almost had Spark set his hair on fire. But I managed to restrain myself for the sake of the hundred grand a year they pay me as a permanent retainer. That's pretty much my entire income.

"The fuck? A little warning first, asshole!"

"Sorry," he said, not sounding apologetic at all. "ID. Retina scan."

"Yeah? What about you? How do I know who you are?"

He produced a thick envelope from his jacket pocket, put it down on my desk. Heavy parchment bound with a gold ribbon and a double wax seal. "This should be enough. Good afternoon, Ms. Simeon."

He turned and left before I could say anything more. I hate these guys, but not only do they pay my rent, there's not much I can do about cutting ties. When you're let in on the secret, they keep track of you. You're either with them or against them, and against them tends not to work out that well. And oh yeah, my mom? She's more than just with them. On their board of directors. Fuck my life.

Right. So there was this fancy envelope on my desk. The first wax seal was the Commission's, a caduceus with the snake in an S around the rod to make a dollar sign. Occult wisdom and profit combined. Cute. The second seal was blank. I put my thumb up against it, and both seals split neatly down the middle. The nicest thing that would have happened if someone else tried to open it was the envelope catching fire.

I read through the enclosed material quickly because the ink was going to fade, or the paper fall apart in a minute or two. Could have scanned it with my phone, but probably that would have cursed the electronics, so I contented myself with making a few notes on a legal pad.

The whole first page was pretentious bullshit. Whoever it was at the Commission liked to pretend they were old-time British admiralty. "Wherefore fail you not in the execution of our commands except at your peril". Et cetera. The meat of the case was distressingly thin. But it was my kind of work. Rogue demon. Broken contract. The creature somehow managed to sever or refute its binding, escaped from the secure sorcery floor of the Goldman Sachs headquarters building on West Street. Geomantic scrying had failed to narrow down its location, but the demon was thought to be in New York City somewhere. My job would be to track it down and then return it, banish it, or destroy it, in diminishing order of preference. My personal preferred order was the reverse. I hate infernals. I had a contact, a vice-president at Goldman Sachs, the creature's supervisor, and that was it.

I'd just finished noting down Ms. Sakashvili's contact info when I felt a sudden urge to turn away from the document. When I looked back it was a sudoku puzzle. It had always been a sudoku puzzle. Fucking Commission. I hate their little games.

When I called, she picked up on the first ring.

"Sakashvili." Cool, clipped delivery, just a hint of an accent.

"This is Nora Simeon. I assume you've been informed who I am."

"Ms. Simeon. Yes, I have."

"I need to speak to you in person. How about in an hour, at your office?"

"Impossible. Staff meeting. I can give you a slot on Tuesday."

Today was Thursday. For me this was one of the few joys of taking on a case from the Commission, pushing people around who normally wouldn't give me time of day.

"An hour from now will be fine," I said. "Or if you like, I can mark you down as intransigent in my report to the board. And I don't mean the board of Goldman Sachs."

A pause. I imagined she was gritting her teeth, trying to control her breathing.

"Just as you say. I'll see you at 2:30. Please don't be late."

I wasted ten minutes getting ready to face the outside world, always a problem for me. I didn't say goodbye to Spark when I left; it was always with me wherever I went if I needed it for something. I didn't smoke, though, so needing it was pretty rare.

It was a sunny autumn day in Manhattan. Not too bad. Ten minutes from my office to Penn Station. Thirty more on the #1 train down to Chamber Street. And another five minutes to walk the two blocks through the mix of tourists and bankers to the hulking, godawful Goldman Sachs HQ on West Street. Right on time. Except for having to pass security. Oh well.

Approaching the entrance plaza, I saw the shiny neo-brutalist skyscraper was practically festooned with security cameras. Lots of plate glass out front, with poster-color murals on the walls; but also lots of square corners and surprisingly simple decor. I suppose they must have made a conscious decision not to show off. I walked up to the front desk, because I knew getting through to Sakashvili wouldn't be as simple as looking her up in a directory. And indeed, I went through two iterations of unenlightened security people before someone showed up who knew who I was, who she was, and was authorized to take me to her.

The man who finally arrived to meet me was 6'6", wedge-shaped, buzz-cut, in a black business suit, and he had a curly wire connected to his earpiece. I was surprised he wasn't wearing sunglasses, but the bulge beneath his lapel was certainly part of the costume. He didn't say a word to me or the regular security guards, just nodded his head slightly, and I followed him into the elevators. We went up to the 25th floor, got out, walked past another security desk with no words exchanged, and entered an elevator for which access to the floor had to be unlocked with a passcard carried by my guy. I was thinking of him as *my guy* at this point, imagining what he'd be like in bed. Domineering at first, probably, but that wouldn't last. By the time we got up to the executive floor, I'd already gotten to the point of our breakup in my little fantasy. It involved a romantic sunset on the High Line and an exchange of gunfire. I was just working out what I'd be wearing at the funeral when we got out and transferred to yet another elevator, this one requiring a key to enter. My guy left me then, and I left off daydreaming for the moment.

This elevator was obviously secured against etheric influences, with planetary amulets embedded in the walls, and what looked like a silver hexagram engraved in the floor. But it was a little too shiny to be silver. I crouched and sniffed the metal. My nose tingled with negative ions. Stabilized azoth warding circle. Fancy and expensive.

A demon who got into this elevator without a sorcerer escort would be banished and incinerated simultaneously.

I went down, down, down, with no indication of the passage of floors except a flashing arrow by the elevator control bank. At last the trip was over, the elevator door opened, and there I was in an underground atrium that practically reeked of magical wards. Sakashvili was waiting for me.

"You're late," she said. Younger than I was expecting: mid-20s, my age. But I guess vice-president is one of the junior grades at a place like Goldman Sachs.

"Blame your security. I was here on time."

She shrugged. Apart from her youth, Sakashvili looked and dressed pretty much like what I imagined she would. Perfect hair and makeup, muted designer outfit in beige, off-white, and black. Nothing pretentious there, but I had the feeling her ensemble probably cost something on the order of a month of my income. She had one distinctive feature you wouldn't normally see in an investment banker, a long leather sheath dangling from her waist, like the case for a conductor's baton, except that from the top poked a symbol-inscribed wooden rod with metal ferrules. Saturnian lead, I expected. Sakashvili was carrying a blasting rod, a sorcerer's tool for punishing unruly demons.

"Whatever," she said. "Let's get this over with." She took me through a couple of boring corridors to her office. Chrome and glass desk, nice but not fancy. Aeron chair, big old laptop, and that was it for her workspace. The visitor chair looked to be conference room surplus.

She walked behind her desk and I pulled up the chair before she could tell me to sit down. When she sat and saw I was already there, she frowned at me. Good.

"So," I said, "you lost a demon. The Commission doesn't like it when that happens. Even human-looking infernals don't understand how to live normally without a lot of training. And most of them are just monsters. They freak out the mundanes."

"You think I like it? Or my bosses?" She opened a desk drawer, pulled out a file folder, tossed it across the desk to me. "It's all there."

I flipped it open. Three pages. First, a printout of a photo. The demon itself. It was sitting at a barebones desk with a MacBook open in front of it. Well, okay, *he*, not it. Most infernals can't do gender very well. I was surprised to see he had a realistic body. They're supposed to be summoned into bodies constructed from materiae like plastic or metal, which the more powerful infernals can alter over time in the direction of the biological. Usually low-level demons like the ones they summon as analysts can't manage it very well. This one was convincingly satyrlike, though. In the photo he was wearing an old-fashioned three-piece-suit waistcoat over an even older starched white shirt with vented sleeves bound by gold cufflinks. Bearded, handsome face, human-looking except for the yellow, bar-pupiled eyes and the cute little horns growing out of his forehead. No pants; any trousers would have to be bespoke to fit his goatlike lower half. The laptop was strategically positioned to hide any view of his genitals, if he had any; but with such a carefully crafted masculine appearance I assumed he did. In the photo the infernal appeared to be engrossed with whatever was on the laptop screen, but I had the sense he was aware of the shot and was posing for the camera.

"Whoa," I said. "*This* is an analyst? Fancy. You guys do happy hours together after work or something? Or happy nights, maybe?"

Sakashvili flushed. "I, uh, I gather he's been summoned before. Not by Goldman Sachs, I mean. For reasons not having to do with financial prognostication."

Next page. The demon's personal data. Name: Barbatos. His personal sigil and magic square as required for summoning and binding rituals. Special talent: finding treasure hidden by magic. Just what the investment banks want in a demon.

"Wait," I said. "Barbatos. *The* Barbatos? The one from the *Lemegeton* and the *Pseudomonarchia Daemonum*? What the fuck is this? You summoned a demon lord as a staff analyst?"

"No," she said, "of course not. It's another demon with the same name. They're not very original down there. Our treaty with the Infernal Powers forbids summoning anyone of earl-level or above."

Last page. Summarized quarterly performance reviews. Barbatos was summoned two years ago, by a group president named Raymond Utgard. Group president of the Goldman Sachs demon-summoning operation was about as powerful a position as you could achieve in the firm without being on the board. And by its nature, this role would always have to be a secret. Probably most of the Goldman Sachs directors had no idea their company's profits were driven by sorcery. All the major investment banks along with the larger hedge and capital firms employed secret cadres of sorcerers and demon analysts. Between them, with a few unaffiliated types like my mom, their board chairs and CEOs made up the Commission that oversaw magic and summoning throughout the city, and indeed, throughout most of the western hemisphere.

Barbatos' reviews were all positive. Surprisingly so considering the demons were worked like slaves. Infernal attitudes toward management typically ranged from passive-aggressive to murderous. But nothing much useful here, except--

"Why am even I talking to you? Where's your group president, this Utgard person who summoned the demon in the first place?"

She hesitated. "Mr. Utgard, is, ah, no longer with the company."

"What? Retired? Headhunted by Deutschebank?"

"Deceased. He screwed up a binding ritual; the demon involved was... recalcitrant."

"I guess that's why they pay you the big bucks. Who's group president now?"

"The position is vacant. Really, I don't see what this has to do with Barbatos. We reported the loss as required by the Commission. Shouldn't you be out there tracking him down?"

I shook my head. "First I want to see the infernals' workspace."

"Why?"

She was being obstructive now. I stood up, put my hands on her desk, encroaching on her space. "It's supposed to be secure, right? I want to hear what you know about how one of them got out, and I want to see the place for myself."

She recoiled from me a little. "Our security protocols... I'm not authorized to allow an outsider to see them."

"For fuck's sake. I'm going to have to write all this up. You think the Commission's going to be happy with 'sorry, it's a secret'? So why not let me decide what's relevant to my job, okay?"

Sakashvili looked like she wanted to argue, but at last she said, "Okay." At least she didn't try to pass the buck, which is what I was expecting.

"I assume you've seen demons in person before," she said. "You know what it's going to be like being in a room full of them?"

"Yeah. My nightmares are not your problem."

"That's for sure. Fine. Follow me."

Out of her office, through an unmarked door that looked like all the others, into another corridor, to a blank steel door. The door was equipped with a near-field phone sensor, a keypad for passphrase input, a palm-print reader, and for retro laughs a mechanical key lock. It took Sakashvili the better part of five minutes to open it up.

She turned to me when she was done, holding the door open to reveal a stairway heading down. "Needless to say, there are hidden cameras here, and everywhere on the secure floor. Someone is watching us right now. If I made the signal, or even if it looked like I might be coerced, armed response would be here immediately."

"Needless to say," I said. "So why didn't they spot a totally inhuman-looking demon sneaking out through all this security?"

She colored. "We suffered a power failure. It was on the weekend. A security officer called me at home within a minute of the event, and I was here in person in fifteen."

"Don't tell me the doors all fail open when they lose power."

"Of course not."

We walked down the narrow staircase to another steel door. This one was equipped with a servo-driven spring-loaded bar. Some security person upstairs had to acknowledge our presence through a camera and microphone interaction, and it was their action that powered back the bar.

"This is it," she said. The door opened.

We were looking into a large room, thirty yards square, with a big structural pillar in the middle that no doubt concealed a skyscraper girder. There was an outer ledge at our level surrounding a carpeted pit full of workstations, little desks with laptops staffed by demons. The whole pit area was fenced off with a cordon like the velvet lines they use for queues in movie theaters, except that each of the brass poles supported a prominent pentacle, and the purple cordon ropes were worked with intricate runes in silvery thread.

A dozen demons were variously standing, sitting, or perching at their workstations in the central pit. Originally summoned into inanimate bodies made out of clay, metal, plastic, or whatever, some of the demons had altered their forms over time. Not to the point of looking like proper living beings though, not even semi-human ones like Barbatos. These things were halfway between piles of trash and people.

The nearest demon glanced our way as Sakashvili opened the door. Its body had originally been a life-sized artist's mannequin, a wooden object with articulated joints allowing the model to be posed as an anatomical drawing reference. But the demon had been altering its body. Flesh mixed with wood, now. The original mannequin structure was still visible, but a clumsy face had formed where a blank had once been; it was more like a sketch of a face than a real thing. I didn't know if it used the hollow pits of its eyes to see or not, but a moment after the thing inclined its head upward towards us, it flinched violently and hunched back down over its laptop. Around the room other monstrosities behaved similarly, pretending they were entirely focused on their computer screens, deliberately not paying us any attention at all.

It might have been a pathetic scene, these hapless slaves crafted into shambling semblances of humanity and forced into servitude by a rich, evil corporation. But I knew from long experience that infernals just aren't deserving of that kind of consideration. It's not just being inhuman. Their fundamentally unnatural existence in our world is creepy, sure. But it's their pervasive malice that really makes me hate them. Low level infernals are stupid; apart from their magical talents, they're just thugs. The higher-ups are villains and fiends. So maybe they're not properly demons at all, not fallen angels or rebels against some divinity, just monsters from some alien plane of existence. But the name fits.

"This is the only way in? What're those?" I gestured at several doors around the sides of the room.

"Conference room," she said. "Summoning chamber, workshop for demon material assembly, and analyst quarters. No other exits."

"I'm going to have to talk to them," I said. "I assume they're all under your control."

"Yes, but..." Sakashvili seemed unhappy with the idea of my going down there.

"Listen," I said. "You've got these things warded up the ass, and the physical security would make Tom Cruise cry. Power outage or no power outage. It's obvious what happened here. Right? You do see it's obvious to me, don't you?"

Sakashvili stared at me for a moment. I wasn't sure what was going on behind her eyes.

"I... I think you're going way beyond your purview, Ms. Simeon. This has nothing to do with finding Barbatos."

I took a step closer to her, and she flinched away from me.

"You're wrong," I said. "I shouldn't even have to explain this, it's so obvious. Someone must have helped your demon get out of here. If it wasn't you, it was someone else high-level at Goldman Sachs who works with infernals. Some or all of these demons must have been here when Barbatos escaped or was taken or whatever happened to him. I assume your internal security people are all over this already, and you were just hoping I wouldn't follow up on it for the Commission. But that's not how it's going to be. Because my reputation is at stake here if I ignore it."

I left unsaid that finding out who the insider was would end their career and maybe their life, knowing the kind of control the Commission's member firms like to exert over magic in the city. That was obvious, too.

"Okay," said Sakashvili after another pause. "So be it. I'm going to have to clear this with security. Hang on. Got to give them some passphrases."

She stepped to the side, far enough to have some privacy from me, and started muttering into her phone. After a minute she put the phone away and returned to where I was waiting.

"I can give you fifteen minutes," said Sakashvili. Then she walked to the top of the steps leading down into the work area, just behind the cordon.

"Listen up, people," she called out, and all the various monstrosities working their laptops looked up, as if they hadn't known she'd been there all this time.

"I invoke your bindings. Code Shemhamphorash. By Anaphexeton and in the name of Abrac Abeor I adjure you; speak truthfully to my servant Nora Simeon and answer her questions. In the name of the Primemeuton. Selah." Then she muttered to me, "Sorry about that servant thing, you know how it goes."

I nodded to her. "May I?"

She unlinked the cordon rope barring access to the three steps down into the demons' work area. Probably it formed some kind of magical ward. "Be my guest."

I have to admit I paused at the top of the stairs. I hate having to be anywhere near infernals. But I'd talked myself into being allowed down there. And the longer I waited, the more likely they'd think I was weak. You don't want to show weakness to demons, even when they're bound to serve you. So down I went. Into the pit.

We appreciate every like, tweet, facebook post and review and we love to hear from you. Please consider leaving us a review online or sending your thoughts and comments to info@mirrorworldpublishing.com

Thank you.